Aloha

Four Romances at a Hawaiian Hideaway

Colleen Coble
Carol Cox
Denise Hunter
Gail Sattler

BARBOUR BOOKS

An Imprint of Barbour Publishing, Inc.

Love, Suite Love ©2002 by Colleen Coble
Fixed by Love ©2002 by Carol Cox
Game of Love ©2002 by Denise Hunter
It All Adds Up to Love ©2002 by Gail Sattler

Cover photo: © GettyOne

Illustrations by Mari Goering

ISBN 1-58660-633-6

Published by Barbour Books, an imprint of Barbour Publishing, Inc., P.O. Box 719, Uhrichsville, Ohio 44683, www.barbourbooks.com

 Member of the
Evangelical Christian
Publishers Association

Printed in the United States of America.
5 4 3 2 1

INTRODUCTION

The four Harrigan brothers have inherited a resort on Maui from their father. Can the brothers work together to make Harrigan's Cove successful—and balance romance in the meantime?

Love, Suite Love by Colleen Coble
As manager of Harrigan's Cove, the last person Barnabas Harrigan wants to deal with is rich and spoiled Liliana Van Cleef. Unfortunately for him, Liliana takes his avoidance as a challenge, but Barnabas is unswayed. And then Liliana begins to see that the true meaning in life is not clothes or status, but a relationship with God. Has Barnabas finally met his match?

Fixed by Love by Carol Cox
Beth feels like a fifth wheel after being invited to Harrigan's Cove by her sister and brother-in-law. The only person she feels comfortable with is the maintenance man, Connor. When she discovers Connor is really one of the owners, she is angry with him for misleading her, as well as feels outclassed by his position. Can Connor convince her that he is just a working person like her and all they need between them is God and a little love?

Game of Love by Denise Hunter
Callie Andersen just wants to lick her wounds after being jilted at the altar. Alex Harrigan, activity director, knows the best bandage for a broken heart is activity; and when Callie notes the lack of children's activities, he's happy to put her to work gathering ideas. But when he starts to lose his heart, he wonders if he will soon be nursing his own wounds.

It All Adds Up to Love by Gail Sattler
Steve Harrigan, the accountant, has seen his three brothers turn into lovesick fools, and because of their sloppiness, the resort's financial records are a mess. When the resort's IRS deadline approaches, Steve teams up with an old friend, Tasha Struchenkowich, to fix things up. Fortunately for him, *he* can keep his mind on his work. Or can he?

Aloha

Love,
Suite Love

by Colleen Coble

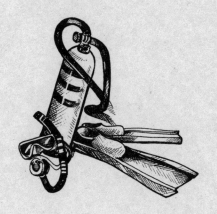

Dedication

For Deb and Bob Green.
Your friendship has brightened our lives for many years.
Love you guys!

Chapter 1

"C ome on, Barnabas, live a little! You're only thirty-four, not sixty. It will be fun." Colin Montreal tossed his light brown hair out of his eyes and leaned over the hotel register. "Harrigan's Cove is a fine resort, and it's time to enjoy the fruits of your labor. You live in paradise, yet you act like a dried-up old man who lives to take his dog for a walk on the beach."

"I stopped believing in your promises when we were nine years old and you promised my bike would be perfectly safe left outside the cinema. Besides, I have work to do." Barnabas Harrigan turned away from his friend's entreaties. With Colin, it was always play time. He didn't know the meanings of the words duty and responsibility—words Barnabas had cut his teeth on.

Barnabas had to wonder if that's how people really saw him—as a dried-up old man at age thirty-four. He didn't feel any older than he had when he first started working here at the resort in his teens. Where had the years gone? Now Dad was retired and the full responsibility fell on Barnabas's shoulders as the eldest of the four brothers. Barnabas was determined to live up to his father's faith in him by working hard.

Colin snorted. "What work? More catering to women like those two coming in the door? Though I wouldn't mind an introduction to the young one. Wowser."

Barnabas turned to see two women approaching the desk. The elder was about seventy with green eyes as clear as glass and white hair styled in waves that softened her sagging chin. She wore a gray suit with a pink blouse. Her gentle smile brought a welcoming grin to Barnabas's face. She reminded him of his grandmother back in Ohio.

His smile faltered as his gaze traveled past her to the other woman. She looked like a younger version of the elder. Her hair rippled down her back nearly to her waist in a black, silken sheen that threw up beams of light from its depths. Her three-inch heels clicked along the tile in a staccato rhythm that announced, "Look at me." Dressed in a red suit that fit her curves to perfection, she was the type of woman that made most men salivate.

Barnabas was not most men. His brows drew together in a scowl. Just the kind of woman he most despised. She would expect to be waited on hand and foot, and he was in no mood for such a hard customer this week. Not when a boatload of responsibility had just been dumped on his already aching shoulders. He had learned one thing early at Harrigan's Cove—a woman's beauty was in direct proportion to how much attention she expected.

He forced a smile to his lips. "Good afternoon. Welcome to Harrigan's Cove. How do you like our beautiful Maui?"

"Oh, it's just paradise," the older woman said. She picked up the pen to sign the guest register. "I am Phoebe Van Cleef, and this is my granddaughter, Liliana Van Cleef. Such a lovely resort you have here. What's your name, young man?"

Barnabas raised an eyebrow. People seldom cared who the staff members were so long as their needs were met. "Barnabas Harrigan," he said.

"Ah, the owner of this fine resort?" Phoebe inquired.

"One of them. My father just retired, but I have three younger brothers who share the business."

"Since my friend seems reluctant to introduce me, let me introduce myself." Colin broke in with an outstretched hand. "Colin Montreal, at your service. If I can be of any assistance in showing you around our paradise, just say the word." He shook Phoebe's hand, then took Liliana's right hand in both of his hands.

A slight hint of color came to Liliana's cheeks, and she pulled her hand back. "Thank you, but we shall be very busy this week."

"Pish-posh, Liliana, you might as well take the young man up on his offer. I don't want you stuck in the room with me when you could be out having fun," her grandmother admonished.

The color in Liliana's cheeks deepened, and she narrowed her eyes as she looked at Colin. "I prefer to stay with you, Grammy. Besides, I want to work on my tan." Her voice dripped with aloof disdain.

Colin shrugged and handed her a card. "If you change your mind, give me a call." He waved to Barnabas, then sauntered away.

Barnabas suppressed a smile as he led the way through the lobby and stepped out into the bright Hawaiian sunshine. A profusion of hibiscus and orchids bloomed along the paths to the hales. The surf pounded along the shore; and far out on the blue water, he could see sailboats scudding by on the white-capped waves.

This was paradise indeed. He sent up a silent prayer of thankfulness to God for allowing him to live on this island of lush beauty and warm, tropical breezes. He glanced at the women walking beside him. Phoebe's rapt expression showed she appreciated the beauty as much as he did, but Liliana walked with her eyes straight ahead without seeming to care about the magnificent beach view.

He indicated a golf cart parked outside. "Hop in and I'll take you to your hale."

"Hale?" Liliana's perfectly arched eyebrows rose. "I specifically said a suite. What is a hale?"

"You'll love it, I promise. It's three rooms, actually, like a little house that's all your own. You'll see." He kept his smile pinned in place, but it was a struggle as he helped the two women into the golf cart. He jumped into the driver's seat and released the brake. He couldn't get rid of the stuck-up young woman any too soon.

They rounded the corner, and the resort hales came into view. Like a cluster of grass huts, the roofs were thatched. The hales were the drawing point to the resort for most visitors. It was like stepping back to the way Hawaii used to be. The hales dotted the landscape, interspersed with more flowers and benches to sit on and enjoy the scenery. He stopped in front of a hale that overlooked the water.

Liliana gasped. "This? Is—is that *grass* on the roof?" She gave an outraged sniff, then turned to her grandmother. "Grammy, I'm sorry. I specifically requested their best suite for our trip away. The Ritz-Carlton is just down the road, and I own stock in it. I'm sure they will find room for us."

Barnabas would like nothing better than to be rid of the beautiful and haughty Liliana Van Cleef, but with the fall-off in tourism lately, he needed the booking. They'd booked for two months, and he wasn't about to let that slip away because of a spoiled, little rich girl. "Looks are deceiving," he said. "Let me show you inside. This is our finest hale, and it has every amenity you could ask for. Most guests enjoy the privacy of our hales. No door slamming in the middle of the night, no loud neighbors. See for yourself."

"Let's at least look at it," Phoebe said. "I think it's rather charming."

Barnabas smiled with relief, then mounted the wooden steps to the deck and unlocked the front door. He stepped inside. Phoebe followed him, and after a brief pause, Liliana stomped up the steps as well.

There was nothing to be ashamed of with these accommodations. He turned expectantly. How could they find fault with this hale? Plush carpeting covered the floors, teak furniture gleamed in the sunshine through the window, and soft green Hawaiian print bedding completed the decor.

"How lovely," Phoebe said.

"This is the joint sitting room. Through that door is one bedroom, and the door opposite it leads to the other bedroom. We've spared no expense to make your stay here a memorable one." He stepped toward a door leading to the first bedroom. "The bathrooms have gold fixtures, and they each have a spa-tub for your relaxation."

Liliana followed him, and he caught a whiff of her perfume, some kind of light, flowery scent that had to cost the earth. She was a lovely creature. Too bad her inside beauty didn't match the outside.

She sniffed. "Very well, I'm willing to give it a try if you are, Grammy. I just want you to be comfortable." But the look she sent Barnabas from her green eyes could have left him bleeding.

Barnabas let out the breath he'd been holding. Maybe he had salvaged this booking after all—if the pristine Liliana Van Cleef didn't find something else to complain about.

Two months might feel like an eternity.

Liliana kicked off her heels and sighed with relief as her toes sank into the sage green carpet. Walking across to the small refrigerator, she opened it and peered inside. "Want a fruit juice, Grammy?" She just wanted to forget the handsome resort owner and her reaction to him. Her first glimpse of him had been like an uppercut to the solar plexus.

"No, thank you, Darling. Get one for yourself and come here a moment. I fear I must take you to task a bit."

Liliana sighed. She knew what was coming. No matter what she did, she never managed to please anyone. She grabbed a bottle of water and sank onto the couch beside her grandmother.

"Liliana, dear girl, I know we haven't spent much time together, and I regret that. It was always my wish to be close to my grandchildren."

Her grandmother sounded near tears, and Liliana had to resist an impulse to take her hand. Though it went against Liliana's nature, she had learned to restrain such actions. Physical contact was discouraged in her family. "It wasn't your fault, Grammy. I know now that Mother forbade you to see us."

Her grandmother shook her head. "I should never have allowed the estrangement to go on. Apologies are hard for your mother. I should have offered an apology myself."

Liliana inched closer. "What happened, Grammy? I was only five the last time we came for a visit, and all I remember is shouting and doors banging. Then Mother took us to the car and shouted that we were never coming back."

Tears glimmered in her grandmother's eyes, then she looked away and cleared her throat. "I'm wise to you, young lady. You're trying to change the subject. Your behavior was appalling. You treated poor Barnabas like he was a lackey."

Heat flooded Liliana's face. "I couldn't help it. He reminded me so much of Jeff, I wanted to slap him."

"Jeff?"

"My ex-fiancé. The one who threw me over for a Holly-wood starlet with a nose job and a fake body." Liliana didn't try to hide her rage. That weasel Jeff had dared to tell her that he needed a woman who incited his friends to jealousy. Did that mean she, Liliana, was the girl next door? She'd made plenty of men turn and take a second look. That Colin What's-His-Name had been positively drooling. Just remembering Jeff's smug attitude when he broke their engagement made her want to throw things.

"Oh, Dear. Well, try to remember Barnabas is not this Jeff. He seems like a perfectly nice young man. I'm glad you found out this Jeff's true character before the wedding ceremony. The Hollywood starlet was not so lucky. But don't blame poor Barnabas for the sins of another."

Liliana sniffed. "We'll see, Grammy." She rose and went toward her bedroom. "I think I'll put on my bathing suit and lie in the sun for awhile."

"I'm going to take a nap. That flight from Phoenix was grueling." Her grandmother yawned.

"It's best to try to stay awake, Grammy. Otherwise, you'll have trouble getting on Hawaiian time."

"I'm an old woman, Liliana. I can sleep and awaken when I like. You run along and play. I'll be here when you get back."

Liliana smiled and closed her bedroom door behind her. She was ready for some relaxation. Though her heart was still sore from her father's death six months ago, her mother's obsessive grief had made her even more critical and judgmental than ever. Liliana was just plain worn out from the ordeal. The thought of sunshine and sand, swimming and sailing held an almost visceral appeal.

She slipped into a black one-piece bathing suit, then pulled on a white cover-up. Two o'clock. Her mother would be expecting a call to let her know they had arrived safely. Glancing around the room, she didn't see a phone. How odd. Maybe it was in the sitting room. But there was no phone there either. Then she noticed that not only was there no phone, there was no television.

That was simply not acceptable. How could any place that called itself an exclusive resort not provide a telephone and television? No Internet access? Her anger surged again. That Barnabas must be like Jeff in more than just appearance. It was clear he held the same disregard for other people that was Jeff's trademark. At these prices, she intended to make sure he rectified the omission.

She slipped on her sandals and exited the hale. Marching across the sand toward the lobby, her indignation rose until she felt she must glow with the heat of it. First he deliberately didn't tell her they had no suites. Then he stuck them in a grass hut with no phone or TV and away from the shops and the excitement. This was not her idea of a vacation.

Grains of sand bit into the tender sole of her foot, and she stopped to shake them out. She lost her balance and teetered for a moment before strong fingers took hold of her arm and steadied her. She looked up into eyes as blue as the ocean behind her.

"Mr. Harrigan," she began. "There is no phone in our—our *hale*. Such a ridiculous name! And not only is there no phone, there is no television. These things are not luxuries; they are normal amenities! For the prices you are asking for these grass huts, I would think we would be able to have contact with the outside world!"

The blue of his eyes hardened to molten steel, and his firm jaw tightened. He really was a most amazing-looking man. Actually much better looking than Jeff—if Liliana was interested, which she most decidedly *was not*. Handsome men only thought of themselves, and she was tired of being an accessory on a man's arm.

He gave a heavy sigh. "Miss Van Cleef, I'm sorry if the accommodations are not to your liking. The brochure I sent you explained that we want our guests to get away from the clatter of normal life and really relax. If you insist, I can bring you a portable phone, but please, try it for a few days and see how free you feel without the intrusion of the outside world."

"Mr. Harrigan, we are going to be here two months! Surely you don't expect us to sequester ourselves away on this island like we're in a monastery. I can understand your point if we were going to be here only two or three days, but I have stocks to keep an eye on and friends to keep in touch with. What you suggest isn't feasible."

"You might be surprised how unimportant those things can become when you get alone with your thoughts and connect with God."

Liliana's eyes widened. She didn't think she'd ever heard anyone mention God outside the elaborate church she attended at Christmas and Easter. Unless it was as a curse word.

Something about the way Barnabas mentioned God, almost like He was a close friend, made her heart thump in her chest in a strange way.

But Liliana hated discomfort. All her life she'd had only the finest of comforts, the tastiest of food, the most lavish of clothing. She didn't have to listen to this man ramble on about peace and connecting with God. She'd come here to spend some time with her grandmother, to work on her tan, and to simply forget her troubles.

"I'd like that portable phone now, please," she said firmly. "And what about the television? What does one do at night without a TV? There's no real night life."

Barnabas smiled, and the glint of white teeth in his bronzed face made Liliana catch her breath. There seemed to be something so solid and dependable about him. But it was just an illusion, just as Jeff's love had been an illusion. She wasn't about to trust another handsome man. She'd find a nice homely man who doted on her.

"I recommend strolls along the beach in the moonlight, reading, or playing a game. Try it, Miss Van Cleef. You might even find your own thoughts enough entertainment. We Americans seem to have lost ourselves in the fast pace of life we lead. We forget how to think, how to commune with our Creator, how to learn who we really are and what we want out of life. We get caught up in the sparkle and tinsel of this temporary life and lose track of the truly important things like faith, love, family, hope."

Liliana felt as though she could burst into tears, and she

didn't like the sensation. He was talking about things she longed for in her deepest soul. But she *never* cried. Mother said tears were for weaklings, for the *bourgeois*. For a moment she imagined walking along the beach in the moonlight with this man. He was unlike anyone she'd ever met. "The TV, Mr. Harrigan?"

"Sorry." His smile didn't seem the least bit penitent. "The phone I can fix, but not the television."

"Fine. Bring the phone to my hale. I have some calls I need to make." Liliana turned on her heels and fled. She'd never run from anything in her life, but she felt as though she were being chased by an unseen force. It was a strange and terrifying feeling, and all she knew was that she had to escape.

Chapter 2

Barnabas fumed as he found one of the portable phones and made sure it was charged. He'd known from his first look at Liliana that she was going to be trouble. The next two months promised to be an exercise in patience, and patience was something he *never* prayed for. God too often sent trials when he did, but this present one had been sent with no warning.

He stopped at the sight of his brother, Connor, repairing a cracked tile in the back hall floor. Connor wore carpenter pants with his tools hung in the loops. A leather work pouch was slung around his hips. Barnabas knew he was happiest when he was tinkering with something.

"Hey, Barney," Connor said.

"Don't call me Barney," Barnabas snapped. "I'm not purple and cuddly."

"Oooh, we're in a good mood today," Connor said, launching into the familiar children's song about Barney.

Barnabas scowled. "Are you through? You know how I hate

that nickname," he said.

"What's put your back up?"

"Oh, that new guest, Liliana Van Cleef. She's bent out of shape about not having a phone or a television. I'm going to take her one of the portables. But she's going to be trouble, I can tell already."

"Beautiful, is she?"

"How did you know?" Barnabas scowled again at his brother.

"Only someone drop-dead gorgeous would bring that look to your eyes. A look of extreme irritation and agitation." Connor chuckled. "When are you going to find yourself a wife and settle down? Women aren't nearly as bad as you make them out to be."

"A lot you know about it. You're a bachelor as well."

"Yes, but at least I date them. I don't understand it. You're not bad looking." Barnabas gave him a withering look, but Connor blithely ignored it and continued with his analysis. "You're financially stable, and women are always flirting with you."

"The wrong kind," Barnabas said. "The only women I see are rich ones who think a man should cater to their every whim. I want a woman whose beauty is inward, someone who loves the Lord as much as I do. Take this Liliana Van Cleef. I suppose she's beautiful." He stopped and shrugged. "No, I have to be honest. She *is* beautiful. But her selfishness mars her outward appearance. Now her grandmother is truly beautiful. You can tell she's a giving, loving woman. Too bad her granddaughter isn't more like her."

A sound came from behind him, sort of a strangled gasp.

He turned and stared into Liliana's stunned green eyes. Her eyes filled with tears, and she turned and fled down the hall and out the door.

"Great. Just great," Barnabas muttered. Guilt smote him. He didn't mean to hurt her. "I should have known better than to be talking like that." He left his brother and hurried after Liliana. How was he going to apologize? Her type would likely throw his apology back in his face, then pack up and leave the resort immediately. His tongue had cost him the booking, but even more importantly, it had hurt a young woman, and he was sorry for that.

His long strides quickly brought him to the beach, and he started toward the Van Cleef hale and thought about what he could say. She had to have heard everything. Unfortunately, it was all true. He rounded the gazebo and saw a shape huddled on the bench. Her shoulders bent in a despondent air, Liliana was crying softly.

Barnabas felt like a brute. Growing up with brothers, he had no idea how to comfort a crying woman. He didn't dare put his arms around her—it would leave him open to a sexual harassment suit. Besides, he wouldn't want Liliana to get the wrong idea. Holding the phone awkwardly in his hands, he mounted the steps to the gazebo and approached her.

She raised her head at the sound of his footsteps. Her face was red and blotchy from weeping, and another pang of remorse struck him.

She tilted her chin defiantly. "What are you doing here? I'm ugly inside, remember?"

"I didn't mean to hurt you," Barnabas said softly. "And I didn't say you were ugly inside." His voice trailed away as he realized, basically, that was exactly what he had said.

"You want a Christian woman with beauty on the inside, isn't that right? Well, I've got news for you, Mr. Harrigan. I want a man whose main object in life is to make me happy. I don't care if he looks like a troll. Does that surprise you?"

He'd already lost the booking, so he might as well speak the truth she needed to hear. "Actually, no, it doesn't, Miss Van Cleef. You say you want him to make you happy. No person can do that for you except Jesus Christ. The rest of it is just an empty heart trying to fill itself with temporal stuff that doesn't matter."

Her tears dried, and she rose to her feet. "I've been here exactly two hours and I've heard more about God than I have in all the rest of my life put together. I would appreciate it if you don't speak to me for the rest of our stay here. You're a fanatic, Mr. Harrigan, and I'll admit that you make me uncomfortable. My grandmother would be happy to discuss religion with you, but it's not a subject I care to hear again." She snatched the phone from his hand, then swept past him and marched down the steps toward her hale.

Barnabas stared after her. For the first time, he'd seen something attractive in Liliana's soul—a lost child looking for love. She needed the Lord, and whether she liked it or not, God was seeking her.

Liliana's eyes felt gritty and tired from crying. What was wrong with her? Weeping in front of that man as though his words had any power to wound her! It must be jet lag. She didn't care a jot for his opinion. Though no woman liked to hear a handsome man thought her unattractive, she wasn't interested in Barnabas, so why had his words brought her to tears? It made no sense to her.

She passed a hand over her eyes, then stared in the mirror. Grammy would take one look at her and demand to know what had happened. And Liliana didn't want to talk about it, so she'd better repair the damage. She carefully applied more makeup, then grabbed the portable phone and her sunglasses and headed outside. Settling herself in a lawn chair, she dialed the phone.

"Van Cleef residence."

"Hi, Molly, it's Liliana. Is my mother there?"

"One moment, Miss Van Cleef. I'll get her."

Liliana rubbed an acrylic nail absently while she waited. She would have preferred to leave a message with Molly, but her mother would have been livid at the supposed slight.

"Darling, how is the weather?"

Her mother's voice sounded bright and happy, and Liliana let out the breath she'd been holding. "Lovely, Mother. It's in the eighties, and the water is as blue as the sky." *And as blue as Barnabas's eyes,* she added silently. She flushed at the direction her thoughts had taken.

Her mother's voice sharpened. "And your grandmother?"

"She's napping. The flight wore her out."

"I can't understand why you insisted on accompanying her

on this ridiculous trip. Hawaii is lovely, but you'll miss the winter ball in February. And all your friends have been expressing their dismay over your absence. Your grandmother will drive you wild with her incessant talking about the old days."

"I like hearing about them, especially about when Daddy was a little boy." Liliana knew she'd made a mistake to bring up her father when her mother gave an indignant sniff and her voice turned as cold as the wind back in Chicago.

"You really shouldn't be neglecting your duties here to cater to an old woman, Liliana. If I were you, I would cut the trip to two weeks and get back in time for some of the winter activities."

"I'm staying," Liliana said firmly. *And you're not me, Mother. You have no idea of the loss I feel from missing all those years with Grammy.* She wished she could say those words to her mother, but the deep freeze rejection would be more than she could bear. Was there anyone who would love her just the way she was? Maybe Grammy would when they got better acquainted. Tears stung the backs of her eyelids again, and she wondered if she was getting sick. She'd never been so weepy.

The long pause on the other end of the line made her grip the phone with tense fingers as she waited for the blast from her mother. "Mother?" she asked.

At first there was only silence, then the dial tone came on. Her mother had hung up. Liliana jabbed the on/off button angrily. That was just like her mother. If she didn't want to deal with something, she just avoided it.

A swim would clear her thoughts. She rose and dropped

the cover-up onto her chair, then loped toward the surf. Her legs were as pale as cream cheese, but by the time this trip was over, she intended to be as brown as, well, as Barnabas. After her swim, she found a place on the beach beside another woman about her age.

"Mind if I sit here?" she asked.

The woman opened one eyelid. When she saw Liliana, she sat up. "You're Liliana Van Cleef, aren't you?" she said eagerly. "I'm Clarissa Winslow. I recognized you when you arrived, but I hadn't had a chance to catch you. I went to school with your cousin Charles and we met at his graduation."

"I thought you looked familiar," Liliana said. How boring to be saddled with someone who prattled. She wanted to close her eyes and get some sun, but now good breeding demanded her to be sociable. She chatted with Clarissa, but her thoughts kept going back to Barnabas.

Why did her thoughts keep drifting to that hateful man? It wasn't his sea blue eyes or curly hair or even his splendid physique. It was the strength and integrity she saw on his face that drew her. He had been grieved to see she was hurt, she realized as she thought back to the encounter. But he hadn't retracted his words. It almost felt like a challenge to Liliana. Right then, she decided she was going to win Barnabas Harrigan. When he was groveling at her feet, she would toss his words back in his face and remind him that he didn't want a woman like her. It would be proof for Liliana that his words were lies.

"Why are you smiling like that?" Clarissa asked.

Liliana's smile deepened as she told her the plan to humiliate Barnabas. The thought of her revenge gave her a delicious thrill. It drove away the strange feeling of wanting to cry, that curious yearning she'd been feeling. The hunt was always fun. But she had to wonder how Barnabas would react to the game.

"I'm going for a swim," she told Clarissa. She jumped to her feet and ran toward the water. With a grin, she ran into the waves, then dove into the surf. The water closed over her head, and she enjoyed the invigorating thrust of the breakers.

The next week flew by, and Liliana discovered Barnabas was right about letting go of the outside world and concentrating on the joy of each day here in paradise. She swam, strolled the beach, and enjoyed her time with her grandmother. Barnabas avoided her, which gave her a few moments of pique. Still, there was plenty of time to put her plan into action.

About ten days after their arrival, Liliana headed out for her afternoon swim. She swam for about half an hour, then reluctantly left the water. At least Clarissa was missing this morning. The thought of spending the rest of the afternoon with the sun and her book was very appealing. Walking back to her towel and chair, she noticed a little girl sitting alone on a sun-bleached blanket about ten feet from Liliana's chair. She appeared to be three or four years old with straight black hair and features that reminded Liliana of an Asian. Or Hawaiian. Liliana looked closer and decided she must be a native of the island. She glanced around. Where was the little girl's mother?

The sand was deserted in this part of the beach except for a young man and woman, obviously newlyweds by the stars in their eyes as they clung together in the water. Alarmed that so young a child would be unattended this close to the water, Liliana approached the little girl.

She wore a pink, several-sizes-too-big swimsuit, which sagged on her skinny frame, and the sun had already left red marks on her shoulders. She clutched a worn and faded "Barney" backpack to her chest. Her hair was full of sand. As Liliana approached, the pitiful-looking youngster looked up and regarded her with a sober stare.

"Hello," Liliana said. "Where's your mama, little girl?"

The little girl pulled her thumb out of her mouth and pointed. "In the water. She said she'd be right back, but she's been gone a long time."

Liliana knelt beside her. "What's your name?"

"Abby. I'm four," she confided. She leaned against Liliana, and her eyes closed.

Within moments, she was asleep. Nonplused, Liliana gathered the child into her arms and carried her to the wooden lawn chair. What was she to do with this little mite? She was beginning to worry about the mother too. If the little girl had been waiting so long that she was exhausted, then maybe something had happened to her mother.

She laid Abby on the chair, covered her with a towel, then pulled on her cover-up. Maybe Barnabas would know something about her. She hesitated. Surely she shouldn't leave Abby alone. A waiter came toward her, and she waved him closer.

"Could you tell Barnabas I'd like to speak with him? Tell him it's Liliana Van Cleef."

The waiter nodded. "Right away, Miss." Still carrying the tray with the bottles of water on it, he strode toward the lobby entrance.

Liliana glanced down at the sleeping child, then out to sea. Shading her eyes with her hand, she studied the waves to see if she could see anyone still in the water. The sea was empty now that the newlyweds had come in to shore. Her unease deepened.

A few minutes went by, then she saw Barnabas striding toward her. His expression was wary, as though he anticipated more trouble from her. But, she suspected, it wouldn't be quite what he was expecting.

"You sent for me?" His tone was polite but reserved.

She indicated Abby, still sleeping peacefully on the lounge chair. "Do you have any idea who she belongs to?"

Barnabas glanced down and his remote expression disappeared. "Abby!" He knelt beside her and touched her cheek. "Abby, wake up." He shook her gently.

Abby yawned and opened her eyes. "Barney," she murmured.

Liliana had to bite the inside of her lip to keep from laughing. She couldn't imagine anyone less like a *Barney*. Her gaze drifted to Abby's faded backpack with the cartoon-character purple dinosaur.

"It's Barnabas," he corrected. "Where's your mommy, Sweetheart?"

Abby sat up and rubbed her eyes. "Mommy went swimming a long time ago," she complained. "She said I would get to see you when she got back, but she never came to get me."

"Did you stay where she left you?"

Abby nodded. "Right there." She pointed to where her sand pail and shovel still sat on the sand.

Barnabas turned and ran toward the lifeguard tower. "Take care of Abby," he shouted back over his shoulder. "I need to find Mary."

Abby started to cry. "I want my mommy," she wailed.

Liliana hadn't had much experience with children, and she felt at a loss to know what to do with the little girl. How did one go about comforting a child? "Um, are you hungry, Abby?"

"Yes," Abby sobbed. "Mommy promised to get me an apple when she got back."

"Well, let's go see my grammy and we'll take you to the restaurant. Stop crying now and you can order anything you want." The promise might be a mistake, but Liliana would do anything to stop the wailing.

Abby sniveled, then swiped at her nose. Her dirty hand left a smear across her face. Liliana certainly couldn't take her to dinner looking like a street urchin. And what could she dress her in? This tattered bathing suit was hardly appropriate. She sighed. She'd gotten herself into more than she'd intended. Why had she gotten involved?

She stood and held out her hand. Liliana turned for a moment and stared at the sea, where frantic movement was occurring as several men and women shoved lifeboats into the waves. It was best to get the child away from the search for her mother. "Come along, Abby. We need to get you cleaned up."

Abby slid the strap of her backpack onto her shoulder

and accepted Liliana's outstretched hand; then, together, they walked to the hale. Liliana's grandmother looked up when they entered.

"Well, who is this, Liliana?" Her grandmother smiled and held out a hand. "Hello there, Sweetheart. Have you come to visit Grammy?"

"I'm Abby. I came for a pineapple boat."

"Well, we shall have to see what we can do about that. I'm not sure what it is, but we will find out."

"Abby, let's get you cleaned up," Liliana said. As they walked past her grandmother, she whispered to her, "I'll explain in a minute."

Her green eyes alert and interested, Grammy nodded. Liliana led Abby to the bathroom. Only a bath could clean this little girl. She turned on the faucets and filled the tub with water. Fishing through her luggage, she found her bath salts and tipped a generous amount into the tub.

"Ooh, bubbles," Abby said. She shucked her bathing suit and scrambled into the water.

Liliana washed Abby's hair in shampoo, then scrubbed her with soap. Abby was reluctant to get out of the water, but Liliana coaxed her out with the reminder of the unknown treat, a pineapple boat. As she wrapped Abby in a large, soft towel, she wondered what she could put on her. The bathing suit was filthy.

"I got pink shorts in my Barney bag," Abby announced. "I like pink."

"Do you mind if I get them for you?" Liliana asked and

waited until Abby nodded her assent before unzipping the sand-coated backpack. A matching T-shirt and shorts set had been wadded into the bag, along with a pair of little girl's underpanties. All of the garments looked like thrift store rejects, but they were clean, albeit stained. The only other item in the bag was a pair of pink plastic sandals.

Abby dropped her towel and allowed Liliana to help her into her clothes.

Grabbing a comb, she smoothed Abby's black hair. "There, you look presentable. Let's get Grammy and go eat."

"Finally!" Abby said.

The three of them trooped over to the dining room. Liliana kept up a steady stream of conversation with the child. She didn't want her looking for her mother. The beach still bustled with searchers, and she felt a sinking feeling that Abby's mother had not yet been found. Maybe she'd drowned. She felt sick at the thought of the child losing her mother at such a young age. Though it didn't appear she had taken the best of care of Abby.

Only four tables were taken in the dining room since it was still early. Liliana led the way to a secluded table in the corner. The waiter brought them menus.

"How about some chicken fingers?" Liliana suggested.

"I want a pineapple boat."

Abby's lower lip trembled, and Liliana hastened to ward off any more tears. "Bring her a pineapple boat," she told the waiter.

His eyes widened. "Now?"

"Now," Liliana said firmly. If it had pineapple in it, it had to be healthy. She hoped. She ordered mahimahi with a baked sweet potato and a salad. Her grandmother ordered grilled swordfish.

The waiter arrived with a tray laden with a pineapple sliced lengthwise. The fruit of the pineapple had been scooped out, leaving a "boat." Filled with three kinds of ice cream and topped with the fruit from the pineapple and chocolate syrup, it looked scrumptious. And much too much for a small child.

Liliana bit her lip. If Abby didn't throw up tonight, it would be a miracle. The waiter set the concoction in front of Abby, and the little girl grabbed her spoon and began to eat it. With the child happily occupied, Liliana leaned over and explained what had happened on the beach in a voice too soft for Abby to hear. "And it didn't look like they were having much luck finding her," she finished.

"Tsk, tsk," her grandmother said with a shake of her head. "Poor child."

Liliana nodded, then her eyes widened as Barnabas entered the dining room. He paused and scanned the room. Lifting her hand to attract his attention, her heart pounded as he came toward them. She just hoped he'd found Abby's mother.

His gaze found hers and he gave a slight shake of his head. Liliana's mouth went dry. That poor child. Her mother must have drowned. Now what were they to do?

Chapter 3

Barnabas slid into the seat beside Liliana and tried not to stare. The perfectly coifed hair of earlier in the day now drooped dispiritedly around her tired face, and stains marred the mussed slacks she wore. But the biggest change was the way she catered to Abby. She seemed to genuinely care about the little girl. It was all Barnabas could do to hide his astonishment. Maybe there was more to the woman than he'd first assumed.

Liliana swept her hair out of her eyes with her hand, and he saw that one of her long acrylic nails was broken, and she didn't seem to care. She rose to her feet. "Grammy, would you take care of Abby for a minute? I need to talk to Mr. Harrigan." Her gaze met his, and he got up and followed her to a secluded alcove.

She barely waited until they were seated at the small table. "What will happen to Abby now that her mother is dead?" she asked.

"We don't know that she's dead," he said. "We haven't

found any sign of her. I'm still hoping she managed to swim to safety somewhere down the coast."

Looking through the window at the lapping waves and extended view of the ocean, Liliana shivered. "That seems impossible."

"It happens, though."

Liliana fell silent, her long fingers toying with the silverware on the table. "What are we going to do with Abby? Does she have any other family?"

Her question caught him off guard, and he became aware that he'd been watching the play of candlelight over her black hair. He mentally shook himself and dragged his attention away from the lovely woman in front of him.

"Not that I know of. Mary never mentioned Abby's father or any other relatives. I'm not even sure where she's from." He had to wonder where this conversation was going. Why would the selfish and self-centered Liliana Van Cleef care about what happened to a little girl she didn't know until a few hours ago?

She finally looked up, and he thought he saw a shimmer of tears in her eyes, but that had to be a trick of the candlelight. "I will keep her until her family is found."

He sighed. "She's not a doll to play with until you tire of her, Miss Van Cleef. She's a flesh-and-blood child with a world of hurt about to descend on her."

"You don't think much of me, do you, Mr. Harrigan? You think I have no thoughts in my head except for fashion and money." Liliana leaned toward him, her cheeks flushed with temper. "I understand more about pain than you'll ever know here in your little paradise." She jumped up and rushed away before he could answer.

Barnabas pressed his lips together. He'd been a jerk and owed her another apology. There had been real pain in her eyes, and he had to wonder what had put it there. Money didn't solve problems, though people often thought it did. He knew better, so why had he assumed she had everything she could want? He followed her back inside. Slowing his steps, he watched her as she reached the table where Abby and her grandmother waited. The child smiled at her with real warmth, and he felt another pang of guilt. He walked slowly toward the table.

Liliana tilted her chin up, but he saw through her obvious show of defiance to the hurt in her green eyes. "I'm taking Abby to our hale and putting her to bed."

"I didn't mention that the sofa makes into a bed," he said. "I appreciate the care you're giving her. I'm sorry I didn't say so before."

Her fierce frown sagged so quickly, he almost laughed. As surprise took the place of defiance, he grinned and held out a hand. "Can we call a truce?"

She slowly held out a slim hand. "I suppose I can forgive you this time. But you seem to make the same mistake a lot, Mr. Harrigan. Are you on the slow end of the learning curve?"

His grin widened. "I've been accused of that before, Miss Van Cleef. I'll try to be a quicker study." Quick and pert. He liked that in a woman.

She smiled, and Barnabas nearly gasped at the way her face was transformed. With her guard down, Liliana was warmth and sweetness. But the haunting loveliness of her expression was quickly covered with that mask of imperious boredom again, and he realized she wasn't about to share whatever warmth might lurk in the depths with him. He had to wonder who or what had caused her to construct that barrier.

Liliana almost skipped as she and her grandmother led Abby back to their hale. That was the first time she'd ever heard a man apologize. Mr. Barnabas Harrigan was quite a guy. She rummaged in her luggage for one of her own pink T-shirts for Abby to use as a sleep shirt, then she pulled the bed out of the couch. After she had Abby tucked in, Liliana followed her grandmother to her bedroom. Kicking off her shoes, she flopped down on the bed and rested the back of her head on her hands.

"I like that young man," her grandmother declared as she took her hairbrush and began to run it through her white hair. "He would make a good husband."

Liliana laughed. "I can see the wheels turning, Grammy, but don't go there. Barnabas Harrigan is not my type. He's much too religious, for one thing. And he can't seem to see past my money and my looks."

"You could do with getting to know God yourself, Darling." Her grandmother turned penetrating eyes on Liliana. "As I've gotten older, I've realized how different my life could have been if I'd given it to God when I was your age."

"What do you regret most about your life, Grammy?" Liliana wanted to get the topic on anything but religion. It left the door open to too much thinking. And she didn't want to face where her thoughts might lead her. This longing in her heart for a place of belonging seemed to deepen at any mention of God.

Her grandmother's hand paused in midair, then she resumed brushing. "Fighting with your mother, for one thing. I missed out on so many things."

"I really want to know what happened between the two of you. Mother won't tell me." Liliana sat up and leaned against the headboard of the bed.

"What do you regret, Liliana?" Her grandmother deftly turned the tables on her.

Maybe she should confess first and see if the fight between her mother and grandmother had anything to do with her discovery. But it was so hard to know how to bring the subject up. It would have to wait. She wasn't in the mood for a discussion like that. She sighed. "Regret? It's not in my vocabulary, Grammy. You can't change anything, so why let yourself think about what might have been?"

Her grandmother gave her a gentle smile. "Regret is how we face our mistakes and vow not to make them again. We give those regrets to God and trust Him to forgive them and wipe the guilt away."

God again. Everywhere she turned, someone brought Him up. She shifted restlessly and got up. She went to the mirror and picked up a hairbrush. Staring at her reflection, she wondered who that woman really was. Her green eyes were stormy and troubled, not the serene pools of love and compassion that characterized her grandmother's gaze. People had always remarked on her beauty. But it wasn't enough, not anymore. Her beauty would fade, then what would people notice about her?

Her grandmother's wrinkled hand touched her shoulder. "What's troubling you, Liliana? I've sensed the distress in your heart. Is there something I can help you with?"

Liliana sucked in her breath and turned to face her grandmother. "What did you argue with Mother about all those years ago, Grammy? I have to know."

Her grandmother's eyes clouded. "I promised your mother it could come from her. It's not my place to talk about it."

"Did—did it have anything to do with my birth, with who I am?" Liliana forced the words out before she lost her nerve. Her heart thrummed in her ears. She had to know the truth. Her mother was too unapproachable, and Liliana couldn't imagine actually asking her mother to tell her the true story.

The pink leached out of her grandmother's cheeks, and she gasped. "Your birth?" she faltered.

Liliana squeezed her eyes shut at the panicked knowledge in her grandmother's face. Pain crashed over her, and she fought to keep her composure. She couldn't cry, not now. "It's true, isn't it, Grammy? My parents aren't really my parents. That's why Mother is never satisfied with anything I do." She opened her eyes and stared at her grandmother.

"Oh, my dear." Her grandmother's voice quivered with pain. "Your mother loves you very much. She's just always had a hard time showing it."

"No, she looks at me and sees—" Liliana broke off. What

did her mother see when she looked at her? Whoever it was, it wasn't the daughter of her heart. Sometimes she glimpsed such rage in her mother's eyes, such loss and desolation. And then Liliana's own failure would sink in again, and she knew she could never be the daughter her mother expected.

"I found a letter," Liliana choked out. "It was from—from my real mother. Marian. Aunt Marian. No wonder Mother flew into a tantrum every time Aunt Marian came to visit. It was her jealousy."

Tears pooled in her grandmother's eyes. "I thought you should know all along, that Marian should have some part in your upbringing. That's what we fought about."

"I knew it," Liliana whispered. "And Dad? What part did he play in all this? But I thought he loved me." In spite of her resolve, her voice quavered again.

"Let's sit down," her grandmother said, rubbing her left arm. "My old bones can't take much more." She pulled Liliana down beside her on the bed.

Liliana's emotions felt as tight as her sunburned skin. Settling onto the bed, she pulled her legs under her. Her grandmother sat beside her and took her hand. "Your father always wanted a daughter. You were the joy of his life, Liliana. You have to believe that. When Marian came to him, he was the one who suggested they adopt you. Marian had planned to get an abortion, but Richard wouldn't hear of it. Marian had always listened to her older brother, and this was no exception. She gladly gave you to him. And the day you were born and the doctor placed you in his arms, he broke down and cried."

Tears welled in Liliana's eyes and rolled down her cheeks. Sobs burst from her throat, and her grandmother enfolded her in a lilac-scented embrace.

"There, there, Darling, it's all right. Just cry. I can tell these tears have been a long time coming." Her grandmother smoothed the hair away from Liliana's face.

"Why did Mother agree when she didn't want me? And she doesn't, Grammy. Sometimes I think she can't bear to look at me. She always tells me I look just like my father's side of the family, especially like you. I can't help that. And Aunt Marian acts like I have the plague. When she visits, she avoids me."

"I know, Liliana, I know. I think Marian is afraid to let herself love you for fear of how your mother will react. But God loves you, dear child. He would heal those hurts if you would let Him."

Liliana pulled away. The thought of God's love enticed her, but the remnants of pride were all she had left. "I'm sorry, Grammy. Let's talk about something else. I can't change who I am or the facts of my birth, not even to please my mother." She attempted a watery smile. "At least I know enough to quit trying to please her. It's an impossible task, and I know that now. Thanks for being honest with me."

Her grandmother patted her arm. "I'm praying for you, Liliana. God has called you as His own, and He will show Himself to be the loving Father you need."

Liliana gathered her composure. "We'll see."

Silence fell over the room for a long minute. Then a knock broke the stillness, and Liliana jumped. She got up and hurried to the door before the commotion could awaken Abby. She threw open the door, and the scent of frangipani drifted past the tall figure standing in the doorway.

"Sorry to disturb you," Barnabas said. "I thought you'd want to hear the news."

Liliana's heart jumped. "News? Did you find Mary's body?" she whispered.

He gave a heavy sigh. "It might have been better if that were the case," he said grimly. "I got a call from her. She's abandoning Abby. She called from the airport in Honolulu and was getting ready to board a flight for California."

It took a few moments for the news to soak in. Abandoned. Abby was abandoned, just as Liliana had been abandoned by her real mother. She glanced back at the sleeping child, and a fierce wave of protective instinct welled up in her. "What will happen to Abby?"

"Mary gave me her mother's phone number over on the island of Kauai, and I called her. The grandmother will come for her, but she said it would be Monday before she could get here to pick her up. I assured her Abby was in good hands with you. She seemed angry at the thought that she might be stuck with Abby. I suppose we should talk about this. Could you step outside with me? I don't want Abby to overhear." Barnabas took her arm and pulled her out into the fragrant night air.

She allowed him to propel her toward the beach. In spite of being at odds with this man, she didn't try to deny the attraction she felt for him. Strong, dependable, caring enough to want to rescue a small girl, he drew her in ways she couldn't explain. More handsome and rich men had sought her out, but Barnabas's square-jawed face, softened by one dimple in his left cheek, made her wonder what she'd ever seen in the others. He had substance, she thought. That was the word. Substance and integrity.

They reached the beach, and Barnabas released her arm. The night air quickly erased the warmth left by his fingers. She focused on the problem at hand. Tomorrow Abby would have to face the news that her mother didn't want her. Impetuous words rose in her throat. "I'll keep her," she blurted. Her offer surprised her as much as it did Barnabas.

"You?" His voice rose incredulously.

She smiled. "I admit I'm as surprised as you are. But I can't let her go to strangers."

"*You* are a stranger," Barnabas pointed out. He glanced at his watch. "You've known her about six hours. Besides, what will you do with a child?"

"You've already pointed out she's not a doll," Liliana said. "It's true I know nothing about children, but I'm willing to learn."

"Why?"

Why indeed. Liliana didn't know herself. She just knew her heart rebelled at the thought of that little girl facing such heartbreak alone. But what did this man know of heartbreak? He lived in paradise with his brothers. She scowled at him. "What business is it of yours anyway?"

"I had hopes of adopting her myself," he said.

"You? They won't let a single man take a little girl."

"Her grandmother didn't seem too happy at the thought of

taking her. I can offer her a good home. My brothers would dote on her as well." He ran a hand through his sun-streaked hair. "At least she knows me."

"She knows me too. In case you didn't notice, she is beginning to trust me." She glared at him, and he glared back. Her earlier attraction to Barnabas evaporated in the adrenaline rush she felt as she realized she would have to do battle with him.

And she shuddered to think of what her mother would say. But that didn't matter, she realized with surprise. Her grandmother's confirmation of all her suspicions had washed away the obsession to win her mother's approval. But saving Abby was something she *could* do. She squared her shoulders. Not even Barnabas was going to stop her.

"Look, we both know your chances of keeping her with you are slim to none. It would be better for Abby if we weren't squabbling over her like a leftover piece of luau pork."

"You don't have the right values for a child," he said softly. "I'm not saying you're not a good person, but Abby needs to be raised by a Christian."

"If her mother is a Christian, I don't want to be." Liliana clenched her fists and glared at him. "She abandoned her child beside the ocean, Mr. Harrigan. Abby could have drowned."

"No, Mary isn't a Christian," Barnabas admitted. "But that doesn't mean we shouldn't strive for the best for Abby."

"At least I'm better than what she had," she retorted. She turned on her heel and stalked back to her hale. "I think even you would agree to that." She slammed the door behind her, and the bang it gave filled her with intense satisfaction. But as she got ready for bed and fumed at his arrogance, she had to wonder if he was right. He would certainly make a wonderful father. Stable, kind, caring. An inner voice told her he would make a husband right out of her dreams as well, but she pushed that thought away. Love didn't last. She'd learned that lesson from her mother's knee. She vowed to do better with Abby.

Chapter 4

Barnabas couldn't remember when he'd had such anticipation upon waking. His goals had been to make Harrigan's Cove the best resort in the islands, but those goals seemed cold and lifeless to him now at the thought that he might have a daughter to raise. His brothers would dote on her as well, and he vowed to bring a smile to that little face. But first he had to get past Liliana. She was right about one thing. Abby's grandmother would be more apt to allow a woman to raise her granddaughter than to give her to a houseful of men living in the hustle and bustle of a resort. But the advantage he had was that at least she would be living on one of the islands. Liliana would take her back to the mainland.

At the thought of Liliana, he couldn't help imagining the tender expression on her face as she tended to Abby. There was more to that beautiful exterior than he'd imagined. If she ever turned that gaze on a man, he'd be a goner. It wouldn't be him, certainly. She'd eat him for breakfast and toss the bones to the sharks. Yet maybe he was all wrong about her. She seemed to have lost all signs of the haughty princess he'd first met. His brother Alex caught him staring at her a time or two and teased him that he was becoming obsessed. His brother was wrong. She intrigued him, nothing more, he told himself. But he wasn't sure if he truly believed it.

The sun and water sparkled like liquid sapphires, and he wished he could get this matter of Abby's custody settled. But he had to cool his heels until Monday. And he hated his day off. He'd much rather be tending to hotel business, but their father had always insisted on taking at least one day off, preferably two. He and his brothers rotated their days, and he had tried to switch with all three of his brothers, but to a man, they had insisted that he take the day and try to relax. *Relax.* Barnabas wasn't sure he knew the meaning of the word.

He could grab his sea kayak and hit the waves, but it didn't sound appealing to do it alone. He could go to a luau, but he hated crowds who pursued a good time with such frenzy. Maybe a luncheon cruise on the resort catamaran. That would be almost like working. He could mingle with the guests and go snorkeling with them. Heartened, he hurried toward the pier.

The wind blew the salt air in his face and took his rattled thoughts with it. It was too beautiful a day to brood about his lovely guest. Not a cloud marred the blue canopy overhead, and the air was fragrant with flowers.

He took the skiff out to the catamaran and boarded the boat. The deck already teemed with tourists chattering excitedly as they milled around the rail and pointed out the bright glimmer of tropical fish darting through the azure water. Barnabas loved living in paradise; he loved the happy tourists, the thrill of sharing his beautiful island with guests.

Growing up with three brothers, his life had been full of the camaraderie of men, but there was a softness he some-times missed when he thought of the way things had been be-fore his mother died. What did God have in store for him? Was a wife and children a part of that plan? Barnabas hoped so, though he didn't know where he would find her. Most of the women he came in contact with passed through here too quickly for any kind of a relationship to develop.

"Slumming today?"

He turned at the sound of a woman's voice. Dressed in a red flowered skort with matching top, Liliana's olive skin glowed with health and sunshine without the artifice of makeup, and her black hair was caught back in a ponytail.

He smiled. "Even I get a day off once in awhile."

"The steady, dedicated resort owner actually knows how to let go and have a good time? I suppose you're an expert at swim-ming and snorkeling?"

"I taught Johnny Weismuller how to swing from the trees into the water when he played Tarzan." The thrill of delight at her appearance startled him. He resolved to be more on his guard. She was a barracuda, and he was a minnow when it came to swimming with the likes of Liliana.

"You weren't even born when he was yodeling and swim-ming in Africa." She laughed and linked an arm through his. "Since we've declared a truce, I'm taking it one step further and hereby claiming your company for the day. Grammy kicked me out of the hale and said she was keeping Abby with her and for me to get out and see something of Maui." Shrugging her elegant shoulders, she wrinkled her nose. "I suppose she's right. It would be a shame to spend this much money on a vacation getaway and spend the whole time inside."

"Today's much too beautiful to spend indoors."

"Every day in paradise is beautiful," she said. "So what are we going to do today?"

The thought of spending the whole day in her company made him feel like a starving man being given the ticket to a presidential banquet. *Better watch yourself, Buddy. You're in danger of losing your heart.* The thought sent a shot of adrenaline through his system. She was not the kind of woman he had any business caring about. Her money and connections made her way out of his league, but even more importantly, she wasn't a Christian. He'd better make sure they spent the day with other people. He didn't want her to get the wrong idea.

"The boat goes out to the island of Lanai, where the snorkeling is fabulous, and the beach is like powdered sugar." He grinned. "And how about a helicopter tour after lunch? That's the best way to see the island's beauty."

Her face paled. "I'm not so sure about the helicopter."

He grinned. "Scared, Miss Van Cleef?"

She tossed her head, and her ponytail bobbed. "Of course not. And don't you think it's time you called me Liliana?"

"Only if you promise not to call me Barney."

She chuckled, and her dimples came and went. "Just don't call me Lily. I hate that."

"It's a deal." He tucked her hand more securely in the crook of his arm and guided her toward the changing rooms. "Let's get changed. We're almost to the island."

While the boat sped toward Lanai, they changed into their swimsuits, and he showed her how to use the snorkel. The boat dropped anchor, and even Barnabas had to admit he'd never seen the island look more enticing. The water sparkled with a deep aqua color and fish swam in bright darts of yellow, blue, and green. But he found Liliana's face much more appealing than the water.

Following her into the warm water, they spent the morning pointing out fish. She prodded a puffer fish and nearly choked with laughter as the fish swelled like a balloon. Barnabas couldn't remember when he'd laughed so much.

When they left the island, they both leaned against the railing and stared at the sea. Liliana's hair hung in wet ropes down her back, but the hot sun and wind were quickly drying it. Barnabas wondered what it would feel like. It hung almost to her waist, and he'd never seen such glorious hair.

Her red-lacquered nails gripped his arm. "Look," she whispered.

He turned to look where she was pointing. "Whales," he said.

A pod of whales was just off the starboard side. They seemed almost close enough to touch. Liliana's fingers dug into his arm with excitement. Then, one of the whales blew water through its blowhole, and she squealed with delight.

"Oh, look," she breathed. "I've always wanted to see that."

He was more interested in staring at her than at the whales.

She'd lost all traces of the imperious Miss Van Cleef. Her bright smile and green eyes shone with enthusiasm and joy. Barnabas thought he could go on staring at her forever.

She glanced up at him, and her smile faded as she stared into his eyes. Unable to help himself, he touched her cheek. He had never wanted to kiss someone so badly in his life, but with a mighty effort, he restrained the impulse by reminding himself that she wasn't a Christian.

Another tourist came up beside them and called to the others to come watch the whales, and the magical moment was broken. Barnabas felt almost glad. His resistance might not have held out much longer. The Bible says to flee temptation, and he had every intention of doing just that.

After lunch, the catamaran went back to the resort and anchored offshore. They caught the skiff back to shore. "I've got my car. You ready for that helicopter ride?"

Her eyes widened, and she paled beneath her tan. "Maybe I should check on Grammy and Abby."

"Coward," he told her. She looked as though he had slapped her, and he had to fight to hide his grin.

"No one calls me that and lives to tell about it. Lead on, Bwana. I'm game if you are. I do get a parachute, don't I?" She gave a sparkling laugh that lifted his spirits as high as the parasail over their heads.

He pointed it out. "That's our next excursion."

He chuckled when she paled again, then he tucked her hand into the crook of his arm. "You'll enjoy it, I promise." He drove to the helicopter pad and paid the pilot. "We want the full enchilada," he said. "The falls and the interior, all the beauty you can throw at us before sunset."

The pilot grinned. "Think you can take your eyes off the beauty beside you long enough to enjoy it?" he asked too softly for Liliana to hear.

Barnabas felt the heat on his face, and he turned quickly away. Good question. He was way too drawn to Liliana. He had to keep in mind that she wasn't a Christian. He hurried over to where she waited and helped her into the helicopter. She looked almost green, but the only way over her fear was to just get in the air and face it.

When the rotors began to whirl, she looked as though she might be sick. Sitting rigidly by his side, she didn't move for the first five minutes. Then, gradually, the color returned to her face, and she began to lean over to the window and look out. While Liliana exclaimed over the beauty of the world below her, Barnabas watched her rather than the terrain.

The helicopter landed in Haleakala National Park near the volcano's crater. The other-worldly feel to it was perfect at sunset and sunrise. As they watched the sun sink below the crater, he felt a pang of regret at the glorious array of crimson and gold. Their day was over, and Monday they might very well have to do battle for Abby.

"I'm almost afraid to breathe," Liliana whispered as she watched the glowing sunset.

"I'll bring you back sometime for the sunrise," he told her. He wanted to offer to do it tomorrow, but he bit back the words. Tomorrow they would be at war again.

They walked in silence back to the helicopter, and Liliana was strangely silent on the flight back to Harrigan's Cove.

The helicopter landed, and he helped her out. "Hey, we should stop and get some clothes for Abby," he said. They stopped at a children's store on the resort complex and purchased several new outfits, as well as underclothing, pajamas, and shoes for the little girl.

Escorting Liliana back to her hale at the end of the day, he couldn't remember when he'd enjoyed a day more. There was something to be said for enjoying the company of a beautiful woman who hung on every word he said.

Every light in the hale was on as they mounted the steps to the front deck. Liliana frowned. "I wonder what's going on. Grammy is such a fanatic about turning off lights that aren't used. I hope Abby hasn't gotten sick." She opened the door.

The sitting room was full of people. Barnabas spotted the resort doctor, one of the women who cared for children, and a waiter who had taken a shine to Phoebe. Phoebe herself reclined on pillows on the couch, her face the color of milk.

Liliana blanched and rushed inside. "Grammy, what is it—what's happened?"

"Nothing serious, Miss Van Cleef." Dr. Parkins put his stethoscope away and straightened up. "Your grandmother just wanted to shake us all up tonight."

"Just a bout of angina, my dear," her grandmother reassured her. "That happens now and again. I made the mistake of forgetting my nitroglycerin at home, and the good doctor was kind enough to bring some for me."

Liliana chewed on her lip. "I should have been here."

"I'm fine, really. And don't think you can hover now. I hate being watched for every twinge. Why don't you check on Abby and make sure the commotion didn't wake her."

Doubt filled Liliana's face, and Barnabas took her arm. "Come on, I'll go with you. The doctor can finish checking out your grandmother without all of us in the way." He didn't think it was serious, but he could tell Phoebe wanted some privacy.

Liliana hung back a bit but didn't take too much persuasion to allow him to lead her to the bedroom. He pushed open the door, and they found Abby still sound asleep, one arm flung above her head. She'd kicked the covers off, and Barnabas tucked them back around her. "What's she doing sleeping in here? Where are you sleeping?"

Liliana blushed. "On the sofa bed. I thought she would settle in better if she had her own space."

Shocked, Barnabas stared at her. Where had the selfish woman gone who had waltzed through the doors that first day? Had she been a figment of his imagination? "You're sleeping on the sofa bed," he said slowly.

She nodded. "I don't mind. It's not too uncomfortable."

"They don't know how to make them comfortable," he said. "You're a remarkable woman, Liliana. I'm sorry I misjudged you."

Scarlet flooded her cheeks, and she turned away. "I'd better check on Grammy."

Liliana watched her grandmother with anxious eyes. She

couldn't lose her now that she had found her again after all these years.

"Quit staring at me," her grandmother said. "I'm not about to evaporate and blow away. The doctor said I'm perfectly fine. There's nothing to be frightened of, Liliana."

"I'm not frightened," Liliana said in spite of the terror that still gripped her.

"Liar." Her grandmother's smile took the sting out of the word. "Death is nothing to be frightened of, Darling. Some day we all face it. When that day happens, remember I'll be in a wonderful place full of joy and light and love. I look forward to the day when I see Jesus face to face and can see all my loved ones again."

"How can you be so sure, Grammy?" Her grandmother's assurance nettled Liliana. How could Grammy discuss her own death so calmly? The thought of facing that unknown terrified Liliana. It was all very well to talk of heaven, but the reality was that no one knew what lay beyond the veil of death. When they'd gone up into the helicopter today, she'd imagined the rotors spinning out of control and plunging them into the canopies of trees far below.

" 'I know whom I have believed and am persuaded that he is able to keep that which I've committed unto him against that day.' " Her grandmother sang the words to the old hymn softly.

The tune strummed the chords of something in Liliana's heart, something that made her want to weep. "I wish I could be that sure," she said wistfully.

"You can be, Darling," her grandmother said. "All you have

to do is trust Jesus."

"What does that mean?" Liliana hated all the Christianese. She didn't understand it.

"Trusting Him is believing He is who He said He was— the only Son of God and God in the flesh. Believe that He died for all your sins and that Jesus is the only way to God."

As her grandmother talked of God's love and how she could have her sins gone and forgotten, something opened in Liliana's heart. Something beautiful and wondrous. She wanted what her grandmother had, what Barnabas had. This was the rest she had been searching for. When her grand- mother asked her if she would like to know for certain she was going to heaven, she bowed her head and took Jesus as her own Savior. They talked long into the night, and Liliana knew she would never be the same, that she had to do something to show her gratitude and love to the One who had given her such joy and peace.

She rose the next morning with a new resolve to show the difference she felt inside. "Can we go to church somewhere?" she asked her grandmother. "Do you feel up to it?"

"Certainly. You get Abby ready while I shower. I feel much better today."

The church down the street was like no church Liliana had been in, although her experiences had been limited to Easter and Christmas. The windows were all open to the sea breezes, and everyone was dressed in casual clothes. She scanned the crowd, and her heart jumped to her throat when she saw Barnabas's familiar curly head. The three men beside him had to be his brothers. They all had that Harrigan dimple. She'd already met Alex, and the four brothers sat shoulder to shoulder in the third pew on the right.

He hadn't spotted her, and Liliana wanted to flee. She hadn't realized how hard it would be to face people who knew the old Liliana. She swallowed hard and led the way to a pew in the back. Maybe they could slip out at the end before Barnabas saw them.

But Abby saw Barnabas and gave a joyous shout. "Barney!"

Several heads turned their direction, and Liliana saw a couple of people snicker. Barnabas turned around with a scowl that lightened to incredulity when his blue eyes fastened on her face. He said something to Alex, who was sitting beside him, then stood and hurried back to them. Abby ran to meet him and clung to his legs. He swung her up into his arms, then carried her toward Liliana.

"Are you the one doing the slumming today, Liliana?"

"No, I—I just wanted to come to church," she stammered. "I didn't know you were here." Was that really what he thought? That she thought herself above church and Christians? Her face burned. She hadn't made her contempt of his faith a secret. Maybe he thought she was chasing him. Then he smiled, and she saw that he was genuinely glad she was there. His smile and the admiration in his eyes made the rush to get ready worth it.

"I'm glad you came," he said softly. "There's room in our pew if you'd like to join us."

"No—no thanks," she said. "I'd rather sit near the back."

His smile faltered, but he nodded. "I'll take Abby to her class, and I'll see you later then," he said. He turned and made his way through the throng and out the hall door, presumably where Abby's class was located. After a few minutes, he reappeared. He smiled at her, then slid into the seat with his brothers.

Liliana drank in the sermon, but she couldn't get Barnabas out of her thoughts as the service drew to a close. She watched the back of his head and castigated herself for her obsession. She should never have gone with him yesterday. He was gaining a foothold in her heart, and she had been hurt enough.

As the offering plate came around, the pastor announced a churchwide effort to help a local homeless shelter. She dug into her wallet for a generous donation, but it didn't seem enough. Merely dropping money into the plate left her feeling vaguely dissatisfied. When the pastor mentioned there was a need for workers, a germ of an idea took root. She wasn't much of a cook, but she could serve the food. She explained her plan to her grandmother, then hurried away before she could make an excuse to see Barnabas. She made sure Grammy was comfortably ensconced in the hale. Then she and Abby changed into jeans and T-shirts and caught a cab to the shelter.

Men and women dressed in dirty clothes with matted hair and a body odor that would make a miner cry milled around the door to the shelter. Liliana gulped and gathered her courage. She'd never been around this class of people before. But pity mingled with love as she saw the hopelessness on their faces.

She made her way inside, but it was a laborious process as so many stopped them to pat Abby on the head or touch her soft cheek with grimy fingers. She checked in with a man behind the counter who told her what to do. She set Abby on a chair behind her to watch while she ladled food onto Styrofoam plates.

"Liliana, what are you doing here?"

She jerked at the sound of Barnabas's voice and slopped a ladle of potatoes onto the tile. "Now see what you've done!" she wailed. She grabbed a paper napkin and scooped up most of it, then deposited it in the trash can behind her.

"You shouldn't be here, especially with Abby," he scolded.

"The people love her," she said, nodding toward Abby, who sat like an enthroned queen with her subjects as various men and women gathered around her. "No one will hurt us."

"You don't know that."

She grinned. "Where's that faith you're always talking about, Barnabas? God expects us to make a difference in our world, or have you forgotten this morning's sermon already?"

His jaw dropped open, and she had to cover her mouth to keep from giggling like a fifteen year old. "You look different," he said. "Happier. I take it your grandmother is doing better this morning?"

"Yes," she said. She wasn't ready to share the news of her new life, so she turned back to her work. "Are you going to just stand there, or are you going to help me? Hand me some plates."

A dazed look came over his face, and he grabbed a stack of plates and began to help her. "The sooner I get you out of here, the better," he muttered. "You confuse me."

Better him than her, she thought. So she'd better keep it that way.

Chapter 5

Today was the day. Dread slowed Liliana's movements as she dressed for the coming interview with Abby's grandmother. Thinking an older woman might be old-fashioned, she dressed carefully in a dress that swirled around her ankles. A delicious silk in a flowered red print, the dress made her olive skin and dark hair glow with health.

Her grandmother had suggested she begin to read her Bible in John, so she read the first chapter before slipping into the bedroom to rouse Abby. "Let's go get some breakfast before your grandma gets here," she told Abby.

Abby stuck out her lower lip. "I don't want to go to Grandma's. I want to stay here."

Liliana knelt and took the little girl in her arms. "I know, Sweetie. But I'm sure your grandma is eager to see you." She didn't want to get Abby's hopes up by telling her she was going to try to keep her.

Grammy was dressed and ready when Liliana got Abby dressed and they came into the sitting room. "I'm actually hungry today," her grandmother told her.

"That's an improvement. You pick at your food like a prisoner on a hunger strike. We need to fatten you up."

"You look nice today, Liliana." Her grandmother's approval shone out of her eyes. "What time is Abby's grandmother coming?"

"About ten. We still have a couple of hours."

When they arrived at Hale Moana for breakfast, she couldn't help the way her heart began to thump against her ribs in a tattoo of anticipation. Barnabas would surely be on duty. Liliana didn't understand why she was so attracted to the man. Saturday he'd seemed so different. His formal, businesslike manner fell away like a discarded cocoon, and a fascinating man had emerged. One who laughed at every one of her feeble jokes and hadn't minded her scream when a fish touched her.

He made her feel things she'd never thought she would. She remembered her earlier desire to make Barnabas care about her, then reject him, and shame welled in her. If only she hadn't said anything to anyone else about that stupid plan. Clarissa would be sure to ask her how the scheme was going. Liliana sighed. She would just avoid the woman.

Barnabas was behind the reception desk and hadn't seen her yet. She drank in the sight of him. Saturday's fun had streaked his hair with more gold lights, but the polite, business expression had taken control of his face again. He looked up and saw her then, and that business exterior fell away with his smile.

She felt the heat of a blush on her cheeks and gave him a

little wave. Maybe their truce wasn't over yet. But once Abby's grandmother arrived, they would be at loggerheads again. The thought pained her.

Barnabas turned and spoke to the woman behind him, then stepped from behind the desk and came toward them. "I've been watching for you. I have a table reserved for us for breakfast." He kissed Liliana's grandmother on the cheek. "You're looking much better today."

"I feel wonderful," she declared. "And I could eat a horse this morning."

His warm fingers gripped Liliana's elbow as he escorted them to their table. "I've got some fresh pineapple that will make you smile," he said. "And eggs and bacon, of course. Will that suffice?"

"A pineapple boat?" Abby asked.

"Not for breakfast, little one," Barnabas told her. He laid his big hand on her head, and Liliana was touched by his gentleness.

"This afternoon?" Abby persisted.

Barnabas looked at Liliana, and she read the question in his eyes. "You'll be with your grandma, Abby," she told the child.

Barnabas gave a slight nod of approval. He had agreed with Liliana that Abby didn't need to be told of their plans until they saw what her grandmother had to say.

They sat at the secluded table on the patio overlooking the water. The sea breeze wafted over them. Another day in paradise. Liliana was beginning to find that she didn't want to leave this island. Ever. But that wasn't possible. She had a life, friends, and family waiting for her back in Arizona.

"May I take your order?"

Liliana looked up into the face of a good-looking young man with a distracted air. He pushed his glasses up on his nose and stared through them with a worried look.

"What's the matter, Steve, you run out of beans to count?" Barnabas asked with a grin.

"Rory called in sick this morning, and I wasn't too busy this morning so I volunteered to fill in," Steve said. "I never thought I'd see the day you left your post to eat a mere meal." The words were almost a reproach.

Barnabas chuckled. "Liliana, this is my brother Steve. He's the controller here and main bean counter." He introduced everyone at the table, and Steve shook their hands, then took their orders and disappeared into the kitchen.

Barnabas's other brothers, Connor, who was the head of resort maintenance, and Alex, the activity director, drifted by to make over Abby and get to know Liliana and Phoebe. Barnabas's dad even stopped by. He brought Abby a book of paper dolls and seemed delighted with her hug of thanks.

"You have a nice family." Liliana couldn't keep the trace of wistfulness from her voice. She'd always longed for the camaraderie of a sibling. Did she have the right to deprive Abby of growing up surrounded by doting uncles? But surely a little girl needed a mommy, someone who would comb her hair and teach her about clothes and makeup and boys. She had to cling to that or she would give up.

"We've always been close," Barnabas said. "Mom died when I was twelve, and we've missed her, but Pop always made sure we didn't lack for attention. I think we've all turned out pretty well."

"I'm an only child," Liliana said.

Barnabas must have caught the regret in her voice, for he reached over and squeezed her hand. "My brothers would be glad to tease you until you howl. They're good at it."

She laughed. "No, thank you. I think I'm beyond howling with frustration. Though we might find out in about half an hour." Her stomach filled with butterflies at the admiration on Barnabas's face.

His face sobered. "Actually, I think she's early. I'll bet that's her right there." He motioned to Alex, who came over immediately.

Barnabas whispered to him, and Alex scooped Abby up and tossed her in the air. "Let's you and me go play, okay, Munchkin? Wait until you see the kiddy yard." He winked at Liliana, then carried a giggling Abby off.

"I think I'll go back to the room and rest. I'll be praying." Her grandmother stood and hurried away.

The woman Barnabas had pointed out stood in the restaurant, her gaze raking the tables. Of Hawaiian descent, her dark hair was peppered with gray, and she wore a shapeless gray sweater over an equally shapeless gray skirt. Black loafers encased her feet, and she looked totally stolid and without a hint of humor.

Liliana's heart sank. Her gaze met Barnabas's, and she saw the same dismay mirrored in his eyes. Barnabas rose and waved his hand. The woman saw them. Her mouth in a humorless line, she walked briskly toward them.

She wasted no time on preliminaries. "Where's my grand-daughter?" She folded her arms over her ample stomach and stared at them.

"We thought we might talk a bit before you see her," Barnabas said.

"What's to talk about? I knew Mary would do this sooner or later. Shiftless, that's what she is. I never could handle her."

"Please, sit down, Mrs. Uma," Liliana said softly. "We have something we'd like to talk to you about. I'm sorry, but I didn't catch your first name."

With a muttered oath, the woman settled into the chair beside Liliana. "I don't got much time. Gotta get home. Some of the girls are coming over to play cards tonight." She scrabbled in her purse and drew out a cigarette. "Mrs. Uma is fine. We aren't likely to be friends." Lighting her cigarette, she blew smoke in Liliana's face

Liliana waved it away and leaned forward. "I would like to raise Abby," she said quickly.

"So would I," Barnabas put in. "I know it would be hard for you to take over the care of such a young child. Both of us love Abby."

A calculating look crept into the woman's eyes. "I didn't know you was married. That would probably be best for the kid to have two parents. How much you willing to pay me?"

"Pay you?" Barnabas sputtered.

"How much do you want?" Liliana put in quickly. She ignored Barnabas's scowl. Money was something that meant little to her. It had bought everything she wanted in life, so this would be no different.

"Looks like a nice setup you've got here," the woman said, her voice dripping with avarice. "You two can't have your own kids?"

"We're not married," Barnabas said. "Look, Mrs. Uma, we're talking about Abby's future. It doesn't all hinge on money."

"These young people are smarter than they were in my day. Marriage doesn't work, and I should know. I've been married five times. Now I just love 'em and leave 'em." She gave a hoarse laugh, the years of smoking obvious with the harsh sound. "Still, you look like a nice couple. Abby could do worse. At least one of you will probably stick around to see her grown."

Liliana felt more adamant than ever. She had to get Abby away from this woman, from a woman who would put a price on her own granddaughter's head. She whipped out her checkbook, letting her large emerald ring flash in the sunlight. "I'm willing to pay for the privilege of raising Abby. How much?" She intended to win this battle, then she would worry about soothing Barnabas. Her action had the desired effect, as the grandmother smiled with an avarice that made Liliana shudder.

"Ten thousand dollars," Mrs. Uma announced. "I have to know she's going to a good home, you understand."

"Ten thousand dollars!" Barnabas jumped to his feet. "That's crazy! I should report you to the authorities. We don't want to buy Abby, Mrs. Uma. We want her to have security, a place where she knows she's loved."

"Fine, just fetch my granddaughter, and we'll be on our way." The woman's chin jutted out, and she glared at him.

He sank back in his chair. "You can't sell a child."

He was right, but Liliana pushed away the stab of guilt. She remembered Abby's reaction at the thought of going with her grandmother. That hadn't been pique, that had been fear, and now Liliana understood why. The smell of alcohol, even at ten in the morning, assailed her senses, and she knew she couldn't sit by while another child, just like her, grew up unwanted by her family.

She held out the check to Abby's grandmother. "There you go. I had my lawyer draw up and fax a temporary custody agreement, which I'd like you to sign." She pushed a sheaf of papers toward the woman. "I'd like to adopt Abby if we can get your daughter to sign the papers. If she calls, would you ask her to call my attorney? Here's his number." She handed a business card to Mrs. Uma.

"Is there any money in it for her?" The woman's tone was sharp with interest.

"I'm sure we can come to some kind of arrangement," Liliana said. She had a sinking feeling this would not be the last of it, but what else could she do? Abby's welfare was more important than money.

The woman carefully tucked the check in her purse and stood. "I'll just get out of your way now."

"Don't you even want to see Abby?" Barnabas asked.

"No sense in upsetting the child and making her cry to go with me," Mrs. Uma said. She turned and scurried away like some giant crab carrying off its next meal.

Liliana felt like she needed to take another shower. She'd

been in the gutter with that woman, but at least Abby was safe. For now.

"That was a mistake. You'll never get rid of the woman. She will be around with her hand out forever." Barnabas scowled and slumped back in his chair.

"I realize that," Liliana said. Weariness pressed her shoulders down, and she fought the tears prickling at the backs of her eyes. Would anyone ever care about more than her money? Money seemed to be all anyone ever thought of. Except for Barnabas. She glanced at him from the corner of her eye. Had he merely been polite over the weekend, or was there any chance of a relationship developing with him?

"You didn't give me a chance to state my case." His mouth was tight with no evidence of the dimple that so charmed her.

"Do you really think she was going to listen? You made it clear you had no intention of paying her. I didn't have any such hesitation. There was no way I was going to allow her to raise Abby. Can you imagine letting that sweet little girl go into that kind of environment?"

"Your money can't buy everything, Liliana. You should have trusted God to take care of this and not depended on your money to bail you out. I can give her a stable home here with a doting grandfather. Are you going to stick in one place and be a real mother or continue flying from place to place and running out to parties?"

Was that still how he saw her? She had changed, and she thought he would notice. Still, he had a point. She was too new at this trusting God way of life. She hadn't even thought to ask God what to do. The deed was done, though, and there was no going back now.

She should try to explain it to him, but she was too tired to try. Yes, money and position had been her life, but she wanted something more, something she thought was in her grasp. She would have to prove to him that she wasn't that society woman he first met. Abby would be safe in her care, in spite of what Barnabas thought.

She stared at him. "You don't really know me, do you, Barnabas? I thought there was real friendship developing between us, but if you think I would make such a poor mother, it's obvious I was mistaken."

He flushed, and pain flashed briefly in his eyes before he quickly masked it. "I'm sorry, I didn't mean that," he said quietly. "You will make a fine mother for Abby. But I would have made a good father." He turned to go. "She needs Jesus in her life."

Liliana wanted to tell him that she would teach Abby about her faith, but her tongue wouldn't work. And her own faith was still so new, she realized he would have a much broader base of knowledge to pass onto Abby. Until last week, Liliana hadn't even known what Christianity was all about, so what made her think she could teach Abby? She squared her shoulders. She would have to learn.

Liliana wanted to stop him. "Wait," she said.

He turned and looked at her. The words that clamored just behind her teeth shocked her. She wanted to tell him he could be Abby's father, that they could marry and raise her together. Marry. Where had that thought come from? There had been no words of love spoken, nothing more than the admiration that shone in his blue eyes, nothing more than the way her heart sang when he walked into a room or touched her hand. If this was love, it was all new to her.

Her throat felt thick, and she wanted to get away to examine this new feeling that swept over her. "I—I'm sorry, Barnabas. You can see Abby whenever you want."

His mouth twisted. "That's not quite the same thing, Liliana."

He swallowed hard, and she saw the emotion that he tried to hide. She didn't know what to say, how to fix it. They couldn't both win. Now that she knew what he really thought of her, she would have to make sure he didn't know how she felt. Once she figured out for herself just what that was. If this was love, why did it have to hurt so much?

Chapter 6

Aman kept his emotions under control at all times. At least that's what Barnabas had always believed. But now his own emotions raged in his heart like a whirlpool of feelings. Hurt, anger, pain, and love. Yes, love. He faced it for what it was. It wasn't curiosity or pity or any other emotion. He'd lost his heart to Liliana Van Cleef, a woman who had no more use for it than she would have for his brother Connor's work belt.

He kept his distance the next week, watching as she played in the golden sand with Abby and came back from shopping excursions laden with pretty new clothes for the little girl. Motherhood seemed to agree with Liliana. She positively glowed when she sashayed through the lobby on her way to the restaurant. It made him question his own judgment that he hadn't seen this side to her when she first checked in. Her inner beauty really did match that ravishingly beautiful exterior.

Several times she acted as though she would approach him, but he quickly turned away. He wasn't ready to forgive her yet.

His heart wasn't some bauble like that emerald she flashed around. Bruised and sore, he threw himself into his work even more, until Alex accused him of turning into a robot that worked all the time and never had time for the rest of the family.

On his day off, he decided to hit the beach at a secluded lagoon he knew. Solitude sounded good after the rat race he'd been trekking the past week. He would just take his Bible and his snorkel and try to get some perspective on his life. Maybe a family wasn't what God had in mind for him. He had to cling to the fact that God knew what was best in this situation, no matter how much it hurt.

The lagoon was empty. A gentle breeze blew across the golden sand. It carried the scent of salt and fresh air, mingled with the sweet scent of hibiscus and orchids that bloomed along the hillside. He spread out his beach towel and dropped his belongings onto it, then kicked off his sandals and ran into the water with his snorkel. The warm waves lapped at his legs, and he plunged headfirst into the blue water.

He swam and snorkeled for awhile, then turned and swam back to the beach. Shaking the water from his hair, he blinked the blurriness from his eyes. A figure rose from a towel laid alongside of his. Liliana stood waiting for him. A red and white beach cover-up skimmed her slim figure. *She should always wear red,* he thought. Her white teeth kneaded at her bottom lip, and he guessed she had reason to be apprehensive since he'd effectively ignored her for a week.

"Alex said I'd find you here," she said. Her slim fingers plucked at the fringe on her cover-up.

He grabbed a small towel from his knapsack and dried his hair. "I come here a lot when I want to be alone."

"And I showed up to annoy you."

"You're not annoying me." She would laugh at him if she knew how her presence made his heart race. She was probably used to lovesick men, but for Barnabas the feeling was entirely new and unsettling. "Have a seat."

She settled herself on her towel and drew her legs to her chest. She'd braided her long dark hair, and the thick plait hung down over one shoulder like a loving caress. "You've been avoiding me. I wanted to apologize. You're right, I'm already regretting offering that dreadful woman any money. She called asking for more. I'm not sure what to do. My lawyer wants me to call in protective services and apply through normal channels to be a foster parent for Abby, then try to come to some kind of arrangement for adoption. But I'm still not sure what to do. I don't want to run the risk that she might have to go to that poor excuse of a grandmother. But I'm trying to trust God in this."

"God?" He'd seen her at church again but assumed it was a brief phase.

"I'm a Christian now. Grammy explained it all to me a couple of weeks ago, and I asked Jesus to save me. I'm so new at it, and it's hard to learn to trust when I've never had the experience of being able to depend on anyone but myself and my money."

A surge of joy straightened his back, and he reached for her hand. "I'm so glad, Liliana! You just have to trust Him with one thing at a time. He loves Abby even more than we do."

She nodded. "That's what Grammy said. I'll probably do it, but it's so hard." She fell silent, her fingers still clutching his. "I haven't talked much about my past, but I found out recently that I was adopted. The circumstances surrounding my adoption explain a lot about why I never felt my mother really loved and approved of me. Abby is like a part of me now. It would destroy me to lose her." She peeked up at him. "Are you still mad at me?"

He shook his head. "No, I'm sorry too. I should practice what I preach. If God allowed you to keep Abby instead of me, I have to realize He knew it was best. A little girl needs a mother, not a single father who works his life away."

"She needs a mother and a father," Liliana said softly. She reached out a hand and touched his cheek.

His face tingled where her fingers rubbed. Her gaze caught his, and he caught his breath at the emotion in them. Maybe she nurtured some feelings for him. The possibility made his heart beat faster. He reached out a hand and wrapped it around her thick braid and drew her to him. He kissed her, and the sweet scent of her breath and the feel of her mouth against his were like another side to paradise he'd never seen here in this tropical heaven.

He could have gone on kissing her all day, but he needed more assurance than a mere kiss could offer. Drawing away, he stared into her face. Her eyes were closed, her lashes black against the smooth skin of her cheeks. She opened her eyes and smiled. His stomach felt like he'd just gotten off a wild ride on the Bonsai Pipeline.

"I love you," he blurted. What ordinary words to describe

how he really felt. Liliana deserved flowery words and romance, but Barnabas had never had any experience with that kind of thing. Still, he had to give it his best shot. "You've called this place paradise, but it won't be that for me again unless you decide to marry me. We'll raise Abby as our own, even if the Lord blesses us with more children."

The words tumbled over one another in his haste to speak his mind. He'd never imagined speaking words of love like this. The light in Liliana's eyes spurred him on. "I don't have nearly as much money as you do, but I can keep you in paradise with me. I even have a suite in the penthouse." He grinned at his reference to her demand for a suite when she'd first arrived. He held his breath, but the promise in her eyes made his heart race.

"Oh, Barnabas!" She flung her arms around his neck, and tears rolled down her cheeks. "Is this really a proposal?" She touched his face, and the love in her face nearly brought him to tears. Wouldn't his brothers laugh at the thought of their staid older brother in such a weak state? But Liliana did that to him. She made him feel vulnerable and open in a way he'd never felt.

The smile on her face deepened, and she opened her mouth to speak, but a backfire from a Jeep racing toward them drew their attention. Loaded with vacationers, it careened to a stop a few feet from them. Five people piled out.

"There you are! I asked at the desk where you'd gone, and Connor told me." Clarissa sauntered toward them, her golden curls in calculated disarray on her shoulders.

She reminded Barnabas of the old Liliana, and he shivered

at the reminder. Liliana was nothing like he'd first thought. He tightened an arm protectively around Liliana.

"We need a sixth for our outing and thought we'd drag you off," Clarissa called.

"No, thanks," Liliana said. "I've got everything I want right here." She gave Barnabas a secret smile that made his head spin.

"We'll lose our spot on the boat if we can't fill it. Come on, it will be fun," Clarissa coaxed. Stopping in front of them, her curious gaze flickered from Barnabas to the arm he had around Liliana. A knowing smile lifted her lips.

"No, really, I'm busy right now," Liliana said. She leaned against Barnabas.

Clarissa laughed derisively. "You've had enough time to have him drooling at your feet the way you planned. Isn't it about time to throw him over? You said it wouldn't take long, and it's taken longer than I'm prepared to wait."

The words she said took a few moments to penetrate Barnabas's brain. It sounded like Clarissa and Liliana had talked about him. Confusion stiffened his back.

Clarissa turned her malicious gaze on Barnabas. "I'll save you from the punch line. Her plan was to get you to fall in love with her, then to tell you to take a hike. Our Liliana is a girl who loves a challenge. But it looks like you have fallen just as she said you would. I have to confess, I'm a little disappointed. I thought if anyone could resist her charms, it would be you. But even the strongest can fall, I guess. You just aren't in her league. Now run along, Barney. This little game is over."

"Barnabas, don't believe her!" Liliana clutched his arm.

"It wasn't like that."

Clarissa laughed, and the mockery in her voice made him wince. Barnabas swallowed the bile that rose in his throat. "Did you have a plan like that?"

Liliana cast her gaze to the sand, then looked back up with a pleading expression. The guilt in her face broke his heart. He dropped his arm from around her. "Did you have a plan like that?" he asked again.

"Yes, but that was before," she whispered. Shame and guilt warred for possession of her face.

Clarissa laughed, and the sound was a blade in Barnabas's heart. He jerked his arm out of Liliana's grasp and turned to leave. He had known it was too good to be true. He'd always known she would chew up his heart and feed it to the sharks. But he hadn't known it would hurt so badly. He kept his head up as he walked to his bike, but it was hard when all he wanted to do was run.

"Barnabas, wait!"

Liliana ran toward him, but he jumped on his bike, kick-started it, then roared away before she could reach him. He didn't look back.

Liliana knew she would never forget the look on Barnabas's face. She didn't know how she could make it up to him, but she had to try.

"Come on, Liliana, let's go. We'll miss the boat," Clarissa said.

Liliana worked to keep her voice calm, but she wanted to scream at her so-called friend. The verse in James she'd read in her Bible that morning was the only thing that kept her from railing at her. "So then, my beloved brethren, let every man be swift to hear, slow to speak, slow to wrath; for the wrath of man does not produce the righteousness of God." She took a deep breath and asked the Lord to help her. To her surprise, she was able to speak to Clarissa without shouting.

"I love Barnabas," she said softly. "And I'm going to tell him so." She turned and walked back to her car. Clarissa's derisive laughter floated after her, but she ignored it. She was done with that kind of life. All she wanted was to spend the rest of her days with Barnabas and Abby and any other children the Lord blessed them with. Money didn't matter. She could give it all away tomorrow and never miss it. Odd how long it took her to realize that.

Her rental car wouldn't start. She pumped the accelerator, but it merely coughed, then died. Nearly weeping with frustration, she shook the steering wheel in a frenzy of impatience. She popped the hood and got out to peer under it. One of Clarissa's friends came to help her, but by the time he'd tinkered with it enough to get it started, nearly an hour had passed. She thanked her helper, then jumped back into the car. There was no way she could catch Barnabas now.

Her foot jammed against the accelerator, she sped back to the resort. She wanted to weep, but she didn't have time. She had to convince him that she hadn't meant any of it. The old Liliana was no more, and she felt such shame that she'd ever been the kind of person who would hurt someone else willingly. Now, she couldn't even imagine having the desire to hurt Barnabas.

Her eyes welled with tears again at the memory of how Barnabas had looked when Clarissa had flung those hateful words at him. The pain and bewilderment in his eyes. She threw on the brakes and screeched the car to a halt. Rushing past the people at the reception area who were just receiving their welcome leis, she scanned the area for Barnabas's familiar head. He wasn't there.

She let out the breath she'd been holding and hurried over to Alex, obviously ready for tennis with racket in hand. "Have you seen Barnabas?" she asked.

The look of dismay in his eyes told her that Barnabas had told him what had happened. "It's not like it looks," she said. "I love Barnabas. I have to tell him."

Alex looked at her steadily, then nodded toward the back doors. "I think he was going to go on the whale-watch expedition. If you hurry, you can catch the boat."

"Thanks." She turned and rushed blindly through the doors.

Barnabas stared at the foaming sea and wondered why he'd decided to go on this stupid whale-watch expedition. He wanted to find someplace quiet to lick his wounds, but he'd been afraid one of his brothers would tell Liliana where he'd gone. Facing her until he had control again was more than he could bear. Stupid, that's what he was. Stupid and gullible. A debutante and someone like him would be like mixing oil and water. Her type of existence was out of his area of experience except as someone to serve in his capacity as resort manager.

He watched the crew begin to cast off. Then a woman

shouted, "Wait!" and he watched in astonishment as Liliana came flying through the air to land on the deck in front of him. Her green eyes wide, she teetered on the edge as though she might slip back into the water, and he reached out and caught her hand. Her gaze bore into his, and his heart stirred at the pleading expression in her eyes.

As soon as she was steady, he released her and stepped back.

"I'm so glad I caught you," she said breathlessly. "Is there somewhere we can talk?"

"I really have nothing to say. Clarissa said it all for you." He folded his arms across his chest. He wouldn't be sucked into her lies so easily this time.

"She didn't speak for me," Liliana said.

Her eyes pleaded with him, but he hardened his heart. He didn't like being made a fool of. The other passengers were watching their exchange with interest, and Barnabas shifted uncomfortably. There was nowhere else to go away from prying eyes. Maybe she would get the hint and leave him alone.

She put her hand on his arm, and the warmth of her fingers matched the look on her face. "I love you, Barnabas," she whispered.

"Maybe until a newer challenge comes along." He wished he could believe that adoring expression on her face and her words. "Just what were your plans, Liliana? Why would you want to hurt me? Is that your usual answer to boredom—just find a sap like me to toy with, then toss him aside like a candy wrapper?"

Tears flooded her eyes, and she shook her head. "Men have always followed me, Barnabas. I can't help the way I look. But no man had ever treated me with the disdain you showed. I was piqued, I admit it. And your opinion hurt, no matter how much I told myself it didn't matter. I thought if I could get you to love me, I could show you that you weren't the astute judge of character you seemed to think you were. But my own plan backfired. I fell in love with you first."

His heart began to thud in time with the pulsing of the boat's engine. "You have a funny way of showing it."

She stepped closer, and the sweet scent of her light perfume wafted up to his nose. "Grammy says I'm a new creature in Christ. Give me a chance to prove it to you," she said softly.

"Yeah, give her a chance," one of the men called.

The tips of Barnabas's ears grew warm, but he tried to ignore the interested stares around him. "I'm not sure you can prove it," he said.

"I'm going to let you adopt Abby instead of me," she said. "If you know what's best for her, you'll find her a mother—a mother just like me. But I'll leave that decision in your hands."

Her lips trembled, and he knew what her words had cost her. She adored Abby. If she was willing to give her up, then she must be telling him the truth. Joy began to fill him. His gaze searched hers, and a smile tugged at his lips.

Her eyes brightened as he started to reach for her. "I want nothing more than to be your wife," she whispered. "I love you, Barnabas."

She loved him. The crowd began to cheer as he took her in his arms. "You can call me Barney," he said as his lips found hers. Love was sweet indeed.

COLLEEN COBLE

Colleen and her husband, David, make their home in Wabash, Indiana, where they are restoring a Victorian home. They have two grown kids, David Jr. and Kara. Though Colleen is still waiting for grandchildren, she makes do with spoiling her "grand-pup" Harley and her "grandcats" Spooky, Damien, and Alex.

She is active at New Life Baptist Church where she sings and helps her husband with a young adult Sunday school class. A voracious reader herself, Colleen began pursuing her lifelong dream when a younger brother, Randy Rhoads, was killed by lightning when she was thirty-eight. She now has numerous fiction titles in print. Colleen's books have appeared on the CBA bestseller list, and they also make frequent appearances on the Heartsong Presents Reader favorites annual poll. Visit her website at www.colleencoble.com.

Fixed by Love

by Carol Cox

Dedication

To the best youth group anyone could work with.
We've laughed, we've prayed, we've grown together.
Thank you for letting me be a part of your lives.

Chapter 1

"Sit up, Beth. You're acting like a sulky child. Anyone else would be thrilled to be here."

Beth Newman straightened from her slouch in the resort shuttle and focused her reluctant attention on the reception building. "It's. . .very nice, Gwen."

"Nice?" Her sister let out an exasperated sigh. "I've heard it described as elegant, luxurious, the most unique resort in the islands, but *nice?* Only you, Beth. Only you. Two weeks at Harrigan's Cove is something most people will never experience. You can have a fabulous time here if you'll just make a little effort. Try, won't you? For Ray, if not for me?"

Beth cast a guilty glance at her brother-in-law sitting behind her. "Sorry, Ray. I didn't mean to sound so surly. It's just. . ." She spread her hands wide. "You two fit in a place like this. I have no idea how to relate to the kind of people who'll be here."

"Give yourself a chance," Gwen admonished. She flashed a brilliant smile at the shuttle driver when he offered his hand to assist her in climbing out of the vehicle.

Beth got out without help and tried to ignore Gwen's indignant huff. It hadn't been her idea to come here. She looked down at her department store outfit, in stark contrast to her sister's and Ray's designer clothing. The two of them belonged in a setting like this. She didn't. And that didn't bother her a bit.

Ray led them toward the entrance. "Are you feeling okay?" Beth asked when she noted his awkward gait.

"Just a little stiff." He twisted from side to side and winced. "I should have walked around more during the flight over."

Beth lagged behind and surveyed the resort's setting. She couldn't deny the beauty of the grounds. The shrubbery next to the entrance was covered with a profusion of blooms that matched those in the lei she'd been given at the airport. "Plumeria," Gwen had told her. Beth breathed in its heavy perfume and felt her tension ease a fraction.

Even in the shadows of early evening, the perfection of the landscaping was evident. Someone worked hard on this. Someone who would probably never be able to afford to stay as a paying guest in this exotic site with its lavish grounds and equally lavish rates. Her discomfort returned, and she headed inside to join Gwen and Ray at the registration desk.

❦

"Isn't it glorious?" Gwen swept her arms wide as if to embrace the room. "Thatched-roof cottages on the outside, five-star accommodations on the inside. Only they're hales, not cottages. How romantic! Just the place to relax and regroup, isn't it, Ray?"

Her husband grunted his approval. "You bet. I'm heading to bed. Jet lag's worse than usual this time." He smiled at Beth.

"You'll feel better in the morning too."

"I'll say good night, then," she told Gwen, seizing the opportunity to make her escape. "See you in the morning." She retired to her own side of the duplex hale and eyed her surroundings with less enthusiasm than Gwen had shown.

Brightly colored cushions padded the white wicker chairs and sofa. Beth tugged on a pair of louvered doors, which opened to reveal a broad expanse of glass she felt sure would display an incredible view in the morning light. She slid one panel of the glass door open before pushing the louvered door back into place. A gentle salt breeze wafted through the wooden slats, filling the room with the fragrance of the islands. Her roommate, Laura, would have loved it. It would be hard to find a greater contrast to their apartment in Wichita.

Beth kicked off her sandals and worked her bare toes into the deep pile of the carpet. She had to admit the room had charm, and the separation from Gwen and Ray ensured her a degree of much-needed privacy. But the expense! She could live for a month on what this place charged for only three nights' stay. She didn't even want to do the math to figure out the total cost for the two weeks they would spend there.

Gwen and Ray could afford it. It wouldn't be any more expensive than any of their other globe-hopping jaunts. But for one of the working middle class like herself, the price seemed astronomical.

Beth pulled on her flowered nightshirt, curled up on a bed wide enough to swallow her, and switched off her bedside lamp. She wrapped her arms around her head and let out a low moan. She must have been out of her mind to let them talk her into coming here.

Through the window came the rhythmic lap of the surf. Its gentle sound soothed Beth's senses and lulled her to sleep.

Sunlight filtered through the slatted doors and cast striped shadows across Beth's face. She threw an arm over her eyes and promised herself the luxury of sleeping in for another five minutes, then remembered she didn't have to get up for work. The knowledge she could stay in bed as long as she liked chased any thoughts of sleep away. Beth grinned at the irony and got up to dress and survey her surroundings again.

By daylight, it looked even more charming than the night before. An unexpected surge of enthusiasm swept through Beth, and she flung open the sliding doors. Clear morning light flooded the room. Outside, the view was even more stunning than she had imagined. Beth stepped through the doors and onto the veranda, where she leaned against the bamboo railing and tried to take it all in. Not twenty yards to her left, a cluster of palm trees fringed the pristine beach.

No wonder I could hear the surf so clearly last night. The gentle wash of the waves continued nonstop. If she managed to free herself from whatever schedule Gwen had planned for their stay, she could picture herself relaxing on the chaise with nothing but a cold drink, a good book, and the sound of the breakers for company.

Beth swung her head to the right, where the beach gave way to a lush jungle studded with myriad bright tropical blooms.

From where she stood, Beth could identify several bird-of-paradise bushes and beyond them more plumeria. Other species abounded. Maybe she could pick up a guidebook and learn the names of more.

"I didn't think to tell Beth what time to join us for breakfast." Gwen's voice carried from the other side of the hale. "I'll just pop over and see if she's awake."

"Don't bother." Beth trotted down the steps and walked around to greet her sister and brother-in-law. "I'm up and ready to go." She tried to put on a cheery expression. Welcome or not, they had made a generous gesture. She could at least attempt to show some appreciation. . .as long as Gwen kept her meddling to herself.

Beth squinted at Ray. "Are you all right?" she asked. His face seemed at least three shades lighter than its usual healthy tan.

He shook his head slowly. "Still a bit tired, I'm afraid. I'll just make a lazy day of it, and I'll bounce back by tonight."

"So where do we go for breakfast?" Beth asked, falling into step beside Gwen. "I don't have a clue about the layout of this place."

"We just follow the main path," Gwen told her, indicating the winding walkway with a lazy sweep of her arm. "It takes us past the other hales to the restaurant. We can eat inside or at one of the oceanfront tables. And all the meals are included, which means they're already paid for. Don't embarrass me by checking the right-hand side of the menu before you order." Her sister's tone was light, but Beth could discern the rebuke beneath her joking. Gwen would check the prices first, too, if she had not married someone as well off as Ray.

"I'll try not to humiliate you," she quipped. Instead of pursuing a conversation that would undoubtedly disintegrate into an argument, she tried to orient herself. Their duplex hale appeared to be one of the last on the north end of the resort. The walk led them past other cottages, each set back among thick stands of trees and shrubs in its own secluded nook. "Amazing how they manage to give each hale its privacy," she murmured.

"I knew you'd love the place if you just gave yourself a chance." Gwen chortled in triumph. "You can't really be as immune to the finer things in life as you like to make yourself out to be."

Beth clamped her lips together and determined to walk the rest of the way in silence. Somehow, she had to get through fourteen days of Gwen's snipping. She would not start out by initiating a battle.

Gwen's hand clamped down on Beth's arm. "Look over there. Do you see those three men? Ray, isn't the one on the left Evan Rogers? Come on." She towed her reluctant sister along the walkway toward her unsuspecting prey.

"What are you doing?" Beth asked through clenched teeth.

"Offering you the opportunity of a lifetime. Evan Rogers is a friend of Adrian Miller, who is on the board of directors with Ray. We met him at Adrian's Christmas party last year. We are talking serious money here, not to mention the fact that he's drop-dead gorgeous."

Beth felt her cheeks flame. "Are you out of your mind? I

am not—repeat, *not*—here on a husband-hunting expedition." She tried to dig her feet into the earthen path, but her sandals offered little purchase.

Gwen's steely voice didn't match the bright smile she had plastered on her face. "I am giving you a chance to meet someone who could take care of all your problems. Don't embarrass me." She drew up to her quarry and gave Beth's arm a tug that reminded Beth of a dog handler ordering his charge to sit and stay. "Evan! What a lovely surprise to find you here."

The men halted their conversation, and one flashed a smile in their direction. "Gwen, isn't it? Gwen Lawson?" His gaze moved past her and fastened on Beth.

Gwen's quick glance followed his. "I'd like you to meet my sister, Beth Newman. We just arrived last night, and we'll be staying for two weeks."

Beth wanted to roll her eyes at her sister's blatant pitch. Next thing she knew, Gwen would hand the man an itemized itinerary, complete with suggestions for romantic outings. She forced a smile. "How do you do?"

"Suddenly much better." He clasped her hand in his and beamed, sky blue eyes sparkling in his suntanned face. "I'm just sorry my time here is nearly over and I'll be leaving in a couple of days. I wish our visits had overlapped more."

Beth slipped her fingers from his grasp and tried to find a more comfortable topic of conversation. "Have you enjoyed your stay?"

"I've been coming to Harrigan's Cove for several years now," Evan told her. "I can't think of a better place to recharge."

Ray came up behind them. "Morning, Evan. Have you had breakfast yet?"

"We're on our way there right now." Gwen's toothy grin made Beth think of a barracuda closing in for the kill. "Would you care to join us?"

"I'm afraid we've just finished eating," Evan told her, "and I'm heading out for a round of golf with these two." He nodded toward his companions. "But I'm sure we can get together for something before I leave." He sent a look at Beth that spoke of his interest.

"I'm certain our paths will cross," Gwen answered.

"Did you see that?" she asked Beth when they'd been seated at a table on the patio facing the cove. "He couldn't take his eyes off you. Now remember, you only have a couple of days to get acquainted, but if you put your mind to it, I know you can work this to your advantage."

"Stop it, Gwen. I know you think you're doing me a favor, but Evan Rogers is not my type. You said you wanted me to come here to get away and relax, so just let me enjoy the trip my own way, all right?" She took refuge behind her menu and tried to ignore Gwen's indignant sputter. Thankfully, Ray maintained his usual easygoing behavior and showed no inclination to get involved in his wife's matchmaking strategy.

Beth ordered a fruit plate and guava juice, while Gwen and Ray settled on omelets and Kona coffee. After a few moments of blissful silence, Ray bunched his napkin next to his half-eaten meal. "I don't think I can finish this," he declared. "Maybe I'll just head back to our cottage and rest awhile."

Beth looked at him with concern. "Are you sure you're all right?" His eyes had taken on a glassy sheen.

"I do feel a bit achy," he admitted. "Maybe I picked up a cold or something."

"I'll go with you and make sure you have everything you need," Gwen said. Her uncharacteristically solicitous behavior raised Beth's level of concern another degree. "You don't need to interrupt your meal." She waved Beth back to her seat. "I'm sure it's something minor, and there's no point in spoiling your morning. Why don't you just run along and explore the resort? There are plenty of things to keep you occupied and lots of new people to meet. We'll get together later and decide what to do."

Beth reached for another slice of papaya and watched her sister herd Ray back toward the cottage. "Plenty to do, huh?" she mumbled between bites. "Like what? Chasing after Evan? No, thanks."

A trio of swimsuit-clad teenagers walked past her on the stretch of sand that fronted the dining patio. The breeze carried the faint scent of coconut oil back to her. At the next table, two couples carried on a lively debate on how to fill their day. The men opted for tennis, while the women wanted to visit the massage center.

Beth tipped the last of the guava juice down her throat and set off down one of the branching walkways. The days—all fourteen of them—stretched out before her like a prison sentence. She remembered her roommate's reaction when she heard about the planned trip.

"A vacation in Maui?" Laura had squealed. "For *free?* Lucky you! I wish I were going."

"That makes two of us," Beth had grumbled. If she could have figured out how to pull off a Leah/Rachel kind of swap, substituting Laura for herself before Gwen was any the wiser, she would have given the idea serious consideration. Her roommate and Gwen probably would have gotten along famously, with Laura showing no opposition to Gwen's attempts to land her a wealthy husband.

Gwen's fixation on financial status had been the cause of more than one heated argument, with Gwen promoting her favorite theme of the importance of economic security.

"But you can't rely on money to make you happy and solve all your problems," Beth would counter. "What happens if the bottom drops out of the market and all Ray's assets disappear? What would you do then?"

What would any of the people here do if they were suddenly left penniless? Beth scanned the beach. No one moved at anything more than a lazy saunter. *Look at them—more money than they know what to do with and nothing better to spend it on but their own enjoyment.* Didn't any of these people think about things like giving to the poor or supporting missionaries instead of indulging themselves? Beth did a quick mental calculation. If only ten of them set aside the money they spent on a week's stay here, the sum could support a missionary family for over a year. It boggled the mind.

With a sniff of disdain, Beth set off down a shaded path with no particular destination in mind. She didn't play tennis, had no interest in getting a massage, and didn't intend to pursue wealthy bachelors. With the rest of the morning on her hands, she might as well explore the rest of the grounds. She strolled at a brisk pace, musing on the shallowness of the wealthy. Tropical scents hung in the air and filled her senses. *Whoever Harrigan is, he's managed to build himself a pretty cushy spot.*

Her steps led her past gardens bright with bougainvillea and bird-of-paradise, then she skirted the edge of a wide lagoon. Points of sunlight glistened on its still waters. All in all, the place was nothing short of magnificent—a setting fit for the wealthy and carefree. . .but not for someone of average means. Not for her. How on earth had she let Gwen talk her into this?

She knew the answer without even bothering to give the question serious consideration. Gwen's unsubtle attempts to find her a successful husband hadn't flagged over the years, but Beth had always managed to fob her efforts off, saying her job at Midwest Appliance kept her far too busy. And it had been the truth; a full day at work left her with little energy for social engagements in the evenings or on weekends.

Then, Midwest closed its doors after twenty-five years in business, and Beth joined the ranks of the unemployed. Gwen's offer to have her accompany them to Harrigan's Cove for a two-week getaway seemed innocent enough and would give her time to pray and seek a new direction for her life.

Sinking onto a bench by a secluded stream, Beth realized she had gone far beyond the resort's residential area. Even the tennis courts and restaurants couldn't be seen. Only the sound of water lapping over rocks met her ears. She stretched out her legs and breathed a deep sigh. The musical splashing brought peace to her soul.

She wondered if the rest of the island held the same sense of tranquility or if it only came in a setting like this, as a paid-for commodity. Maybe she could rent a car one day and explore the island. She wouldn't mind discovering more of this serenity in a natural setting done by God rather than a landscaper.

Beth leaned her head back and closed her eyes. Without question, she could use more of this laid-back feeling, this sense of release from the hurried pressure of the lifestyle she'd left back in Wichita. Back where she scrambled forty hours a week just to cover living expenses and put a bit aside for emergencies—and thank goodness she had—without an income, she could at least draw on her modest savings to tide her over for awhile. But she wouldn't have had that if she hadn't learned years before how to live frugally.

Enough. Jesus said not to worry about tomorrow. Today she was here in paradise, according to Gwen and Laura at least. She might as well enjoy it and use the time to seek direction, not fret over things that weren't under her control. Maybe in this place of peace she could discover what God had planned for her future.

Could it be that Midwest Appliance shutting down wasn't the disaster I thought? Maybe this is the Lord opening a new door in my life.

"God, could we talk? You know I've appreciated having a steady job, and I've enjoyed it for the most part. But this time I think I'd like to find something I *want* to do, not just something expedient, if that's okay with You."

Beth rose and retraced her steps, smiling when she realized her stride had slowed to a more relaxed pace. Maybe the concept of leisure wasn't so bad in itself. A group of sunbathers lay on the beach, working on their tans. A part of Beth wished she could enjoy inactivity as much as they seemed to. No cares, no worries. It sounded appealing, especially compared to the uncertainty of her own situation.

On closer inspection, though, their faces didn't reflect contentment but emptiness. Not one of them looked truly peaceful. The old cliché really did hold true: Money couldn't buy happiness.

"Beth?" A lean, tanned figure jogged toward her, and she recognized Evan Rogers, Gwen's intended victim, wearing gleaming tennis whites. "We're getting up a game of mixed doubles. How about being my partner?"

Her earlier tranquility fled. "I don't think so, but thanks."

"How about a game with just you and me, then?"

"I'm sorry. I don't play tennis."

"Not at all? No problem. I could just as easily be persuaded to spend the afternoon snorkeling. Care to join me?"

"I'm afraid I don't snorkel either."

"A walk along the beach, then? You do walk, don't you?" His lazy smile took any sting from his words.

Beth brushed a strand of hair back behind her ear. "I appreciate the offer, Evan, but I've been having a pretty stressful time back home. Right now I'm just enjoying the solitude."

His white teeth gleamed against his suntanned skin. "All right. I'll let you off the hook this time. But be forewarned, I can be very persistent." He raised his tennis racket in a brief salute and loped away toward the courts.

Chapter 2

Back inside her hale, Beth kicked off her sandals and padded out to the veranda. She stretched out on the chaise and closed her eyes, trying to recapture her earlier serenity. Instead, a vague feeling of discontent settled over her. Relaxation had its place, but she couldn't be still *all* of the time, and encouraging Evan didn't fit her concept of productive activity.

Maybe Ray was feeling better. Beth swung her feet to the deck and slipped her sandals back on. Even listening to Gwen would be better than inactivity.

Gwen answered her knock with a pinched expression that deflated Beth's hopes for a sisterly chat. "You're not going to believe this," she wailed. "Ray has chicken pox!"

"He can't. You get that as a kid."

"Ray didn't." Gwen sniffled and dabbed at her eyes. "The poor thing started feeling so bad, we had to call a doctor. He left just a few minutes ago. He said it's a lot harder on adults than children. Ray probably isn't in any danger as long as he takes care of himself, but he's going to be miserable for awhile, and I don't see how I can go off and leave him. And I was so looking forward to making sure you got acquainted with the right people."

"That's okay. I'll be fine." Boredom might not be so bad after all.

"Are you sure, Beth? I wanted this to be such a special time for you." The sincerity in Gwen's voice reminded Beth that, in her own misguided way, her sister meant well.

"I'll be fine," Beth repeated, wondering how on earth she would manage to fill the next thirteen days. "Can I get you anything?"

"I can't think of a thing right now. Maybe later." Gwen cocked her head toward the bedroom. "I think Ray is calling me. I'd better go see what he wants." She fluttered her hand in Beth's direction and closed the door.

Now what? If spending two weeks in Gwen's domineering presence had seemed depressing, the prospect of being completely on her own in a setting like Harrigan's Cove made her feel like the proverbial fish out of water. True to its promise to provide its guests with a quiet haven, the hales came equipped with comfortable furnishings and exquisite views, but no TVs or telephones. She didn't even have the option of flipping through the local television channels. Right now, even a mindless game show would offer some relief.

With the sense of embarking on a quest, she retraced the path toward the restaurant. If she remembered correctly, she'd seen a gift shop just past it. Maybe she could find a newspaper, a book of crossword puzzles, anything to keep her occupied.

Thirty minutes later, she emerged victorious from the gift shop, armed with a dozen mystery novels. If nothing else, she could relax on her lanai and indulge in her passion for reading. Feeling marginally more cheerful, she returned to her hale and selected a book to read. She perused the choice of beverages in the hale's mini-refrigerator and settled on another guava juice. *Might as well get into the island frame of mind as long as I'm here.*

Out on the veranda, she positioned the chaise to give her a view of both the beach and the tropical forest, then settled down with her book. Little by little, her tension ebbed, swept away like the surf lapping at the shore. By chapter 3, she had forgotten her irritation with Gwen for trying to run her life and became immersed in the story. By chapter 5, she'd developed definite suspicions of who might be behind the string of show-dog thefts. When droplets of rain spattered dark circles on the first page of chapter 10, she looked up, startled at the reminder she was relaxing at a luxurious Hawaiian resort instead of chasing suspects across coastal South Carolina.

A glance at the sky told Beth she needed to move indoors. She tucked the book under her arm, picked up her empty juice bottle, and carried them inside. If rain showers would be a regular feature of her days here, it made her appreciate the hale's large windows all the more. She raised the wooden blinds on the window opposite her bed, plumped up the pillows, and prepared to continue reading. Clouds dimmed the natural light, so she reached for the bedside lamp and twisted the switch on its base.

A flash of blue light erupted from the lamp, accompanied by a loud popping sound. Beth shrieked and leaped from the bed. The lamp continued to make ominous buzzing noises. She yanked the plug from its socket and stared wide-eyed at the smoking remains, trying to decide what to do next. How did you let a five-star resort know it had an exploding lamp in one of its rooms?

She thumbed through the guest services information folder and learned that while the hales didn't have telephones, each came equipped with an intercom that communicated with the front desk. "You'd think a place that charges this much could keep its equipment in working order," she muttered during a brief search in which she located the intercom next to a light switch. The voice on the other end assured her someone would take care of the problem in short order.

Beth moved her book to a chair beside the window and settled in for a long wait.

Within twenty minutes, she heard a brisk tap at her door. *Maybe that's one perk of being around the moneyed class,* she thought grimly. *They aren't kept waiting like the rest of us.* She swung the door open to find an athletic-looking, sandy-haired man on her doorstep.

"Good afternoon," he said with a broad grin. "I understand you have a lamp that's giving you trouble." A quizzical frown crinkled his forehead when she didn't respond right away.

Beth tore her gaze from his deep blue eyes and tried to re-member whom she'd called and why. "The lamp!" she stammered, feeling like a world-class idiot. "It's over here." She led him to the offending appliance and hoped he would attribute the flush she felt creeping up her neck to sunburn.

He surveyed the blackened base and pursed his lips in a soundless whistle. "That must have shaken you up."

"It did." Beth chuckled at the memory of her flying leap off the mattress. "Do you mind if I stay while you fix it?" Her stomach knotted the moment the words left her mouth. The resort's other guests undoubtedly had better things to do than hang around the repairmen while they worked, but she'd finally found someone here she could relate to, and she didn't want to lose the connection.

His raised eyebrows confirmed her suspicion that he didn't often receive requests like hers, but he nodded, and the easy grin returned. "That would be fine. I'll try not to take too long."

Take all the time you want. Meeting another working person in the midst of all this opulence was a pleasure not likely to be repeated. Beth perched on the brightly patterned cushion of her wicker chair and watched him while he examined the plug on the lamp's cord.

"I brought a replacement just in case," he told her. "And it definitely looks like you need it. I'll go get it out of my golf cart." He left the hale and trotted down the steps with an easy grace that Beth admired. Here was someone who stayed in shape because he worked hard, not because he lived on the tennis courts or spent time in a gym. He returned with a lamp identical to the one that had shorted out. "Let's try this and see if it works." He plugged it in and turned the switch, but nothing happened.

"Looks like it blew the breaker. I'll go out and reset it at the panel. Back in a minute." When he came back, he tried the lamp switch again. Nothing.

"What's wrong now?" Beth asked.

"It's probably shorted out the outlet. I'll get another one and replace it for you." After another trip to his golf cart, he settled himself on the floor with the new outlet and his tool pouch. "My name's Connor, by the way," he said over his shoulder. "I'm the maintenance supervisor. Normally, Kai would be doing this, but his wife's having their first baby today, so you're stuck with me instead."

"Can I do anything to help?"

Connor raised his eyebrows and regarded her thoughtfully. "Sure. I left my voltage tester on the seat of the cart. Would you like to get it for me?"

Beth jumped up, elated at having something productive to do, even something as small as playing fetch-and-carry. She scooped up the tester and carried it back to Connor.

His eyes widened when she handed him the small box with its dangling leads, but he made no comment. He inserted the metal probes into the socket and nodded when he read the meter. "Yep, it's fried, all right. I'll turn the power off again and have this new one installed in just a moment." With a few deft motions, he loosened the screws that held the cover plate and removed the faulty outlet. "You aren't exactly one of our typical guests," he said over his shoulder.

Beth kept silent, not sure whether he meant it as a compliment or not.

"I have to admit I didn't really expect you to know what a voltage tester was, much less be willing to go get it for me." He wrapped the wires around the screws on the sides of the new outlet, fastened the outlet in place, and replaced the cover plate.

"Oh, that." Beth grinned. "I worked at Midwest Appliance in Wichita for nearly eight years. Theoretically, my job was answering the phone and scheduling service calls, but when the phone wasn't busy, I used to watch the guys work on equipment they'd brought back to the shop. Sometimes they'd let me help with the repairs." She shrugged. "I enjoyed it. It's hard for me to sit around and do nothing."

Connor chuckled, a rich baritone sound Beth decided she'd like to hear again. "Like I said, not our typical guest." He plugged in the new lamp and twisted the switch. "There you go. Good as new."

Beth extended her hand. "I'm Beth Newman. Thanks for both the repair and the visit."

She watched him steer the golf cart along the path, wishing the resort had a few Connors among the guests. Being in the presence of someone with a regular job had been refreshing after the rarefied atmosphere she'd existed in the past couple of days.

Now she could finish her book. She walked back to the lamp and turned the switch off, then on again. Maybe something else would need repairing. Her spirits lifted at the thought, then she remembered that Kai would be back on the job soon. She wondered if he could possibly be as nice as Connor.

Connor Harrigan tallied the final column on his worksheet

and winced at the total. Steve would have a fit when he learned what replacing the steam tables in the kitchen would cost, but it had to be done. He'd have to remind Steve to look at the bottom line. Their father had spent his life making Harrigan's Cove a prosperous concern. He'd succeeded admirably, and he hadn't done it by pinching pennies. Steve would just have to get used to the idea that they couldn't run a resort like this on a shoestring.

He put the worksheet in a folder with a batch of invoices he planned to give Steve tomorrow and rolled his shoulders to loosen his muscles. He detested paperwork as much as he enjoyed working with his hands and spending time outdoors. It was a good thing his brothers thrived on indoor work and interacting with the guests.

He picked up his tool pouch from the corner of the desk where he'd tossed it earlier and set it on top of a file cabinet. The recollection of his earlier repair call brought a smile to his lips. What brought someone like Beth Newman to Harrigan's Cove? Even though he'd said it jokingly, she truly didn't fit the general profile of their clientele. She had portrayed herself as an office worker, so how could she possibly afford the prices they charged?

Connor wondered briefly if she really were the type of person she represented herself to be. He passed off the notion with a chuckle when he remembered the way she'd appeared with his voltage tester in her outstretched hand. She knew her tools, all right. He thought it highly unlikely she'd gone to the trouble to pick up that kind of knowledge in an effort to appeal to blue-collar types. Whatever the reason that brought her there, he was glad her lamp had shorted out. Meeting her had been like a fresh breeze from the afternoon trade winds.

Too bad they didn't get more visitors of her type. With all the time he spent trying to keep the place running, supervising his maintenance crew, and staying on top of his paperwork, he didn't have much opportunity to meet women away from the resort. The pampered types he encountered there didn't fit the profile of a woman with whom he wanted to spend time.

This woman, though. . . Connor's smile broadened at the thought of her curly russet hair and saucy brown eyes. Too bad he couldn't expect to make any other service calls to her hale.

Chapter 3

Beth strolled along the well-worn path, trying to decide which direction to take. She stopped to trace the edges of a scarlet hibiscus blossom with her finger and marveled at the diversity of God's creation. In the short time she'd spent on Maui, she'd encountered a profusion of new plants, new sights and smells, but breathtaking as she found it all, it lacked a sense of completeness without someone to share it with.

She had to admit her plan to spend her time reading and relaxing hadn't worked out well. Over the past few days, she'd managed to make her way through half the books she'd purchased before the novelty of uninterrupted reading time palled. Even having to fend off Gwen's tireless machinations began to sound good. At least it would give her someone to talk to and a purpose for her days.

Beth continued on, this time choosing the employee access road that bypassed the hales on the way to the center of the resort. Maybe she'd run into Connor. The thought brought a sniff of self-reproach. According to the information packet in her hale, Harrigan's Cove offered a multitude of activities for the pleasure of its guests. How lonely did someone have to be to go seeking out the maintenance man?

Really lonely. She knew Gwen would have been astonished at the thought that anyone could feel alone in the midst of one of the most desirable resorts on the islands. But that's exactly how she felt. The enjoyment Connor's visit had brought only served to underscore how out of place she felt with everyone else. She'd tried to strike up a conversation with some of the other employees, hoping they would prove to be as easygoing as the maintenance supervisor. She found them polite enough, although clearly startled at her efforts to talk to them. Even so, after a few friendly phrases, they excused themselves and went about their business.

Can you blame them? They have jobs to do, and that doesn't include hanging out with the paying customers, who are supposed to be able to find plenty of entertainment here.

Evan Rogers would have been more than willing to fill those empty hours. Before he left, he'd invited her to join him on a catamaran dinner cruise, an excursion to Lahaina, and an early morning drive to watch the sun rise over Haleakala Crater. All of which she had turned down, feeling more churlish with every refusal.

Gwen's patience, never long-suffering at the best of times, had grown increasingly taut with her duties as caretaker and nurse. "What's wrong with you?" she'd demanded the night before Evan left, when Beth stopped by to check on Ray's progress. "The man has everything a woman could want—looks, charm, and a bank account that would solve your financial worries forever. And don't try to tell me about some silly scruples and say you don't want it to look like you're chasing him. *He's* the one who's showing interest here. What could it possibly hurt to get to know him? He may be just the man you're looking for."

"Only one problem," Beth said. "I'm not looking for anyone, and I don't feel any need to. Your ideas of security and mine are worlds apart, remember? I'm not worried about my future; you don't need to be either."

Gwen crossed her arms and glared. "Maybe you think Ray and I will come to the rescue whenever you get in a bind, but it isn't that simple. You need to have someone of your own you can rely on, someone you can depend on to—"

"I do. God hasn't let me down yet, and I don't expect Him to quit taking care of me now. I may not know what I'm going to do for a job, but I believe He already has things all worked out. All I have to do is find out what He has in mind and follow His leading. I'll be fine."

Gwen shook her head. "You make it all sound so easy, but wait until that little savings account of yours runs out. You have no idea what peace of mind a decent bank balance and a solid portfolio can give you."

"And if some kind of shakeup comes along and your money is suddenly gone? Then what happens to your peace of mind?"

The skin stretched tight across Gwen's face, bringing her already thin features into harsh prominence. "That won't happen. We've spent years getting our investments in order. Ray may not be the most handsome man who ever walked the earth, but he has a good mind for business. We're going to be fine."

"Just think about it, will you?" Beth urged. "You may be right and you'll never have a moment's worry about money. But when you come to the end of your life, all the portfolios in the universe won't buy your way into heaven. Having a Savior who already paid the price for you is what real security is all about."

Beth could still picture the anger on her sister's face when she stepped back and shut the hale door with a decisive click. She shouldn't have let Gwen's comments get to her. Being cooped up with Ray couldn't be any fun for her, and she might have known what reaction her words would bring. They'd had plenty of similar conversations over the years. Gwen knew exactly where Beth stood, and vice-versa. Still, she couldn't stand the thought that all her sister's trust lay in something as temporary as earthly goods.

The access road forked, one branch going to the fitness center, the other toward the beach. Beth hesitated and started to take the path to the beach when she caught sight of a golf cart coming from the direction of the maintenance area. She shaded her eyes and felt a grin split her face when she recognized the sandy-haired driver. He answered with a grin of his own and pulled the cart to a halt beside her.

"Don't you know this is a luxury resort?" Connor asked, wagging his finger at her like an old-time schoolmarm. "You're supposed to be out enjoying the fruits of our labors, not wandering the back roads." The welcoming gleam in his deep blue eyes belied any implied criticism.

Beth couldn't very well say she'd been hoping to catch sight of him, so she settled for a slight shrug of her shoulders. "Off on another repair job? I thought Kai was supposed to be back by now."

"He wanted a little more time off to get used to being a daddy. That's okay with me, though. I'd rather be doing this kind of work than sitting behind a desk any day. One of the dryers at the guest laundry is acting up, so I'm going up there to check it out."

"Mind if I tag along?" The words slipped out before Beth could stop them, and she braced herself for him to say no. To her delight, he patted the seat next to him.

"Hop on," he said. "It isn't often I get an offer for an assistant who's as knowledgeable as you are. Besides," he added, his eyes crinkling with laughter, "you're a lot prettier than Kai."

Beth climbed on before he could change his mind. The breeze stirred her hair, and she sniffed, reveling in the combined scents of sea air and tropical blossoms. She stepped out when Connor pulled up to the thatched-roofed building, then followed him inside the empty laundry room.

He laid his tool pouch on a shelf and went to examine the dryers. Beth wandered around the sunny room, her nose wrinkling at the heavy smell of laundry soap and bleach. *I guess a Laundromat is a Laundromat, no matter how beautiful the setting outside.* Her right foot slid out from under her, and she grabbed a nearby washing machine to keep from falling. Looking down, she saw a small puddle of water on the floor in front of the washer.

"Hey, Connor, it looks like you have a bad water pump

here." She pointed to the offending puddle.

Connor left the dryer and inspected the wet spot. He grinned and shook his head. "I'll mark it on my calendar. This is the first time a guest has diagnosed a repair problem."

Beth beamed back at him. She liked the way his eyes crinkled at the corners when he smiled.

"I have some spare water pumps back at the storeroom," he told her. "I'll pick one up while I'm getting the heating element for the dryer. Do you want to ride along, or would you rather go back to your walk?"

Beth glanced at the tool pouch. "How about if I take the water pump off while you're gone? It'll be ready to replace by the time you get back."

Connor gave her a speculative look, then handed the tool pouch to her. "She knows her tools, she repairs washers. What else can this woman do?" He gave her a wink, then headed outside.

Beth set to work, feeling happier than she had in days. For the first time since her arrival, she had something useful to do. She chuckled to herself at the incongruity of the situation: Everyone else came to Harrigan's Cove to forget work and do nothing, but she found pleasure in repairing a broken machine. The thought of Gwen's reaction if she ever learned of this brought an outright laugh.

She pulled the washer forward slightly, then tilted it back to lean against the wall so she could remove the two screws holding the front in place. Setting the front panel aside, she squatted in front of the machine and felt a wave of satisfaction. Sure enough, water seeped from the pump. Humming softly, she pulled the belt off and sorted through the tool pouch for a nut driver. She had just finished loosening the water pump when she heard footsteps outside. She stood, ready to show off her accomplishment, but the face that met hers wasn't Connor's.

The newcomer stared at her quizzically, then his expression cleared. "Oh, it's Miss Newman, isn't it? I'm Barnabas Harrigan."

Beth recognized the man with the sun-streaked brown hair from the reception area the night they checked in. "That's right." She shook hands with him, noting the difference between his smooth, uncalloused palm and Connor's work-hardened grip.

Barnabas still appeared puzzled. "Steve told me Connor was up here, but it appears he was wrong."

"He'll be right back. He just went to get a replacement water pump." Beth gestured toward the washer, then realized she still held the nut driver in her left hand. Now she understood Barnabas's bewilderment. She glanced up at him, feeling sheepish. "You probably don't get many guests who enjoy taking your machinery apart."

A slow smile spread across his face. "Come to think of it, we don't."

"I hope you don't mind. . . ." Beth let her voice trail off, wondering if she had broken some unwritten code of behavior. Gwen would be sure to know exactly what degree of transgression she might have committed.

Barnabas hesitated, then said, "You do know, don't you, that we have a wide variety of activities available for the enjoyment of our guests?"

"I know," Beth wailed. "I've read the brochure. It's just that I *like* doing things with my hands."

Barnabas spread his arms in resignation. "You sound just like Connor," he told her. "If this is what makes you happy, Miss Newman, have at it. Our sole purpose here is to serve you." He walked toward the doorway, then turned. "Would you let Connor know I'd like to see him whenever he has a free moment?" He gave her another curious glance, then sketched a wave and was gone.

Thank goodness Gwen wasn't here to see that. At the thought of her sister's reaction to waving a workman's tool at one of the resort's owners, Beth erupted into a fit of giggles. What a sight that would have been!

She had a feeling Connor would have enjoyed the whole scene thoroughly. She knew her sister would surely prefer Barnabas, with his spotless clothes and impeccable manner, to his down-to-earth employee.

Beth had to admit he'd been abundantly gracious, despite his obvious surprise at her unorthodox activity, and she appreciated his willingness to accept her for who she was instead of making her feel foolish. But if she had to choose between the two men, she'd pick Connor every time. Barnabas seemed nice enough, but he made his living by charming people. Connor had plenty of natural charm, and it wasn't even in his job description.

The object of her thoughts returned laden with the new water pump and heating element. Beth relayed Barnabas's message, expecting him to get back in his golf cart and leave.

Instead, he shrugged and said, "I'll catch up with him later."

He surveyed her progress, then gave her a long, appraising glance. "Not bad. You really do know what you're doing." He knelt and bolted the new pump into place, then set the belt back onto its pulleys. "Want to put the front panel on while I replace this element? Then maybe we could go enjoy a cold drink as a reward for all this manual labor."

"Are you sure you can take the time?" It might be all right for him not to jump and run immediately at his employer's beck and call, but he probably ought to be a little less casual about responding to his boss's desire to see him. "What about Barnabas?"

"He can wait," Connor told her with a slow wink that made her knees tremble. "I don't take many breaks. I'll tell him I'm averaging things out."

Beth sipped her iced fruit punch and walked beside Connor. "I'm glad you talked me into this. I didn't expect a guided tour along with the drink."

"Only the best for our honored guests." Connor bent low in an elegant bow. "After all, you spent a good part of your afternoon helping me, so it's only fair I show you what you've been missing."

The only thing Beth had missed had been spending time with Connor, but she wasn't about to tell him that. She let another swallow of punch trickle down her throat and waited for him to point out the next item of interest.

"The fitness center is over there." He gestured with his glass. "Have you tried it out yet?"

Beth shook her head. "I'm more inclined to get my exercise outside instead of on a bunch of machines."

"Soul mates," Connor declared. "When you have this kind of scenery around you, who wants to spend a moment more than necessary cooped up indoors?"

"Exactly." Beth tilted her head back and spread her arms wide as if to embrace the beauty around them. "If the rest of the island is as gorgeous as this, how could anyone in their right mind choose staying inside?"

Connor gave her an approving look that sent shivers along her spine. Their gazes locked, and their steps slowed. He took her arm and linked it through his before they went on.

"To your right," he said in a mock tour guide voice, "is our noteworthy lagoon. And just beyond. . . ," he swept his arm out in a dramatic gesture, "is the imu."

"The what?"

"Imu. Not emu, the bird—*imu*, the cooking pit. For the kalua pig. Luaus every Friday night, you know."

"Ah. Imu." She gazed around at the lush grounds. "You really have done an amazing job here. I'm trying to find a word to describe it, but it goes beyond anything I can think of."

Connor followed her gaze. "God gets the credit for that, not me. He did the work of creation; everything I do is stewardship."

In a few more moments, they reached the point where they'd started. Beth spotted the golf cart and realized with a shock that the "brief tour" she'd expected had taken up a significant part of Connor's work day. She stopped short and turned to face him. "I completely forgot about your still being on the clock. I hope you won't get into any trouble on my account."

"Not to worry. I'll make it up another time." He took her hand and smiled down at her. "Thanks for making my afternoon such a pleasant one. Can I give you a lift back to your hale?"

Beth shook her head. "I've taken up enough of your time. You'd better get back to work. Even supervisors have to answer to somebody."

Two hours later, Beth answered a knock to find a stocky young Hawaiian boy on her doorstep. He handed her an arrangement of brilliant crimson blooms. "For you, Miss Newman. They're anthuriums."

Beth set the vase on a low table and studied the waxy heart-shaped flowers. A tiny envelope peeked out from behind one of the blossoms. Beth opened it and extracted the card.

> *Unique blooms for a unique lady.*
> *C*

A tender smile curved her lips.

Chapter 4

Tropical fish swam across a sea-blue background on the reservation center's computer screen saver. Connor leaned against the desk and looked around to reassure himself that the area was indeed empty. He huddled before the computer and watched letters appear on the monitor as he typed them on the keyboard: N-E-W-M-A-N. He pressed *Enter* and scanned the information that appeared on the screen.

"She's traveling with her sister and her husband, and they're booked until the twenty-second," he murmured. "Only eight more days."

"Looking for something?"

Connor whirled to face Barnabas and planted himself directly in front of the computer. He gave a nonchalant nod while he reached back and groped for the backspace key, hoping it would remove the telltale screen. "Just checking out some information. I understand you were looking for me earlier."

His older brother folded his arms and leaned against the door frame. "Quite a bit earlier, actually. As I recall, it was while you were busy repairing laundry equipment with the help of a certain guest. Just before you went for an extended walk around the grounds with the same mechanically inclined and very attractive female." He shifted to one side and peered over Connor's shoulder. "It wouldn't just happen to be that same guest you were checking up on, would it?" A mischievous grin lit his face.

"I didn't mean to put you off so long," Connor replied. "What did you need to see me about?"

Barnabas responded with a resounding laugh. "You aren't going to sidetrack me that easily, dear brother. Not after the ribbing I took from you when I first met Liliana." He gave Connor a light punch on the shoulder. "Actually, it's great to see someone's taken your fancy. But really, Connor. . .a guest who fixes washers?"

Connor gave up on diversionary tactics. Barnabas knew him too well. "She's not exactly your average guest."

"Yes, I can see that." Barnabas settled back on one corner of the desk. "So. . .is she anything special? Aside from her mechanical aptitude, that is?"

"Come on, Barnabas. I just met the woman."

"That isn't exactly what I asked. Sometimes things happen a lot more quickly than you'd expect."

Connor wadded up yet another loose paper from his desk and lobbed it toward the wastebasket. Those receipts Steve wanted had to be here somewhere. Connor could have sworn he'd given them to him days ago, but Steve said no and Connor believed him. Steve had always had an organized mind and incredible memory. He could find any piece of paper in his office, neatly filed away, with his eyes shut. It must be a gift, one that hadn't been doled out equally to the four of them.

If Steve wanted to know about changing out the walk-in freezer's compressor, Connor could give him a blow-by-blow account of the whole process, but things like that never seemed to interest his younger brother. Or Alex, or Barnabas, for that matter. For brothers, they had widely divergent interests. None of the other three, for example, would have looked past Beth's friendly smile to discover the inner qualities that made her different from any other woman he'd ever met.

And those amounted to far more than just the mechanical aptitude Barnabas mentioned the night before. Funny how he had automatically assumed Beth's proficiency with machinery made her a match for his brother.

Connor snorted and delved into another stack of paper. Yes, he'd enjoyed his time with Beth, but that "love at first sight" mentality belonged in romance novels and tearjerker movies, not in real life. Not in the kind of relationship Connor wanted—one that would last a lifetime. Building a bond like that required plenty of time for two people to get to know each other. Time to see if their likes and dislikes meshed at all. Time to find out whether they were in tune spiritually.

All he knew about Beth Newman could be put in a thimble, and a small one at that. After all, they'd only been around each other a couple of times, barely enough to get acquainted. But long enough to know he found her refreshingly different from the other women he'd met, either at the resort or away from it.

Rather than being focused on indulging herself, Beth seemed genuinely interested in the people around her, a quality lacking in most of the women he knew. Maybe if he weren't so busy helping to run the resort, he'd have time to meet women more his type. But with the kind of hours he and his brothers had to put in just to keep the place operating at a profit, spare time would be in short supply for quite awhile to come.

Not that he was complaining. Continuing their father's legacy had a higher priority at the moment. Barnabas had managed to find the love of his life right there on the grounds, but Barnabas had always had more than his share of charm. Alex, with his good looks and outgoing personality, never had a problem attracting female admirers. And Steve. . . Well, somewhere behind those glasses, Connor felt sure thoughts of romance lurked within that analytical brain.

As close as he felt to his family, Connor had long considered himself the odd man out, being so strongly geared to physical labor. For him, the perfect mate wouldn't be likely to pop up under his nose. Unless that woman happened to be someone like Beth.

He yanked open his bottom drawer and upended it on the desk, letting loose a flurry of screws, wire nuts, and assorted old memos. He extracted a month-old invoice. Steve would be sure to want that too. The rest of the papers joined their fellows in the trash can. He ought to search for receipts more often. His desk hadn't been this paper-free in ages.

Who would have thought he could run across a woman like this, someone not only easy to talk to, but who understood the difference between an adjustable wrench and a socket set?

A search of the middle drawer revealed a pile of parts catalogs and flyers. . .and the missing receipts. Eureka! That would get Steve off his back for at least a week.

And in just one week, Beth Newman would go out of his life. His elation at finding the receipts dimmed. Seven days. Would it be possible to find out whether this budding friendship might grow into something more special in so little time? He'd never believed anything so critically important could be determined over such a short term. But then, he'd never experienced an attraction as strong as this one before.

Maybe he should just enjoy the time Beth would be at Harrigan's Cove, cling to the knowledge that such women existed, and after she left make more effort to spend time off the resort looking for someone like her. But he had the uneasy feeling that a woman *like* Beth wouldn't do. What he wanted was not a copy but the original.

Connor didn't know how much one person could learn about another in only a week, but he planned to find out. Starting today.

Beth tapped softly on the door of Gwen's hale, not wanting to disturb either her or Ray if they happened to be resting. Gwen swung the door open almost before Beth finished knocking.

"How's the patient today?" Beth asked. She stepped inside and took a better look at her sister. "How are you, for that matter? You look awful."

"Thank you so much. That's just what I needed to hear."

"I'm not kidding, Gwen. You look exhausted. Why don't I stay with Ray this afternoon? You can go walk along the beach or relax by the pool. I really think you need a break, and it would give me something to do."

Gwen closed her eyes and gave a hollow laugh. "Only you could wind up at a place like this and say you have nothing to do."

Beth winced. "But I don't. Nothing practical, anyway. Come on, Gwen, you planned this vacation and you aren't getting to enjoy any of it. I'm the one who's out of place here; you're in your element. Get out and have some fun."

"It's okay," Gwen said with a feeble attempt at a smile. "Really. Ray needs me, and I wouldn't feel right about leaving him now." She leaned her head against the door frame, then took a closer look at Beth.

"Something's happened. You don't look like you're at loose ends anymore. You must have learned how to fit in after all, or else. . ." Gwen let the comment trail off and a speculative gleam glittered in her eyes. Her voice dropped to a whisper. "Have you met someone?"

Beth could feel the telltale flush rise from her neck to her cheeks.

"I knew it!" Gwen crowed. "I knew you could find someone here if you just put your mind to it. This is wonderful! It almost makes being cooped up in this sickroom worthwhile." She clasped her hands. "So who is it? Evan?"

"Not exactly. He's been gone for days, remember?"

"You mean you actually got acquainted with someone here on your own? That's even better. Who is it? Come on, give!"

Beth swallowed hard. "His name is Connor—"

"Connor." Gwen rolled the name around on her tongue as though sampling its flavor. She nodded. "Beth and Connor. Yes, it sounds good together." She grasped Beth's arm and propelled her out to the veranda.

"So how did you meet him? Come on," she prompted when Beth hesitated. "I have to have some compensation for being stuck here watching Ray's spots multiply. Let me guess—you met him playing tennis. No, I forgot you don't play. Walking on the beach? That would be so incredibly romantic!"

"Actually," Beth began, "you may have gotten a glimpse of him a few days ago." She squeezed her eyes shut and delivered the blow. "When he came by to fix my lamp." She braced herself for the explosion, but none came. She opened her eyes again to find Gwen gaping like a stranded fish.

"You don't mean. . .you *can't* mean. . ." Gwen's voice went higher up the scale with every syllable. "Don't tell me you've gone and gotten mixed up with a maintenance man?"

"He's the maintenance supervisor. It's more of a management-level position."

"Oh, he's a *supervisor*. I see. That makes it all right then. Instead of wearing a greasy uniform, he fixes things while wearing a tie."

Beth tried—and failed—to squelch the flash of anger that shot through her. "That's just like you to see the position instead of the person. Connor is a decent, hard-working man. He also happens to have a wonderful personality and is even better looking than Evan, not that it matters. On top of that, he loves God."

She paused for breath, her chest heaving. "Can't you see? All the things you consider so important don't matter a bit to me. I'd a hundred times rather care for someone who knows what it is to work for a living and has his priorities straight than decide who I want to spend my life with based on the size of his bankroll."

"Then I hope you and Mr. Fix-It have a lovely time together. If the sink stops up, I'll know just who to call."

Beth flung up her hands and stomped off the veranda. She started up the steps to her hale, then stopped. Right now she wanted more than just a wall separating her and Gwen.

A shower of sand sprayed into the air. Beth watched the particles scatter in the wind, then aimed another kick at a different spot on the beach. The curved edge of a shell popped up above the surface of the sand. She bent to retrieve it and held it up so its pearly surface could catch the sunlight. Only God could have combined such delicacy and strength.

"Do clams and starfish have problems getting along, Lord, or is it just people who rub one another the wrong way? I hate letting Gwen get to me like that."

"Don't tell me you've been reduced to talking to seashells." Connor emerged from the fringe of palm trees.

"It might be better than talking to some people. Not you," she hastened to explain. "My sister and I just had a spat, and I was trying to sort things out. With God, not the seashell."

"That's the best place to take a problem." He scooped up a handful of sand and let it trickle through his fingers. "How would you like to get away from the resort for awhile? I thought we might go hiking in the Iao Valley tomorrow, if you're interested."

Beth's remaining irritation melted away. She grinned. "What time do I need to be ready?"

Chapter 5

It's going to be a great day.

Connor opened the door to the registration area and let Beth inside. She smiled her thanks. He linked his fingers with hers and led her down the hallway to his office. "I'll only be a minute. Barnabas wanted me to drop off these revisions of the plans for the new fountain before I left." He crossed the hall to his brother's office, intending to toss the folder on the desk and be on his way.

Barnabas rose from his desk and crossed the space between them. Connor held the folder out, but Barnabas ignored his outstretched hand and walked past him to where Beth stood waiting. "It's good to see you again," he said with a smile.

Connor tried again. "I just wanted to give you the—"

"Ready to head out?" Steve emerged from his office down the hall, followed by Alex. They stopped beside Barnabas.

Connor waved the folder in Barnabas's direction one more time, then gave up. No one had any interest in the new fountain. Not with Beth in the room. All three of his brothers grinned at her with the same inane expression.

"It's about time Connor took a break," Alex told her. "We all think he needs to get out and have more fun."

Beth nodded and smiled, not seeming to be put off by the group inspection. Connor knew his brothers, though. He had to get her out of there before they went into playful mode and started recounting some of his childhood exploits best left forgotten.

He circled the trio and came up behind Beth. "We'll be leaving now," he told them. He shoved the folder at Barnabas. "Here are the revisions you wanted." He placed his hand in the small of Beth's back and guided her outside. At the door, he glanced back over his shoulder. All three of them still stood there, watching. Alex gave him a wink and thumbs-up. Connor cringed. They hadn't gotten out of there a moment too soon.

"I assume those were the rest of the Harrigan brothers?" At Connor's rueful nod, Beth chuckled. "They seem nice."

The tension in his shoulders eased. If he'd had his way, he wouldn't have arranged a meeting with his family until he felt more sure of where their relationship was headed. . .if they even had a relationship, he reminded himself. Apparently, his brothers hadn't seen it the same way. Wait until he found a way to repay Barnabas for setting him up like that.

Beth didn't seem upset by their blatant scrutiny, though. His spirits lightened. It could have been worse. Lots worse. At least that hurdle had been cleared.

"This is incredible." Beth looked up from her position on the valley floor and stared at the impossibly steep slopes above her. A lush green carpet blanketed the mountains and lent a hush to the valley that cradled them like the hollow of a giant hand.

Connor reached into his day pack and handed her a water bottle. "It's quite a sight, isn't it?"

"That has to be the understatement of the year." Beth sipped her water and perched on a rock at the edge of the trail. Ahead of them, the Iao Needle towered into the air, its emerald spire pointing to the heavens. Green light filtered through the leafy canopy, softening the vibrant blooms around them. She breathed deeply, savoring the scents of ginger and plumeria. Up the slope to her left, waterfalls drenched the mountain walls. Connor knelt behind her, and she felt him lean close.

"Look up there." He stretched his arm over her left shoulder to point out a spot farther up the trail where a rainbow glistened in the mist of a waterfall. "Beautiful, isn't it?"

"Amazing," Beth murmured, resisting a sudden desire to brush her cheek against his arm. "No wonder people call this paradise."

"I'm glad you like it." Connor's husky whisper caressed her ear. "Ready to hike farther?"

Beth only nodded, not wanting to break the stillness of this wondrous place. She followed him along the trail.

"I hope you worked up an appetite."

Too relaxed to bother with putting her thoughts into words, Beth merely murmured her assent and watched Connor thread his Jeep through the bustle of Lahaina's Front Street. Shoppers of every description strolled at a leisurely pace from one wooden waterfront store to another.

Connor managed to find a parking place and came around the Jeep to let her out. He laced his fingers through hers, and they joined the throng of sightseers. Her hand felt comfortable nestled in his grip, safe—as though it belonged there. They ambled along Front Street past the massive banyan tree and the green and white Pioneer Inn, where a carved wooden sea captain grinned at them from the porch. Beth's stomach rumbled, and she flattened her hand against it, hoping Connor hadn't noticed. Maybe they could stop in one of the ubiquitous burger places before long.

Instead, they continued walking to the end of the next block, then turned up a side road. "Ready for dinner?" Connor asked.

Beth stared at the open-air restaurant before her. Even with its relaxed island motif, it in no way qualified as a burger joint. Connor couldn't be serious. She glanced at him, expecting him to laugh. Instead, he took her elbow and led her up the porch steps. "How about a seat on the veranda?"

In a daze, Beth let him seat her at a table in the shade of a mango tree. Her first glance at the menu confirmed her suspicions. The prices were every bit as high as she feared. She shot another glance at Connor. Maybe she could offer him a graceful way out. "I think I'll just have a salad."

"Is something wrong? You don't like the selection?"

His worried expression shot a twinge of remorse through her. He didn't have to impress her by bringing her to this expensive place. She knew all too well how tight a workingman's budget could be. Still, she couldn't bring herself to hurt him by disparaging his gesture.

"Not at all. It looks wonderful."

"Great." He grinned at her over his menu. "Order anything you want. They do a great job with mahimahi here. The sword-fish is good too."

Beth blinked at his familiarity with the restaurant's offerings. Her discomfort eased a bit, and she scanned the menu with interest. "How about the chicken long rice?"

"Sounds good. I'll have the lomi salmon."

A smiling waiter took their orders and their menus, and Connor stared at her with eyes as blue as the deep pools they had passed along the trail. A crease formed in his left cheek when he smiled. He reached across the table to cover her hand with his own.

"I had a wonderful day," he said.

"Me too." Another understatement. "Wonderful" didn't come close to describing the contentment she felt in Connor's presence.

He gave her a slow wink that made her tingle. It would be easy to get used to that wink. And those eyes. And that smile.

But she'd be going home in a few days. She would do well to remember that. No matter how wonderful Connor might be, no matter how comfortable she felt with him, he made his home on this island and hers lay on the other side of the vast Pacific. People didn't commute between Wichita and Maui.

She took advantage of the waiter's return to pull her hand away.

Connor didn't seem to notice. "How's your chicken?"

"Delectable." Beth sampled another forkful and sighed with pleasure. "I love the ginger flavor. It's times like this I regret not having my own restaurant."

Connor set his fork down and stared. "And here I thought I was sitting across from an accomplished repair person. You mean you're actually a chef in disguise?"

"More like a chef in my dreams." She nibbled at her sweet potatoes and sipped her iced tea. "I started college with the idea of getting a degree in culinary arts."

"So how did you go from fine cuisine to replacing water pumps?"

Beth polished off the last of her noodles and swirled her tea in a gentle motion. "My dad got sick at the end of my freshman year—a heart problem he'd never suspected. It was serious enough that my mother had to scale back her work hours to part time so she could take care of him at home. That meant someone else had to help take up the slack."

"So you and your sister had to drop out and go to work?"

"Not my sister. Just me." Beth pressed her lips together and tried not to let the long-standing resentment show. "Gwen had just finished her junior year. She was majoring in communications and had her whole career mapped out. The way Gwen planned it, she'd be a nationally known news anchor by the time she was thirty. Money, prestige, recognition."

Connor whistled softly. "An ambitious lady."

"To put it mildly. Anyway, she only had two semesters left. It made more sense for me to take a break and get a job than for her to quit when she was so close to finishing school. At least that's what Gwen said. Everyone thought I'd have plenty of time to go back and get my degree later, after Dad got better."

Connor's smile disappeared. "How long did it take him to recover?"

Beth shook her head. "He didn't. He only lived another year and a half, then it was just Mom and me. After awhile, Mom went back to work full time and had enough to support herself. By that time, I was so busy just making ends meet, I didn't have any time for school."

"What about your sister's big career?"

"It didn't happen. She met Ray just before she graduated. Marrying him gave her the kind of status it would have taken her years to come by in the communications world—and with a lot less effort. They had the wedding four months later. She's never had to work a day in her life."

Beth didn't know when Connor's hand wrapped itself around hers again, but she welcomed its steady warmth. She returned the pressure of his fingers and hoped he understood how much she appreciated his silent sympathy.

"I take it the two of you have reconciled, since you're traveling together."

Beth gave a short laugh. "This trip is something of a mission for Gwen. Her goal in life is to marry me off to someone in Ray's income bracket. She thinks I'll be happy if I'm just like her."

"I'm glad you're not." His smile returned, warming her even more than his handclasp.

After supper, they rejoined the parade on Front Street. Connor draped his arm lightly over her shoulders, as if to protect her from the crush of tourists.

"What about you?" she asked. "How did you wind up overseeing the maintenance at Harrigan's Cove?"

Connor shrugged. The action lessened the distance between them. "It isn't much of a story. My dad felt strongly that all his kids should have a college education. I got my degree in mechanical engineering at Cal State, then got a job redesigning production equipment for an injection molding factory." Two vertical lines appeared between his brows. "Too much time in the office and not enough outside. It only took a few months for me to know I'd rather be back on Maui. I do plenty of office work at the Cove, but I still have the opportunity to go out and get my hands dirty, and it would be hard to find a prettier place to do it in."

"You said 'back on Maui.' You mean you were born here? You're not a transplant?"

"No, I'm a Maui native. My whole family's still here. We all had the chance to take off and spread our wings, but all of us wound up coming back home."

They took their time meandering past the shops, eyeing the multitude of souvenirs in the windows, and sometimes going inside to investigate further. Beth found herself enthralled with one shop featuring everything from inexpensive trinkets to fine handmade crafts. Connor followed with an indulgent grin while she browsed its aisles.

She picked out a coral necklace for Laura and a set of

monkey pod bowls to send her mother. After some thought, she selected a box of chocolate-covered macadamia nuts for Gwen and Ray. They ought to have something to enjoy on this trip to counter spending the better part of two weeks in the confines of their cottage.

Beth carried her finds to the counter and pulled out her wallet. Her gaze fell on a string of cobalt blue lampwork beads. Their color fascinated her. Blue as a Hawaiian lagoon. *Blue as Connor's eyes.* She added it to her other purchases. It would serve as a keepsake of this magical evening when those unforgettable eyes had stared across the table into her own.

Ships' bells clanged in the harbor, their music carrying clearly on the evening breeze. Beth slowed when they passed a stand where a lei vendor had draped his wares over a wooden railing. Her gaze rested wistfully on the exotic blooms.

"How about some flowers for the lovely lady?" the seller called.

Connor tucked her hand into the crook of his arm and halted to peruse the selection. "Is there any special one you'd like?"

Beth shook her head, not wanting him to feel pressured to buy her anything more. He'd already spent enough on dinner.

"Then let me choose for you." He handed a bill to the vendor and lifted a string of plumeria from the rail. "Like it?"

Beth traced the edge of one of the creamy five-petaled blossoms and leaned forward to inhale its heady perfume. "Very much."

Connor lifted the lei over Beth's head and settled it on her shoulders. He cupped her chin in one hand, and his thumb stroked her cheek. "Aloha," he whispered.

Chapter 6

Beth towel-dried her freshly shampooed hair. After a quick perusal of her closet, she pulled on a flowered top and a pair of khaki shorts. Yesterday's outing with Connor had renewed her desire to see more of the island. First, though, she would enjoy a leisurely breakfast. *Macadamia nut pancakes. . .mmm.* If Gwen insisted on putting her up in style, she wouldn't pass up the chance to indulge in the Harrigans' luscious recipes.

She ran her finger along the inside of her waistband. Maybe she shouldn't indulge too much more. The slack that had been there when she arrived seemed to have disappeared. If Connor had some spare time, she might see if he wanted to go hiking again. How much activity would it take to counteract those delicious extra calories?

Then again, it wouldn't do to get too used to Connor's company. In less time than she cared to think about, she would be headed back to the mainland. Back to the reality of finding a new job and resuming her usual routine. Unexpected tears stung her eyes at the thought.

Beth pressed her fingertips against her eyelids. *What is wrong with you? You didn't want to come here in the first place. You've had a nice break, but your real life is back at home waiting. Nothing has changed.*

Nothing except Connor becoming a part of her life. *A temporary part.* Hadn't she heard enough about the perils of a vacation romance? She might feel more at home here with Connor than she ever had back in Wichita, but that didn't mean a thing except that she'd allowed island sunsets and soft breezes to dull her good judgment.

Enough. She ran her fingers through her damp hair, scrunching the russet waves into shape, then added a dash of lipstick. She'd been given a taste of paradise, but paradise couldn't last forever this side of heaven.

Beth gave a tentative smile to the woman at the reservation desk and breathed a sigh of relief when no one questioned her walking down the hallway to Connor's office. She hated disturbing him during work hours, but she'd only take a moment of his time.

She darted a quick glance at the other office doors along the hall. Good, they were both closed. The Harrigan brothers did seem to have a lot of respect for Connor. Still, it wouldn't do to create any reason for them to find fault with him.

Connor looked up with a pleased expression when she slipped into his office.

"I won't keep you long," Beth said. "I just wanted to know if you'd like to go for another hike after you get off work today."

"How about a counter offer? My family is having a cookout this evening. I was planning to look you up later to see if you'd like to come. We could go hiking again tomorrow afternoon, if that's all right with you."

Beth drew her eyebrows together. "Won't they mind having a total stranger barging in?"

The crease in his left cheek deepened. "I wouldn't call you a stranger. They're all hoping you'll come."

So he'd told his family about her. Beth's lips parted in a surprised smile. "All right, I'd like that."

"And you'll keep tomorrow open?"

"Are you sure you can take this much time off?"

The corners of Connor's eyes crinkled when he smiled down at her. He reached out to smooth back a stray curl, and the backs of his fingers grazed her cheek. "I consider it time well spent."

"What about Barnabas and Steve? Will they mind?"

"They're fine with it. I'll pick you up at seven, okay?"

"Fine." *Fine?* Another evening with Connor would far surpass "fine."

"Do I look okay?" Beth peered over her shoulder at the mirror behind her.

"Stand still," Gwen ordered. "I can't tell with you twisting around like that." She tilted her head to one side, then nodded her approval. "You'll be fine. It's just a family gathering, right?"

"That's what he said." Beth ran her hands down the sides

of the dark blue hibiscus-patterned sundress she'd bought that afternoon. Connor might see the occasion as a simple family get-together, but she felt the need to wear something special, even if it meant a bit of a splurge.

"How formal could it be? He's a maintenance man, after all. The whole family's probably made up of nothing but blue-collar workers."

"Maintenance supervisor, Gwen, with a mechanical engineering degree. He oversees the whole physical plant, everything from fixing lamps to keeping up the grounds to maintaining the buildings and equipment. It's a lot more than the menial job you make it out to be."

Gwen sniffed. "I still can't believe you've been given the opportunity of a lifetime and you've thrown it away dallying with a—"

"*Gwen.*"

"All right. I'll even wish you a good time. Have a lovely evening." She turned toward the door and glanced out the window. "Here comes your Sir Galahad now, driving his white charger." She waved to Beth, managed a cool nod in Connor's direction, and returned to her own side of the hale.

Connor parked his golf cart and bounded up the steps. The appreciative look on his face dissolved Beth's doubts about the wisdom of her purchase. He reached for her hand and helped her down the steps. "Ready, Milady? Your steed awaits."

Beth expected him to steer the cart toward the lot where he parked his Jeep. To her surprise, he turned up an access road that led to the back part of the resort.

"Where are we going?"

"To see the family, where else?"

"Your parents live on the resort?"

"It's just Pop now, but yes, he lives here. He says he likes being close to all the action, even if he is retired."

Beth hadn't considered the possibility of others in Connor's family being employed at the Cove. His father must have worked here for a long time to have been able to make special housing arrangements.

The cart glided up to a long, low house set back in a mango grove. Connor pushed open the front door without knocking and ushered her inside. "We're pretty informal here," he told her.

They entered a tastefully furnished living room. A little girl about four years old ran into the room and stopped when she saw them.

"Hi, Sweetie." Connor squatted down and put himself on her level. "I've brought someone for you to meet. Say hello to Beth."

The little girl's dark brown eyes focused on Beth with a solemn gaze, as if taking stock of the newcomer. A shy smile parted her lips, and she wiggled her fingers at Beth in greeting. With a soft giggle, she ran back out the door she had come through.

Connor chuckled and got to his feet. "That was Abby. My brother and his wife adopted her. She's quite a kid."

Beth grinned, thoroughly charmed by the dark-haired sprite.

"I hear voices," Connor told her. "Let's head this way."

They followed the sound of Abby's happy chatter and entered a spacious, airy kitchen. A tall woman greeted them with a smile for Connor and an outstretched hand for Beth. "Welcome," she said before Connor had a chance to speak. "You must be Beth. And I hear you've already met Abby." She turned a loving look on the child who clung to her mother's silk slacks. "I'm Liliana. The rest of the family is out back. Why don't you join them? We have a little cleaning up to do." She pointed to Abby's grubby knees and led the little girl off.

"Are you sure I'm dressed for the occasion?" Beth asked. The dress that had seemed so right a few moments before now struck her as downright dowdy in comparison with the other woman's elegant tunic outfit.

"Don't worry. That's just Liliana's personal style. We have an agreement with her: We don't have to dress in designer suits, and we don't make her wear aloha shirts." He grinned broadly.

"Let's go introduce you to the rest of the clan." He pushed open the back door to reveal a lush tropical garden filled with vibrant blooms. A portly man with graying hair detached himself from the group in a shadowed corner of the yard and came to greet them.

"Beth, I'd like you to meet my father. Pop, this is Beth Newman."

Connor's father beamed and clasped Beth's hand in both his own. "So this is the lovely lady who's made such an impression on my son. Welcome, Beth."

The warmth of his greeting put to rest any embarrassment Beth might have felt about being the topic of family discussion. She returned his smile with pleasure and studied his features.

He had hair a couple of shades darker than Connor's and his eyes were brown, not blue. Still, she could see a resemblance in the shape of his jaw and the crease that lined his cheek.

"Let me introduce you to my other boys." He turned.

Connor put his hand on his father's arm. "She's already met them, Pop."

Beth swiveled her head toward Connor and started to speak. Behind her, the door flew open and Abby hurtled across the yard toward the group of three men. "Daddy, I'm all cleaned up!"

She wrapped her arms around the tall man in the middle, who scooped her up and turned toward Beth. Barnabas Harrigan carried his daughter across the yard and put his arm around Liliana's waist. "It's good to see you again," he told Beth. "Pop, I think those steaks are about ready."

"Great. Tell Alex and Steve to light the torches, and we'll be ready to eat. Connor, can you give me a hand putting those tables together?"

"Sure, Pop. Excuse me," he said to Beth. "I won't be but a moment."

Chapter 7

Beth watched the two men walk away and tried to shake off the feeling she'd just been punched in the stomach. Barnabas, Alex, and Steve were brothers, that much she'd known. But Connor? A Harrigan?

Why hadn't he told her? For that matter, why hadn't she asked his last name? Back at home, she'd never dream of spending time with anyone without knowing something as basic as that. But here the thought had never crossed her mind. Maybe the feeling of existing in another world had been to blame. Maybe she'd just lost her head. He'd simply been Connor, and she hadn't needed to know more. She'd never considered the possibility of his working at Harrigan's Cove as part of a family business. . .his family's.

Fragments of conversation drifted through her mind: *My whole family's here. Pop likes being close to all the action.* The clues had been there, but they'd been only that, clues. A sense of betrayal mounted within her. Why hadn't he come right out and told her instead of resorting to this masquerade?

Her first instinct was to walk back through the house, out the front door, and back to her hale. Instead, she forced her legs to carry her toward the tables set up on the lanai where the Harrigan clan stood waiting. Connor seated her between himself and Liliana and clasped her hand while Pop asked the blessing.

Beth had no idea whether the meal lived up to the standards of Harrigan cuisine. She had trouble enough trying to form coherent responses to the comments the family addressed to her. If she could only get through this interminable evening, she would spend the remainder of her stay keeping to herself and away from a certain Connor Harrigan.

At last the meal came to an end. Beth helped Liliana clear the table with her mind on autopilot and didn't wait for Connor to ask twice if she was ready to leave. They walked back to the golf cart in silence.

Connor steered the cart through the darkness and congratulated himself on a successful evening. He hadn't been sure just how his family would react to him finally showing an interest in someone, but their reception of Beth had surpassed his hopes. Another hurdle conquered.

His plan to get to know Beth better seemed to be working admirably. He'd never been so relaxed with anyone, never enjoyed a woman's company more. If only he could think of a way to keep her here on Maui.

He kept the cart at its slowest speed, not wanting to end their time together any sooner than necessary. Maybe now wouldn't be a bad time to test the waters and see if Beth might be willing to consider prolonging her stay. He let the cart drift to the side of the path under the sheltering arms of a shower tree. A quiet conversation, uninterrupted by family or resort guests, seemed in order.

Connor slid his arm along the back of the seat and cupped Beth's shoulder in his hand. He let the moment stretch out, not wanting to break the comfortable silence.

Beth stiffened under his touch. "Why didn't you tell me?" she demanded in a tight voice.

Connor blinked. "Tell you what?"

"That you're a Harrigan." Beth swiveled in the seat to face him, pulling out of his grasp. Even in the moonlight, he could see the tension etched on her face.

Connor spread his hands wide. "You mean you didn't know?"

"How could I have known? All you ever said was, 'Hi, I'm Connor, the maintenance supervisor,' not 'Hi, I'm Connor Harrigan, part owner of this resort.' You left out that one little detail."

He cast his mind back over their times together. He couldn't remember whether he'd introduced himself by his full name or not. "Maybe you're right. I'm sorry; I guess it just didn't come up. But it's no big deal. What difference does it make?"

"Plenty. You let me think you're just an ordinary person like me. Not a Harrigan. Not one of them."

Connor knit his brows together. "Them? What do you mean?"

Beth crossed her arms and stared past his shoulder into the darkness. "One of the moneyed class. The *haves*, as opposed to the *have-nots*. Not someone who understands what it's like to have to scrimp and save to get along."

"Is that what you think, that we live the good life and don't have a care in the world?" He reached out to touch her shoulder. "Come on, Beth, you've watched me work. Have you seen me sit around on my hands? Running a place like this is hard work, and lots of it, for all of us. It took Pop years to build it up out of nothing, and it's going to take everything my brothers and I can give to keep it going. So far, it's made a nice living for us, but we'll have to stay on top of every detail to keep it that way. Nothing's been handed to me on a platter."

"Just a regular working guy, right?" She waved her arm in a half circle, taking in the luxuriant grounds. "I thought this was your workplace, Connor, not your home. It makes a lot of difference."

Beth closed her hale door with a resounding thump. She hadn't taken more than five steps toward the bedroom before she heard a peremptory knock. She marched back to the door and swung it open, ready to give Connor Harrigan a piece of her mind.

"I didn't expect you back so soon." Gwen breezed past her and curled up on the white wicker sofa. "It didn't take long to sweep those stars out of your eyes once you met the rest of the family, did it?"

"You'll never believe this—"

"It doesn't matter." Gwen waved her hand as though shooing away a pesky insect. "I have some good news. Ray is much better. Not only is he better, he feels so badly about me missing the time I'd planned to spend with you that he wants to make it up to us both. He's made arrangements to stay on a few extra days. Isn't that wonderful?"

"Gwen, I—"

"I know what you're going to say. You're worried about the cost and you need to get back and start looking for a job." She dismissed the notion with another wave of her hand. "Ray is more than willing to pay for it, and you're not out a thing. Think of it this way—you'll have that much more savings still in the bank when you get back."

"That isn't it. It's Connor." Beth drew in a deep breath and hoped her voice wouldn't break. "I found out tonight he's one of the Harrigans."

Gwen's prolonged silence expressed her shock more clearly than any words could. Eventually she found her voice. "Connor. Your Connor? The same Connor you've been spending all this time with?"

Beth nodded dismally. "One and the same. Can you believe it?"

Gwen stared in wonder. "No one would." Her crimson lips widened into a broad smile, and she jumped up to fold Beth in an exuberant hug. "Way to go, little sister! You managed to snare one all on your own. Who'd have thought?"

She took a step back and held Beth at arm's length. "This changes everything. I definitely don't want to get in the way. I'll think of some romantic places Ray and I can visit instead." She leaned forward to peck a kiss on Beth's cheek. "Don't blow it, Sweetie. You don't have much time to set the hook."

Beth watched a shaft of moonlight creep its way across her bed. She rolled over and slammed her fist into her pillow. She thought she knew Connor. But her new friend—the man who made her glad she'd let Gwen drag her along on this trip and dread the thought of leaving Maui, the one "real" person she'd encountered on the resort—turned out to be less real than she'd thought.

The blazing anger she'd felt earlier rose up again and flooded through her. She ought to arrange for the shuttle to take her to Kahului Airport in the morning and catch the first flight back to the mainland. If it weren't for the fact that Gwen held her ticket, she'd do just that.

While Connor's duplicity shocked her, Gwen's 180-degree turnaround in attitude didn't surprise Beth one bit. Just like her sister to assume Beth would go full speed after the Harrigan bankroll.

Beth got up and padded across the floor. Sliding the glass door open, she stepped out onto the veranda. The moonlight painted a silvery pathway across the water and silhouetted the palm trees on the beach. The pounding of the surf continued its ceaseless rhythm. A perfect setting. Paradise.

Did paradise always contain a serpent to mar its perfection? Beth rubbed her arms and leaned against the bamboo rail, wondering how she would be able to avoid Connor for the remainder of her stay.

And knowing in her heart she didn't want to.

Chapter 8

"Y es!" Connor grinned at the new departure date on the Newman/Lawson entry. He thought the one-sided discussion he'd overheard about extending a party's stay might concern Beth and her family, but he had to make sure. Stealthily, he set the reservations computer back to its main page and hurried to his office before anyone spotted him.

He leaned back in his desk chair and steepled his fingers. He'd been given more time to show Beth what really mattered to him. To let her know that God, not money, received the honor in his life. To convince her that leaving him and returning to the mainland would be the biggest mistake she could ever make.

Connor checked the calendar on his desk. Nothing there that couldn't be put off a few more days. He headed out toward the restaurant. Beth ought to be eating lunch right about now.

She shouldn't be here. Beth watched the sugarcane fields roll by as Connor steered his Jeep along the highway. It had all happened in a flash of flustered impulse. If she'd had a grain of sense, she would have turned down his offer and not set herself up for more disillusionment. She could have gone back to her hale, taken a tennis lesson, or gone for a swim. Anything but agree to accompany Connor on his mysterious outing.

"So where is it we're going?" she asked.

"I want to show you something."

The road wound higher, now skirting rolling hills that reminded her more of Midwestern ranch land than any Hawaii travel poster she'd ever seen. Connor let the Jeep drift to a stop beside a towering eucalyptus and led Beth to the top of a low rise. Stands of Norfolk pine dotted the grass-covered slopes. Farther ahead, she could see horses grazing in fenced pastures.

She shook her head. "I never imagined anything like this here."

Connor smiled. "Maui wears many faces. You can't judge the whole island by any one area." He shot her a quick glance and added softly, "Any more than you can judge a group of people by the attitudes of one individual."

Beth chose not to respond.

"Look over there. You can see the West Maui Mountains from here." He pointed out the peaks in the distance, then turned to indicate the brooding volcano behind them. "And on the other side of Haleakala is Hana. You haven't seen even a fraction of Maui yet. You could stay on this island for years and still learn new things about it."

He turned to her and held her gaze with his own. Even across the short distance that separated them, she felt its caress.

"Do you think you could do that, Beth? Spend time getting to know it. . .and me?"

"It wouldn't work." The words stuck in her throat. She tried to see Connor's face through the tears that blurred her vision. "You can't build a relationship based on moonlight and palm trees. There's something about all this tropical splendor that warps your thinking. It's easy to believe something that isn't based on reality can last. . .but it can't."

Connor peeled a strip of bark from a eucalyptus trunk and twisted it in his hands. "I'll grant you that Maui can fill your senses. But how do we know there isn't any hope for us unless we take the time to find out if this is something God wants?"

When Beth didn't respond, he sighed and helped her back into the Jeep. They covered half the distance to the valley before she spoke again.

"There's more to it than that."

"Are you telling me you don't feel the same way I do? That you don't sense something very special between us?"

"That isn't it."

"Then what? The fact that I'm a Harrigan?"

"You can't serve God and money, Connor. I've seen what it does to people, and I don't want any part of that."

"Why? Because your sister chose to put money first? That doesn't make sense. Not everyone is like her. Would it make a difference to you if I gave up my job? I'd still be the same person, whether I worked at the Cove or not. No," he amended, "I wouldn't be the same, because I wouldn't be nearly as happy. And it has nothing to do with money. It's about family, about my place in life."

He slowed to ease the Jeep around a sharp curve. "Sure, we've done well. But the income isn't what's important. The main thing is I'm part of something my father started years ago, and you have to admit it's a great family venture. Being part owner doesn't change who I am. I'm just a guy who loves his work, his family, and his Lord, not in that order." The Jeep picked up speed again. "Remember what the book of James says about not letting a person's financial status change the way you treat them? Maybe you're the one who needs to check your priorities here."

"Are you saying—"

A loud bang exploded under her feet. The Jeep lurched to the right, then pivoted into a spin.

"Hold on!" Connor yelled, fighting to regain control of the wheel.

The world seemed to shift into slow motion. The Jeep teetered at the edge of the roadway, then slid over the embankment and landed with a sickening thud.

Time moved back to normal speed. Beth allowed herself to breathe again. "At least we're right side up," she said in a shaky voice. She released her white-knuckled grip on the armrest, forcing her fingers open one by one. "I'm okay, how about you?"

Connor didn't answer. Panic clutched at Beth's stomach when she saw him slumped against his window with his eyes closed. She yanked her seat belt off and knelt on the seat next to him.

"Connor? Can you hear me? *Connor!*" Fear threaded its

way through her limbs. She took hold of his shoulders, then pulled away again, afraid to move him. Instead, she looked him over as best she could. She couldn't see any blood. Could he be bleeding internally? She ran her hands through his hair, careful not to jostle his head. Her fingers touched a bump the size of a golf ball just above his left ear.

She needed to call for help. Beth scrabbled through the debris on the floor until she located Connor's cell phone. She turned it on and checked the display screen. No signal.

She pushed open her door and clambered up the slope to the roadway. Still nothing.

"What am I going to do, Lord?" Her breath came in short, ragged gasps. She scanned the road in both directions. Of all the times for there to be no traffic! How many miles was it to a phone? And did she dare leave Connor alone for the time it would take her to walk that distance?

"Beth?" At the sound of Connor's voice, she scrambled back down the slope, nearly falling in her haste.

Connor leaned against a flowering tree, one hand pressed to his head. "Are you all right? I was getting worried."

"*You* were worried?" Relief made her knees go weak. "I didn't know how I was going to get you out of here."

Connor held out his free arm, and she slipped into his embrace without a moment's hesitation. He smelled of eucalyptus and sunshine. He pulled her close, and she pressed against his side, calmed by the steady sound of his heartbeat.

"So what do we do now? You're going to need some medical attention."

"I just got a knock on the head. I'll be fine."

Maybe that bump had been harder than she thought. "Connor, you were unconscious. You could have a concussion. Let me look at your eyes." She placed her hands on either side of his face and drew him close. The pupils looked normal, but she was no medical expert. Except for the swelling over his ear, he looked all right. She checked his eyes again, looking deeper into the blue pools that made her think of plunging into the warm waters of a Maui lagoon.

His cheeks moved under her palms when he smiled. "What do you think, Doc? Do I pass?"

"Mm-hmm." Her thumb traced the crease in his cheek. "I was so scared." She linked her hands behind his neck.

Connor chuckled. "I should get hit on the head more often." He brushed the curls back from her face and cradled her head in his hands. He lowered his lips to hers.

A shower of blossoms drifted down around them, brushing against her face and shoulders with the touch of a butterfly's wings. Connor plucked one of the blooms from her hair and held it out to her. Beth twirled it between her thumb and two fingers, marveling at its delicacy.

"That's an ohia blossom," Connor whispered. "Did you know that?"

She shook her head and watched a gentle smile cross his face.

"See how much more you need to learn about Maui?"

Beth started to turn loose of the flower, then changed her mind and tucked the red blossom into the pocket of her shirt.

Connor straightened and held out his hand. "Looks like we'll have to walk for help. Ready for another hike?"

"Are you sure you're up to it?"

"The way I'm feeling right now, I could fly all the way home." He helped her up the slope, and they set off down the road hand in hand.

A mile farther along, Connor cleared his throat and put his arm around her shoulder. "Barnabas and Liliana are having the rest of us over to their suite this weekend," he told her. "They asked if you'd come too. What do you think? Want to give us another chance?"

Beth hesitated, then said, "Okay. No promises, but I'll come."

Footsore and more than ready for bed, Beth pulled on her nightshirt and wondered what she had gotten herself into by agreeing to attend another Harrigan gathering. She picked up her clothes to toss them into the laundry hamper. A red blossom fluttered to the floor. Beth picked it up with a sense of wonder, reliving the tenderness of Connor's kiss under the ohia tree.

She knew why she'd agreed, even against her better judgment.

"See anything you like?"

Beth turned from her survey of the buffet table and smiled into Barnabas Harrigan's eyes. Blue eyes like Connor's. Why hadn't she noticed the similarity before?

"I was just admiring the way you have everything arranged. It looks lovely, just like everything in your home."

"Ah, yes. Connor said you had an interest in food." He flashed a smile at her, and a dimple appeared in his left cheek at the same spot a crease would have formed in Connor's. "A woman of many talents. I can well understand why my brother finds you so intriguing."

A week ago the comment would have made Beth bristle. Tonight she returned his smile, surprised at what a difference her change in attitude made in her perception of Barnabas. Instead of seeing him as a professional host whose friendliness ran surface deep, she now saw him simply as Connor's brother. In that light, he didn't appear any different than the people she knew in Wichita.

She turned to look at the family group gathered around the low coffee table. Neither did Alex or Steve. Even Liliana, once Beth got past her outer elegance and expensive clothing, had a charming personality and obviously adored her daughter and husband. She could have been having dinner with the family of one of her friends back home.

Sleep eluded Beth that night. Kicking off the wadded sheets, she got up, slipped on a shirt and a pair of shorts, and let herself outside. The pathway to the beach warmed her bare feet. She sat in a secluded spot on the sand and drew her knees up under her chin.

Stars glowed in a black velvet sky. Curls of foam formed scallops on the shore only a few yards from her feet, reminding her of the vastness of sea and space and her own tiny spot in the universe.

Her sigh mingled with the night sounds. She tried to picture her position on the beach from the perspective of heaven. How insignificant she must look to the Creator of heaven and earth! Yet God saw her, knew her as an individual inside and out, with all her weaknesses. . .and loved her just the same.

Beth rested her forehead on her knees. "Connor was right, Lord. I judged too quickly."

Worse, she had been guilty of doing the same thing she'd accused Gwen of for so many years—looking at the position rather than the person. The knowledge shamed her.

Her Father's grace beckoned. "I'm sorry, Lord, so sorry. Please forgive me." His peace washed over her like the waves that lapped at her feet.

"So what kind of progress are you making?" Gwen sipped her iced mocha and leaned across their beachside table. "You don't have much time."

Beth shrugged. "I'm learning a lot about Connor—and his family. But I can't make a lifetime decision based on knowing someone just a couple of weeks." She drew a deep breath. "I've learned some things about myself too. You and I tend to see a lot of things differently. We always have. I haven't changed my mind about what I feel is important, but I want you to know I'm sorry for being so hard on you."

She reached out and laid her hand on her sister's arm. "At the same time, a relationship with Jesus really is the only hope for true security. I promise I won't badger you anymore, but think about it. Please." She left the table before she lost her resolve to let God work things out with Gwen without her interference.

Beth tossed a shell into the ocean and pondered the irony of it all. She had balked at coming to Maui in the first place; now she couldn't bear the thought of leaving the island. Or Connor.

She closed her eyes and let the balmy breeze play across her face. All her preconceived notions seemed to have been turned upside-down with the advent of Connor Harrigan. She found the prospect of going back to Wichita to start a job hunt utterly depressing.

She wiggled her feet down through the warm sand to the cool moisture beneath and considered what kind of job she ought to look for. For the first time, she had the opportunity to pursue a whole new direction.

Beth walked back to her veranda and sank onto the chaise. What did she really want to do? She reached for the snack tray she'd set out earlier and speared a pineapple slice. Halfway to her mouth, her hand froze in midair. An idea—a wild, impossible idea—took shape in her mind.

Chapter 9

She's leaving today. Connor steered his Jeep through a picture-perfect setting that wouldn't be perfect any longer without Beth.

How could his life have changed so much in such a short time? Only a few weeks ago he hadn't known Beth Newman existed. Now, he knew he couldn't live without her.

He didn't have much time left to convince Beth of the same thing. Somehow between Harrigan's Cove and Kahului Airport he had to make his case.

He parked in front of the reception building and rubbed his palms down the sides of his slacks. At least she had agreed to let him drive her to the airport instead of accompanying Gwen and Ray in the resort shuttle. At this point, every moment counted.

Beth walked up the path from her hale. Connor caught his breath. She looked so right in this place. *Lord, don't let me lose her.*

Seated beside him, Beth rode quietly, gazing at the scenery as it rolled by. Fields of sugarcane made a patchwork on the mountain slopes. On their right, Haleakala loomed, wreathed in a circle of clouds.

Say something! He racked his brain for the right words. What would convince her? He glanced at Beth, wondering if she felt the same sense of urgency. Her hands lay loose in her lap, and she gave no indication of her nerves being stretched to the breaking point. If he had read her wrong, if she didn't really feel the way he hoped she did. . .

He pulled into a parking space at Kahului without uttering a syllable of all he wanted to tell her.

The moment they entered the terminal, Gwen appeared with Ray in tow. "Everything's set. Our luggage is checked and we have our boarding passes." She waved the printed cards.

Connor's stomach knotted. If she left, he'd catch the next flight to Wichita and plead his case there.

The four of them walked toward the gate. Gwen stopped at the security checkpoint and turned to Connor. "I guess it's time to say good-bye. We've enjoyed our stay. I'm sure we'll be back."

His resort training notwithstanding, he couldn't frame a coherent reply. The woman he believed God had placed in his life was about to board a plane, and he hadn't done a thing to stop her.

"Would you excuse us?" Without preamble, he took Beth by the elbow and led her a few steps away.

"Beth, I don't know the right way to say this, but I don't want you to go. I know you have a life back on the mainland. But I'm asking you anyway. Stay here. Please."

Tears pooled in her eyes. Instead of answering, she turned away and walked over to her sister.

Beth blinked back the tears of joy. If she had needed any confirmation of her choice, Connor had just given it to her.

Gwen took both Beth's hands in her own. "I think you're absolutely crazy. You know that, don't you?"

The corners of Beth's mouth quirked up. "I kind of got that impression." Her smile faded and she added, "Whether you think I'm crazy or not, think over what we've talked about, okay?"

Gwen's expression grew serious. She locked gazes with Beth, pressed her lips together, and gave a quick nod. "I will." She pulled Beth into her arms and held her close.

The loudspeaker crackled. "Flight 291 will be boarding in fifteen minutes."

Beth gave her sister one last hug. "I guess it's time. Have a good flight. You too, Ray. And thank you both for everything."

Gwen and Ray went through the checkpoint, waved goodbye, and proceeded to their gate. Beth turned to face Connor. "What do you want to do today? Another hike?"

Connor's mind reeled. He caught Beth's shoulders in a gentle grip. "What just happened here? Did I miss something?"

She linked her arm in his and started walking toward the parking lot. "I've done a lot of thinking about what I want to do with my life. I decided it's high time I finished my education."

Things still weren't meshing. "And. . .?"

She stopped beside the Jeep. "It turns out Maui Community College has a program in culinary arts. I can't think of a more beautiful place to pursue the dream of a lifetime."

He couldn't control the grin that split his face. Then a thought sobered him. "I can't believe I'm asking you this, but have you thought this through? How are you going to live while you're taking classes?"

Beth leaned back against the Jeep with a Cheshire cat smile. "It so happens that I've been offered a job in the food services field."

Connor brightened. "Where? With school and a job, I know you'll be busy. But you might as well resign yourself to spending your spare time with me. And it doesn't matter when that is. I'll adjust my schedule to fit yours."

"I'm sure we can work something out. And you won't have to drive very far." She laughed at his puzzled expression. "Barnabas offered me the job," she explained. "I'll be right there at Harrigan's Cove. Barnabas thinks it's a great idea, by the way. So do Alex and Steve. Nice people, those Harrigans."

Connor pulled her close and shook his head in wonder. After all the arguments and counterarguments he'd rehearsed, God had made it all fall into place without a bit of help from him.

He rubbed his cheek against her hair. "So you're going back to school and you have a job with the nicest bosses in the world. What happens next?"

Beth tilted her head, her brown eyes inches from his own. "We'll have to wait and see," she whispered. She pressed her palm against his cheek and ran her thumb along the crease. "Everything seems right, but we both know we need more time to find out if this is really what God has planned for us.

You said I needed to get to know Maui. To get to know you." Her hands linked behind his neck. "I want to give us a chance."

"Yes!" Connor whooped. He wrapped his arms around Beth and whirled her in circles across the asphalt. His lovely island had become paradise again.

CAROL COX

In addition to writing, Carol's time is devoted to keeping up with her college-age son's schedule, home schooling her young daughter, and serving as a church pianist, youth worker, and 4-H leader. The Arizona native loves any activity she can share with her family in addition to her own pursuits in crafts and local history. She also has had several novels and novellas published. Carol and her family make their home in northern Arizona.

Game of Love

by Denise Hunter

Chapter 1

Callie Andersen came to a weary stop at the white door and dropped her duffel bag by her suitcase. Fighting the colorful lei around her neck, she fished the key from her shirt pocket. A warm wind ruffled the curls hanging past her shoulders. She could hear the roar of the surf crashing on the Maui shores just beyond the hale.

She slipped the key into the door and pushed it open, then turned to retrieve her luggage. The duffel caught on the door-knob, and she stifled a sigh. She shouldn't be doing this. She shouldn't be here alone.

Tropical light poured in through the French doors on the other side of the room, and she could see the perfection of the view beyond. She flicked on the light switch and kicked off her sneakers. All she wanted right now was a bed and some peace and quiet. She scanned the tropical hideaway. A huge bouquet of orchids protruded from a cut-glass vase, and beside it, a green bottle rested in a bucket of half-melted ice. Champagne? She walked closer and read the label. Sparkling Grape Juice.

An envelope leaned against the bucket, the words "Mr. and Mrs. Fischer" splayed across it in red ink. She peeked inside and found gift certificates for two free massages.

Her heart clenched and sent unpleasant tingles through her veins. Her gaze swept across the floor to the huge bed that dominated the room. It was only then that she really noticed the room's red and pink decor. The bed's two plump pillows lay at the head of the bed, a red rose angled across one of them.

An ache started in her stomach and spread through her limbs until they quaked. She told herself it was fatigue. After all, she'd hardly slept in the past forty-eight hours. Her trip had taken a full day of travel from Grabill, Indiana, with two connecting flights and the bus ride to the resort.

Still, it wasn't fatigue that made her heart feel hollow. It wasn't fatigue that made her eyes sting.

Tearing her gaze from the romantic decor, she slipped on her shoes and grabbed her luggage. Her back protested against the weight, and her feet already dreaded the long walk back to the registration building. But there was no way she was staying in this room.

On the walkway, her roller suitcase bumping along behind her, memories of the past forty-eight hours flashed in her mind like a bad slide show.

She saw herself standing in her bedroom, trying on the dress one last time. She heard the phone ringing, heard the giddiness in her voice as she answered it.

She saw her mother's face as she'd told her. Saw the disbelief—the refusal to believe—then the compassion as she pulled her daughter into her arms.

She saw the guilt on Shaun's face as she confronted him at his home. She saw the stubborn set of shoulders when she'd tried to change his mind.

She saw very little after that. The details of the guests and the food and the flowers had been shouldered by her sister and mother.

On what was supposed to be the most wonderful day of her life, in what had to be the most beautiful place on earth, she was completely and utterly alone.

As the suitcase bumped over the cracks in the walkway, it seemed to echo the word. *A-lone, a-lone, a-lone.* This wasn't supposed to be happening. She was supposed to be here celebrating love and marriage. She was supposed to be happy. She was supposed to be starting a wonderful new life with a loving husband.

Alex Harrigan walked through the open-air reservations building on his way to the volleyball court, the soles of his tennis shoes squeaking on the tile floor. He tossed the florescent yellow ball in the air, nodding hellos to guests as he went.

"Alex!"

From behind the check-in desk, his brother Steve waved him down.

Alex approached the desk. "Hey, Steve."

Dressed in business attire and sporting a serious-looking pair of glasses, Steve couldn't look less like a brother of Alex than Bill Gates—except that they shared the renowned Harrigan dimple.

"Those receipts from the luau? I asked you to leave them in my office."

"I did." He gestured past Steve to the hallway behind him. "I put them on your desk."

"I looked on the desk; they're not there." His eyes narrowed.

"No way, Bro, I put them there. I even stapled them together." He walked around the desk and past Steve, through the open doorway.

Steve mumbled something behind him.

"Hey, now, I've been doing much better about keeping track of things, haven't I? Did I not turn in every receipt last month?" Alex began looking under stacks of paper.

"Don't mess those up."

"I wouldn't dream of it."

A raised voice sounded from the check-in desk. "I don't care, I want another room," the female voice stated emphatically.

"Hey, Steve, isn't the girl at the desk new? Maybe you should go help her out. It sounds like one of the guests is unhappy."

Alex watched Steve teeter on the threshold of his office as if worried about leaving it to his mercy. "Don't worry, I won't mess up your system here."

Steve left, and Alex continued shuffling through papers. He distinctly remembered putting them on the desk. Okay, maybe he'd tossed them on the desk, but they still had to be here somewhere. He looked under the stacked trays and in the center drawer, all the while vaguely aware of the distraught guest at the counter and his brother's low-pitched voice. He pulled out the chair and looked under the desk. Voila! There they were, all stapled together. They must have fallen between the desk and computer station. He collected them, grabbed his ball, and started out the door.

The scene at the desk stopped him.

"I know the room is not under *Andersen*. It's under *Fischer*. It's not under my name, it's under my. . .look, there was a change in plans."

Steve's hands played over the keyboard and waited for the information to display on the screen. He tapped his blunt-cut fingernails on the mouse while he waited, a sure sign he was flustered.

Alex's gaze trailed to the guest across from Steve. She looked a lot like many lovely young tourists; but unlike most of them, this one wasn't wearing a smile. In fact, her eyes, as clear blue as the bay outside the door, were red-rimmed. Her ivory skin stretched tautly across her face, except where two little lines puckered between her brows.

"I don't understand, Mrs. Fischer—"

"Andersen. Miss Andersen." She crossed her arms and glared at Steve.

"Sorry, yes, Miss Andersen. We have you booked for the honeymoon suite, is that not right?"

"It is right, but I saw the room. I was just there, and I just can't—"

"It's our nicest hale, Mrs. Fischer. I'm sorry if you're—"

"Miss Andersen!" She fairly hissed the words. "Why can't anyone around here understand—"

"Excuse me, Miss Andersen," Alex soothed. "I'm Alex Harrigan, and I couldn't help overhearing your situation. Perhaps I could be of help." A little charm never hurt. And at least he had gotten her name right.

Steve stepped aside with a shrug. Alex handed him the receipts and turned his attention to the guest.

"It's quite simple." Her voice reminded him of violin strings. Really tight ones that were about to snap. "I want a different room. A different room, is that so much to ask?" Her voice escalated with each word.

"Not at all, Miss—"

"Is it not bad enough that I've been humiliated in front of every friend and relative I have? Is it not enough that I'm alone on my wedding night? Is it not enough that I have a silk nightgown in my suitcase that I will never get to wear—" Her chin quivered and her nose began to run. "But I arrive here and get a room that looks like an exploded Valentine card, and now I can't seem to find anyone who understands that I just want a different room." She wiped at the tears that ran down her cheeks.

"A different room, is that so hard?" Her hands trembled on her face.

Alex pulled a tissue from the box under the counter and handed it to her. "Not at all, Miss Andersen." He punched a few keys and started the transaction. Other guests in the lobby had stopped to stare, but Alex concentrated on the one who obviously needed help—possibly more help than he could provide. "I'll take care of it right here, and we'll get you in another hale in a jiffy."

While he waited on the computer, he glanced up and offered one of his famous smiles. She blew her nose and shifted her weight, seemingly oblivious to it.

The poor woman needed a vacation, though obviously this was not the way she'd wanted to take it. Maybe he could cheer her up.

The computer assigned her a hale, and Alex grabbed a key from slot number twenty-three. "Here you go. It's on the other side of the resort, but I'll call the shuttle to come pick you up. The hale has an ocean view and is tucked back away from the pool. I think you'll like it. The difference in the cost will be refunded to your account." He handed her the key along with another showstopper smile.

She took the key without looking him in the face. "I'm Alex Harrigan, by the way, and I'm in charge of activities at the resort. Maybe I'll see you at one of them."

She picked up her bags. "I don't plan on doing much while I'm here. But thank you, Mr. Harrigan." With that, she turned and walked away. He watched her go, her honey curls swaying around her shoulders.

He looked back at the monitor. One whole month. That wasn't cheap. He wondered if her fiancé had funded the trip. Regardless, the resort was booked, so some other lucky guest was going to benefit from this swap.

"Thank you, Mr. Harrigan." The new employee tilted her head and smiled. "I didn't know what to do."

"Alex," he corrected. "Not a problem—" He looked at her

name tag. "Melanie. Oh, and see if you can find some honey-mooners that are coming on a budget. We can upgrade them to the honeymoon suite. No sense wasting all that romance."

"Sure thing, Alex."

He smiled broadly and took heart when she smiled back. At least someone was not immune to his charms.

Chapter 2

Something pulled Callie from the deep haze of sleep. She didn't want to go. She wanted to stay right where she was, snuggled in the dark land of the oblivious.

A tap sounded at the door.

"Housekeeping," a voice called.

Arrgghh! Go away! She started to pull the cover up over her head, then realized housekeeping would open the door and waltz right in if she didn't answer it. The clock read 8:10.

She pulled herself up and treaded across the cool tiles. She looked through the peephole to see a lady who looked old enough to be her grandmother. A glance down at the shorts and T-shirt she'd pulled on the night before reassured her she was decent. She eased open the door and squinted in the bright light.

"Aloha! I can come back, *Naupala.* When would be a good time?" The woman's eyes crinkled behind her glasses.

Callie tried to smile. "Actually, the room's fine, I won't be leaving today."

"No problem. You call housekeeping if you need anything. Ask for Api."

"Yes, thank you." Callie started to shut the door, but the woman's words stopped her.

"If you do not wish to be disturbed, it is customary to place a coconut outside your door." She gestured toward the ones lying at the base of trees just outside the hale.

"How quaint. Thank you."

After the woman left, Callie plucked a hairy coconut half from the ground and placed it on her stoop. Inside, the room seemed dark after the harsh light from outdoors, and she flipped on a light. She grabbed the resort's directory from the desk and slunk back into bed. The resort offered everything from parasailing to restaurants. But then she knew that.

Her mind flashed back five months ago to the day when Shaun had booked the resort.

"We'll never even have to leave the place," he'd said. "We could stay the entire month and barely have a chance to try everything. What do you think?"

He looked at her with those green eyes she'd known since she was seven, and she could see them frolicking on the beach together the way they'd done at the lake all those summers. It was perfect. "It's so expensive."

"You know that's not a problem. Besides, we're only going to do this once."

She saw a flicker of something in his eyes, but it had disappeared so quickly, then he'd started talking about all the fun they would have on their honeymoon.

Some fun. She was alone, and she didn't like being alone. Wasn't that the whole purpose of their marriage pact?

Good-bye marriage, good-bye family.

Where are You, God? How could You let this happen?

Callie tossed the guidebook aside and fell back onto her pillow. She felt tired and drained. More sleep was what she needed. She reached out for the other pillow, pulled it to her chest, and clutched it tightly.

Alex high-fived the teenage boys on the winning volleyball team. "Awesome save, Jon."

"Not so bad yourself."

Alex grabbed the ball and glanced at his watch. He had a half hour until surfing lessons, and his gaze was compellingly drawn to the trail that led to Callie Andersen's hale.

He tossed the ball absently. She'd said she hadn't planned on participating in any activities, but it was her third morning here, and he had yet to see her at all. In fact, when he'd passed her hale on his way to and from the pool the past couple of days, a coconut had announced her desire for privacy. Had she been holed up all this time or had he merely missed her?

He remembered the look of misery in her clear blue eyes and the lonely tears that had streaked her ivory face. Had she been distressed enough to do something desperate? He held the ball. But why would someone come to paradise if she wished to harm herself? She could do that just as easily at home. Then again, what did he know about Callie Andersen? Virtually nothing, except she was distressed about losing her fiancé. He felt a hard lump coagulate in his gut and turned toward the path that led to Callie's hale.

"Housekeeping!" Three hard taps followed.

Callie looked up from her copy of *Early Childhood Today* and glared at the door. With a sigh, she tagged the corner of the article she was reading and went to answer it.

"Hi, I really don't need the room cleaned, Api, but thanks."

"Towels? You need towels?"

"Sure, I could use some."

The woman grabbed a stack of fluffy white towels from the cleaning cart.

She had to put an end to these daily interruptions. "Look, Api, I really came here for some time alone; and if it's all the same to you, how about if I just call when I need something? You don't need to come back every day."

The woman handed her the stack of towels. "All right, *Naupala*, if you are sure."

"Yes, thank you."

After depositing the towels on the bathroom counter, Callie sank onto the bed and opened her magazine to the marked page. The article on children's learning styles had managed to distract her from her troubles for a little while, and anything that would help her teach her kids was something—

A knock sounded on the door.

Frustration welled up within her. She'd come here to escape, to heal, to pray. And it seemed she was spending half her time answering the door. Another insistent knock sounded, and she flung her magazine on the couch and marched to the door. Nice as Api was, she was not following the resort's own rules about privacy, and she'd been more than clear. . . .

She flung open the door. "Do you not see my coconut?" It was not Api's dark eyes gazing back, but rather a wide set of familiar brown ones. "Oh. It's you." Her heart flipped in embarrassment when she realized it was Alex Harrigan of Harrigan's Cove—witness to her embarrassing front-desk fiasco.

"Sorry to bother you, but I hadn't seen you around, and I was getting worried." The surprise had left his face, replaced with a smile that was like a friendly hug.

She recalled the scene she'd made at the check-in desk and the meaning of his words snapped into place like Legos. At the same time, she noticed the tanned skin revealed by his neon tank. Not to mention the muscles under it.

Her face turned red. She didn't have to see it to know. It always turned red when she felt as she did now. Pathetic. Stupid. Embarrassed.

"I'm fine, I just—I'm going to hang around in here a lot."

"We have a surfing lesson at four o'clock. It might help you get your mind off things."

She clenched her teeth. Who was this man to suggest he knew what was best for her? "Listen, Mr.—"

"Harrigan."

"Fine. Harrigan. This is what I came here for. To rest. But it seems like your little coconut thing is not working at all because I have done nothing but answer the door since I arrived, and I would really appreciate it if you would—"

A white hanky waved above his head, and she saw him peeking out from behind a volleyball.

For the first time in days, she felt a lightness of spirit blossom from under the thick layer of muck. A smile almost made it to her lips. "Sorry. Didn't mean to snap."

He reached down to get three plastic-encased papers she hadn't noticed before, shoving aside the empty room service platter with the toe of his tennis shoe. "I don't want to be a pest, but all the activities are listed in these each day." He put the yellow one on top and handed them to her. "This one is today's. Would you at least promise to look at it?"

She opened her mouth to say no. Then she noticed his smile. It was wide and bracketed with a dimple on the left side. She nodded her head.

He tucked his hanky in his cargo shorts. "Hope to see you around."

She shut the door, clutching the slippery plastic sleeves in her hand.

The afternoon passed in peace, and around five o'clock, she felt herself drawn to the French doors leading to the beach. "Harrigan's Happenings" listed the surfing Alex had mentioned, and Callie knew it would be finishing up soon. She pulled open the heavy draperies, and sunlight stung her eyes. She hadn't realized how dark her room had been.

When her eyes adjusted, she took in the scene that, even in her current state of mind, could only be described as paradise. In the glimmering heat of the afternoon, sun-lovers of all ages dotted the beach. If she laid her forehead against the cool glass pane, she could see Alex riding a board on his belly, several wannabe surfers trailing behind him.

The ring of the phone pulled her away from the scene. She'd requested a phone for her room, knowing her family would want to keep in touch. The phone rang again. Probably her mom was calling her back.

"Hello."

A slight pause, then, "Callie?"

His voice, as familiar as the air she breathed, sounded in her ear. The voice she'd heard nearly every day of her life since his family had moved in across the street.

"Callie?"

"I'm here."

"You okay?"

Okay? She'd practically been jilted at the altar by her dearest friend and confidant.

"I'm sorry, Callie. This is so unfair. You don't deserve it." His voice caught then, and she could almost see him pinching the bridge of his nose. "We never should have agreed to this."

"You just met her. You don't even know if it will work out."

"Of course I don't. But I know enough to see there's something missing from what you and I have."

"How can you say that?" She hated the way her voice wobbled.

"You know I love you, Callie—have ever since the day you shoved Buddy Fitzer on the ground for poking fun at Sarah."

Callie remembered the day well. She wouldn't let anyone make fun of her sister's stuttering. Especially not Buddy Fitzer.

"But you deserve better. You deserve to be loved the way a wife should be loved."

"You humiliated me." She tossed the pillow against the headboard. They'd had a deal. She'd made it to twenty-eight years without a promising prospect and so had he. She'd thought this had been a sign. Hadn't she prayed for the right man to enter her life if it was God's will? And now she'd been jilted in front of the whole town of Grabill.

A knock sounded at the door. "I have to go, Shaun."

"Are you sure you're okay?"

His compassion grated on her nerves. After all, he was causing this whole mess. "I need some time alone. I'd really rather you didn't call back."

She could almost feel his hurt across the wires.

A more insistent rap sounded on the door. "I have to go."

They said a stiff good-bye, then she hung up the phone and went to answer the door. Coconut or not, she was glad for the intrusion.

Chapter 3

"Hi there." Alex put on his nicest smile as Callie's door opened, but he faltered at her appearance. Her red-rimmed eyes shone with some undefined emotion.

She crossed her arms over her T-shirt. "Hi."

Okay, so she wasn't thrilled to see him. When had that ever stopped him? "Did you get a chance to look at the activities schedule?" He quirked a brow.

"Um-hmm."

He cleared his throat. "Well, I can see you're excited about the possibilities. Was it the sunset cruise tonight or the morning tennis that's got you all worked up into a lather?"

Her lips twitched, just the slightest bit, and he felt a ridiculous surge of satisfaction.

"Ah-ha. It's the tennis, isn't it? Can hardly wait to swing that racket."

She leaned against the door frame, tilting her head. "Actually, I've never played tennis in my life."

He sucked in his breath, clutching his chest. "That's shameful."

"Story of my life."

His brows shot up. "Now there's an intriguing statement."

"Did you say something about a sunset cruise?"

"Do I detect a little interest?"

"Anything's better than tennis."

"You wound me. However, since it's the cruise you're interested in, I happen to know we have three spots open. And the guide is incredible. He knows a wealth of information about the area's history and has an uncanny knack for sharing it in an entertaining yet provocative way."

She tucked in the corner of her lip. "You?"

He smiled broadly.

"What time?"

"Boat dock at six-thirty."

She nodded once. "Thanks, Alex." She began to shut the door.

He stuck his foot in. "Hey, wait, does this mean you're coming?"

"Do I have to sign a contract or something?"

"No. A promise will do." He winked. "Wouldn't want those slots to fill up, now would we?" On the other hand, maybe that was exactly what she wanted to happen. "Tell you what. You want to go, I'll go sign you up. How's that for service?"

She sighed loudly. "Fine, fine, sign me up."

He removed his foot from the door.

"There, was that so hard?"

Something flashed in her eyes. "I'll let you know later." With that, the door clicked into place.

A short time later, Callie changed into a new outfit, a melon-colored sleeveless sweater and floral shorts with the same shade of melon. She had to pull the price tags off both items, which she'd bought in anticipation of her honeymoon.

None of that, she told herself. She wasn't going to think about Shaun and his infuriating phone call. She swept her hair up in a twist and held it with a big white clip.

After a quick touch of makeup, she left through her French doors and made her way across the beach for the first time. A few steps later, she removed her sandals, dangling them in her hands, and relished the feel of the warm sand squishing under her toes.

She knew from looking at the resort map that the docks were a long walk away, so she edged closer to the water where the sand was wet and packed.

She passed children and couples, families and teenagers, some drawing in the last rays of the day, others playing in the breakers. One brave soul surfed the waves, his arms flailing out for balance.

Okay, God, here I am, all alone on my honeymoon. I have a whole month to put the pieces back together, but I don't even know where to start. I don't understand why You've let this happen. I asked You to bring a man into my life. You know I wanted to marry young and start a family of my own. And here I am at twenty-eight, a jilted bride.

She talked to God as she walked and realized it had been a long time since she'd done so. Not that she hadn't prayed at all, but she acknowledged that her relationship with Him had faltered over the recent months.

She watched the seagulls that seemed to hover at the shoreline. She breathed in the salty tang of the air as she listened to the squeals and laughter of children playing at the edge of the water. The stimuli almost seemed overwhelming after the dark, quiet confines of her room.

Soon she reached the dock that jutted about fifty yards out into the water. Several boats bobbed alongside, held in place by thick cords of rope. Already a crowd of tourists had lined up, entering the boat one by one. Hawaiian music floated from the craft.

Callie took her place at the rear of the line, slipping her sandals on her feet as she waited. She couldn't help but notice most of the others were couples. There were a couple of families, though, their children ranging in age from preschoolers to adolescents. One little girl, around four, she guessed, clung to her mother's leg like she was Velcroed onto it.

When Callie reached the entry point, Alex was there offering a hand to steady the guests as they stepped aboard the rocking boat.

His brown eyes seemed to light when he met her gaze. "Callie." He smiled, showing his dimple, and offered her his hand.

A charge of excitement zinged through her body at his contact. He held her hand as she descended the two steps, then squeezed it gently before letting go. Her thoughts jumbled in her head. How odd that she should react like this when her own wedding had only just been canceled. She chided herself for her fickleness. It wasn't like her at all.

Somehow, she found herself on one of the benches that stretched across the boat. The family with the clinging girl sat to her left, and Callie had an aisle seat. A trio of musicians graced the far corner, playing their instruments and cooing the Hawaiian song.

The boat was filling fast, and she noticed many of the guests getting drinks at an open bar behind her. *Oh, no, not one of those party cruises.* Why hadn't she thought of that? Her uncle had gone on a cruise in the Caribbean and come back with stories of those party boats.

The last guests boarded, and the music stopped as Alex's voice came over the intercom system.

"Welcome aboard the *Hawaiian Honu*, ladies and gentlemen. *Honu* is Hawaiian for the green sea turtle, a species native to the islands. If you wish to see them up close and personal, sign up for snorkeling on Tuesday or hang around the beach, where you might get lucky and see one basking in the sun. My name is Alex Harrigan, and I am activities director for Harrigan's Cove, as well as your tour guide this evening."

His voice was deep and melodic, a rich timbre that tickled her vocal cords. He introduced the crew, making a few jokes along the way that made the tourists chuckle. When he gave locations of the amenities aboard the *Honu*, Callie was relieved to hear the bar was actually nonalcoholic.

As the tour got underway, the girl beside her continued to cling to her mother, her face buried in the woman's neck. The boat left the shore, and after Alex's brief and entertaining history of the area, the Hawaiian band began to play again.

Callie struck up a conversation with Megan, the girl next to her. After a few minutes, she was actually sitting upright on her mom's lap and smiling at Callie. She had an unusual combination of deep blue eyes and dark brown hair, which had been pulled back into two ponytails. The wind whipped them, and Megan brushed them from her eyes.

Callie couldn't help but be aware of Alex as he made rounds, chatting with guests. The teenage girls sitting three rows up stared and giggled, watching his every move. And she'd seen at least two single women flirting with him—not that it was anything to her.

Megan was sitting beside her on the bench playing "See, see, my Playmate" when Alex approached, taking a seat at the edge of the bench. Megan's mom took the opportunity to take Megan to the rest room, and Callie scootched over to give him room. Even so, their legs touched, the hair on his knee tickling hers.

"You look like you're having fun," he said, that wonderful smile of his spreading across his face.

"So do you."

His eyebrows popped. "What can I say? I have the most fun job in the world."

A strand of hair had come loose from her twist, and she brushed it back with her hand.

"You look better," he said.

"A little makeup does wonders."

"That's not what I mean."

She looked away. "Well, I haven't cried in the last two hours. That helps." The check-in scene flashed uncomfortably in her mind. He felt sorry for her. *Poor Honeymoon Girl, here all by herself, ditched at the altar, and left for—*

"I'm glad you came."

She looked at him then and read sincerity in his eyes. Or pity, she really couldn't tell which.

"Can I get you a drink?"

It wasn't part of his job, she knew. She hadn't seen him fetching drinks for anyone else. "No, thanks. My buddy'll be back soon, and she'll keep me busy."

"You like kids."

She allowed a smile. "I should hope so, they're my job."

"You're a teacher?"

She nodded. "Preschool."

"So you're on summer break?"

"Um-hmm." She and Shaun had planned it that way. That's the only way she could take a whole month for a honeymoon. "I've noticed quite a few young families at the resort."

"Yeah, we get a good mix of ages here."

Megan and her mom returned, and Alex stood up to give them room. "I'll let you get back to your new friend."

She was surprised at the disappointment she felt. "Sure."

"Tennis tomorrow morning, right?"

She cocked her head. "I never agreed to that."

"But you will now?" His big brown puppy-dog eyes squirmed

their way into her heart. He wasn't leaving until he had an answer. She suspected he wasn't leaving until he heard a yes.

"All right, but I'm warning you, I have no experience whatsoever."

"We'll have you whopping that ball in no time." He winked and walked off, joining two teenage boys by the rail. Callie's heart clenched in her chest, and she recognized the feeling for attraction. *This cannot be happening.*

Chapter 4

Callie's legs pumped harder, her feet digging into the cool, damp sand until she worked her way to a slow jog. She'd woken early to the surf pounding the shore and knew she needed to start exercising again. She did not want to gain back those seven pounds she'd lost for the wedding.

The beach was mostly deserted, though she passed a walker or jogger every minute or so. Seagulls pierced the salty air with their high-pitched squeals. Strangely, her mind drifted to Alex and yesterday's excursion. He'd insisted on walking her back to her hale in the evening's dim light, though she wondered again if it was only pity that made him offer.

Ahead, another jogger approached. This one with an expansive chest and a long-legged stride. The gap closed, and she recognized him at the same time he recognized her.

A smile stretched across his face. "Callie." He made a U-turn and fell into step beside her, shortening his stride to match hers.

Suddenly she was aware of her knotted curls and sleepy face. "Hi."

"You're a jogger?"

"Usually." *When I'm not sulking in my room like one of my preschoolers.*

They moved in silence for a moment, their feet pounding the sand almost in unison. She was too aware of his breaths, coming evenly, too aware of his size, dwarfing hers. "Jogging on the sand is harder," she said to break the silence.

"True, but you can't beat the view. Where do you jog at home? Don't tell me a treadmill."

She shook her head. "Only in winter. Otherwise, I just jog on the street."

"Is that safe?"

She laughed. "In Grabill, home of one stoplight? Home of 751 citizens—most of whom were invited to my wedding?" She clenched her jaw. *Now why did I have to go and say that?*

Another awkward silence followed.

"I'm sorry," he said. She knew he was looking at her, but she didn't have the courage to return his gaze.

"You have nothing to be sorry about." She forced a tight smile on her face.

She was ever conscious of his body moving next to hers. His arms pumping rhythmically. His bare feet splashing through foamy water. "Whoever he is, he needs to have his head examined."

They were kind words, but Callie couldn't help thinking of the pitying stares she'd received on her last day in Grabill. Mrs. Koogle at the drugstore hadn't said a word when she'd paid for her sunscreen and Dramamine, but the look on her face said it all. Now, Alex was probably looking at her with the same expression.

"Hey, look," he said. "I need to get back and take a shower before I head over to the courts."

"Sure, see you later."

He turned and jogged in the other direction. "See you at the courts," he called.

She said nothing, mainly because the dark quiet of her room was sounding better all the time.

Alex rushed through his shower, throwing on his resort T-shirt and shorts and running a hand through his damp hair. He'd seen the look on Callie's face when he'd mentioned tennis. She wasn't going to show.

But he wasn't going to give her that option. Draping a whistle over his head, he started off for Callie's hale. What was it about her anyway? Ever since he'd checked her in, he'd thought of little else. And that was ridiculous. She was heart-broken over another man. She was on her honeymoon alone, for crying out loud.

And yet, he knew it wasn't pity that drew him. Sure, he felt bad for her, wanted to help her. And she obviously needed help. She seemed determined to hole up in her hale like a caterpillar in a cocoon and nurse her wounds. But he knew from experience that would do no good. She needed to keep busy, and that's where he came in.

When he came upon her hale, he wasn't surprised to see the

coconut lying on her stoop again, next to a tray of empty dishes. He shook his head. He should've steered her clear of the wedding topic this morning. Now she was all depressed again.

He knocked loudly on the door and waited until he heard the door opening.

"Tennis, anyone?" he asked.

She cocked her head, and he noticed a light smattering of freckles on her nose. "Do you escort all your guests to their activities?"

"Only the special ones." He gave his most charming smile. It didn't work. "Listen, I don't really feel like tennis today—"

"No, no, no. I signed you up. You have to go."

"My clothes—"

"Are fine."

"My hair—"

"Is beautiful."

She harumphed and crossed her arms.

"Come on, now. You're going to make the teacher late for class." He poked his head in the door and spied some tennis shoes. "There. Throw those on and you'll be all ready."

She narrowed her eyes, and for a moment, he thought she was going to balk. Then she turned and grabbed the shoes. He couldn't stop the smile that spread across his face, even when she turned a mock glare on him.

By the time they were at the courts, Callie was actually starting to enjoy the morning warmth from the sun and the fragrance from the hibiscus growing along the paths. She'd watched

Alex's serving technique and figured she could manage that. They were merely warming up and would divide into teams of two. With the four courts and sixteen guests, that made for a full activity.

Alex walked over to her, handing her a racket. "Ready to try?"

She shrugged. "Sure."

He followed her behind the service line and showed her how to hold the racket. His hand was warm on hers, and when he stood behind her, taking her through the motions of a serve, she was very aware of his presence. His musky scent, his bulky form, his gentle hands.

The kids on the next court squealed as they played, but Callie was only vaguely aware of them. Alex was virtually a stranger. How odd that she should react so strongly.

"Ready to try on your own?"

Did his voice sound raspy? "Yeah, think so."

He stepped back, giving her space. A teenage boy waited for her serve on the other side of the net.

"Ready, Josh?" Alex called.

"Bring it on," he said.

Callie tossed the ball in the air and brought the racket around in the same smooth motion Alex had demonstrated. The ball sailed over the net.

"Hey, not bad, Callie," Alex called.

Josh returned the ball easily, and Callie ran toward it and smacked it back.

After two more returns, she missed a zinger to the corner of the court.

"I thought you said you never played before," Alex said, hands on hips.

She shrugged. "I haven't." She had played volleyball and baseball in high school. She'd always been athletic.

Alex nodded his head approvingly and moved on to help the kids on the court next to hers. Before she knew it, they were paired off into teams. Callie matched up with a nine-year-old girl, and they played a team of adolescent brothers.

She had so much fun with the kids, she realized she'd forgotten her troubles for almost an hour. They switched around after the first match, and Callie found herself playing against Alex and an older man. The man's dark belly hung over his Hawaiian shorts and bounced as he chased after balls. He was too slow to return most of them, but when he did get hold of one, he had a knack for smashing into the corner on Callie's side of the court.

Alex, on the other hand, played easy, sending her shots she could usually return. His shots to her partner were always gentle and placed right next to her. His partner got disgruntled a couple times. "Come on, Man, what kind of wimpy hit is that?"

Alex ignored him and continued to play noncompetitively. Callie was glad when the game ended and they moved on to another team.

By the time tennis was over, Callie was starved. The bagel and juice she'd ordered from room service were long gone, and it was now lunchtime. The sun beat down from a blue sky, and she could feel the sweat trickling down her back. A shower was definitely in order.

She'd had a great time, especially with the kids. She was surprised so many had turned out for tennis. But then, their parents probably liked having a break while they were on vacation.

She wondered why the resort didn't have a children's program. One of her student's moms had told her about their spring break trip to the Caribbean. Their resort had had a children's program that the kids had enjoyed, and the parents actually got a little quiet time in the sun.

Her stomach gurgled a complaint. She was already planning her call into room service when Alex caught up with her on the path.

"Wait up, Callie."

She slowed until he fell in step with her, then gave him a smile. Her heart flipped when he returned it with interest.

"You had a good time."

"Um-hmm."

"You're good at tennis. Not bad with kids either."

She fished in her pocket for her key as they approached her hale. "I was just wondering, with all the kids around here, why haven't you started a children's program?"

He raised his brows. "It's not like it hasn't occurred to me, but there's hardly enough hours in the day for the activities I already have going. Besides, little kids aren't really my thing."

She remembered the way he'd handled her partner on the courts. "You're good with them."

"Oh, I like them and all. I guess I just feel more at ease with teens and adults."

They reached her hale, and she unlocked her door. "I'm the

opposite. Kids make my clock tick."

He smiled at the expression.

"Maybe you could hire someone else to do it. I'd think it would draw more families."

He considered that for a moment, his brows drawing together over those brown eyes. "Maybe I'll give it some thought. How 'bout we have lunch together over at the cafe? It's on me. You can give me some ideas of what kind of things young kids like to do."

She studied his eyes. Was this just another pity tactic to get her out of her hale? His sparkling eyes gave nothing away.

"I know you're busy and all," he said. "Probably have room service ordered already and everything."

She smacked him playfully on the arm. She wasn't about to mention that had been the next thing on her schedule. "Let me get a shower, and I'll meet you over there."

He quirked a brow, suspicion lining his face as if he was remembering this morning, when she'd changed her mind about playing tennis. "Maybe I should swing by here and pick you up."

"I'll be there." She tucked in a corner of her lip.

They set a time, giving them both time for showers, and Callie let herself in her hale. Her heart was pumping vigorously, and she couldn't even blame it on their leisurely walk. She could only attribute it to anticipation of spending time with Alex. Her heart was starting to get involved here, and the thought caused a niggle of fear to work its way into her belly. The last time she'd given her heart to someone, it had been royally rejected.

Alex slipped a clean shirt on over his damp shoulders and finger-combed his wet hair. He was too excited about this little lunch he'd planned with Callie.

"I'm only trying to improve the resort's activities schedule," he said to himself. The kids' program was a great idea and doable if he could find someone else to take it on—and convince Steve to allocate the funds for it.

Who are you kidding? His conscience pricked him. Okay, maybe this was more about spending time with a great lady and less about the resort, but was that such a bad thing?

Are you forgetting about Lana?

Alex sighed and mopped the water off of his face, then tossed the towel into the hamper. How could he forget about Lana? He'd thought he and Lana had something. But he'd learned the hard way that, while tourists might like a little vacation romance, dropping their lives and moving out here was a different story. He'd learned his lesson. Hadn't he steered clear of romantic entanglements with guests for two years?

Until now.

Yeah, yeah, but Callie's different.

Sure she is. She's just off a broken engagement.

That inner voice again. But he knew it was right. Number one, after Lana, he was committed to dating only island girls. Number two, Callie was in no shape for a budding romance. She needed time to heal from the one she was coming off of. Just because she was getting out of her hale more willingly was no indication of a healed heart. These things took time. It had taken months to get over Lana, and he'd only known her a few weeks. Who knew how long Callie and her fiancé had been involved?

He stuffed his wallet in his pocket and grabbed his key. Yep, this was a business lunch, pure and simple. If he said it to himself often enough, perhaps his heart would believe it.

When Callie arrived at the Hale Moana, she spotted Alex, seated at an outdoor table just off the beach. The aroma of food from the buffet reminded her of her empty stomach. She wove through the tables toward him. He rose from his seat at her approach, and her heart gave a heavy thump at his wide smile.

"Hi again," he said.

"Hi." He seated himself as she did, and her gaze took in the beautiful setting of palm trees and hibiscus growing around the dining porch. The warm breeze ruffled her hair, and she pushed it behind her ears.

"This is really lovely. The pictures on the brochure just don't do it justice."

A waiter filled their glasses with water, and Alex introduced them before the man walked away.

"I take it by that last comment, you really have been existing on room service for the past three days."

She felt her face growing warm and knew it had nothing to do with the sun high overhead. "I suppose I have been a bit of a hermit." She sipped her water, and under the table, her sandals flipped on her heel as she bounced her leg up and down.

"How long had you known him?"

Her leg stopped bouncing. She wasn't sure she wanted to talk about it yet. Or with Alex.

"Sorry, we don't have to go there. We came to talk about kids, didn't we?" He gestured to the buffet. "Why don't we grab some lunch, then you can tell me everything I always wanted to know about children."

She couldn't resist his boyish smile. She followed him to the buffet, where he filled her in on his favorites, recommending the cold cucumber soup, fresh Hawaiian fruit, and shellfish.

When they returned to their seats, he asked if she would like him to bless the food. Her heart warmed at the words. In all the dates she'd been on, a man had never prayed with her. Her mind stirring, she missed the words of prayer but appreciated so much his effort.

"So," he said after his first bite of kiwi, "tell me what kinds of things little kids like to do."

She filled him in on some of the activities at her preschool that were big hits, adding that the sand on the beach added a wonderful learning opportunity for small children. A sand castle building lesson would be a big hit, she thought. "And a competition among the older kids would go over great. Boys especially love a good competition."

"That's a great idea. I should've brought a pen." He patted his shirt pocket.

"Here, I have one." She gave him one from her purse, and he jotted on a napkin. "I'll bet little girls would love to have hula lessons. Of course, that would require hiring somebody from the outside. Unless you. . ." She drug the word out suggestively.

He laughed and held up his hands. "Oh, no. I don't do hula skirts." He picked up the pen. "So, how old would a child have to be to participate in the program without parents?"

"Preschool children still need a lot of help with motor skills and socialization. Probably a parent would need to be present to help one-on-one with their children. I'd say around six years is a good age for children to participate independently."

"What about a maximum age? Where do teens fit in?"

"Hmm." She chewed a bite of salad. "The cut-off age for children's activities should probably be twelve. But that's not to say there couldn't be some activities for six to twelve year olds and some specifically for teens. Snorkeling and water sports would probably go over well with teens."

"Yeah, they often join in those adult activities. In fact, the water sports are usually predominantly teenagers."

She sipped her water and took a cool bite of her soup, enjoying its delicate flavor. She was enjoying this. The food, the atmosphere, the company.

Slowly, she became aware of the silence growing between them and looked at Alex. He was staring. That's the only way to describe the intense way his gaze studied her face. His gaze zeroed in on her eyes, caught.

A flush crawled up his neck and into his cheeks. He cleared his throat, his gaze swinging to the food on his plate. It was the first time she'd seen him ill at ease, and she wondered what he'd been thinking while he stared at her so.

"I was in second grade when we met." The words startled her. She didn't realize what she'd been thinking until they slipped past her lips.

He looked at her then, his brows pulled together low over his eyes.

"Your question earlier. You asked how long I'd known Shaun."

He sat back in his chair, nodding his head. "Second grade?"

"Actually, the summer before. He moved in across the street."

"You grew up together?"

"Umm-hmm. Best buddies. There were no other boys on our street, see, and I was something of a tomboy anyway." She shrugged.

He smiled, his dimple catching her heart. "I can see that."

He pushed his plate back and folded his arms in front of his chest. His shoulders were almost as wide as the table, and she couldn't help but notice his tanned forearms that bulged with muscle. A picture of Shaun's lean frame flashed in her mind. They were very different men, not only in appearance, but in personality.

"When did you begin dating?"

"Dating?"

His smile widened, and he winked. "That thing men and women do together when they want to get to know each other better?"

She could feel the heat working its way into her face. "Shaun and I know each other about as well as two people can. There was never a need to date."

She couldn't miss the confusion on his face. The furrowed brow, the drawn lips. But suddenly, she didn't want to think about Shaun, much less talk about him. And she had an uncomfortable feeling it had something to do with the man sitting across from her. Which was ridiculous. Here her heart had just been broken, and she was attracted to the first man to show her a little attention. She'd never been a fickle person, so what gave?

"You mind if we talk about something else?" She tried for a smile but knew it came up short.

"Not at all." He was staring again, but this time he did not seem ill at ease. He picked up his pen again. "So, you think this kids' program will go over?"

She shrugged, glad the conversation was back on comfortable ground. "I don't see why not. Lots of other resorts offer them. The main thing will be finding a good person to head it up."

"Any chance of snagging you away from Grabill, Indiana?" He winked again, and her heart tumbled. Those puppy-dog eyes and boyish dimples tugged at her. Did a man really have a right to look so cute?

She considered his question, which really seemed more like a rhetorical one with the wink and little chuckle. "I have a lot happening in Grabill, you know. Teaching at Knowling Creek Preschool, summer readings at the library, nursery at Grabill Missionary, family. . ." She let the sentence drag out. He'd only asked to be polite. Or maybe to make her feel wanted. So why did her stomach do a little flip at the thought of coming here to stay?

Later that day as Alex put away the snorkeling equipment, he admitted to himself that he was in the dumps. Not that he'd allowed the guests to see that. He was too professional for that. But the fact that he wanted to slam the equipment shed door shut and retreat to his room was all the evidence he needed that he was out of sorts. He was a people person. He thrived in social situations. But right now he wanted to go to his room and sulk. And he knew why. She had curly hair the color of honey and eyes that matched the ocean he'd just swum in.

He'd drawn her out, spent time with her, telling himself he was trying to distract her from her pain. And then he'd talked with her to get her input on the kids' program. And now he wondered if that was a bunch of baloney. Had it all been an excuse to spend time with her? Because when he'd asked her about taking over the kids' program, he hadn't been joking. Sure, he'd tossed the question out casually. But he knew it was really his way of finding out if Callie would ever consider coming here to stay.

You're falling for her, Harrigan.

He clenched his jaw and made his way back to the path that led to his hale. He'd told himself this wasn't going to happen. He'd learned after Lana, hadn't he? Apparently not. Callie would be here for more than three weeks, and if he wanted to keep his heart intact, he would avoid her like a jellyfish.

Which was exactly why he'd invited her to the luau Friday.

Chapter 5

Friday rolled around slowly, but Callie was beginning to wonder if Alex had even been sincere about the invitation to the luau. It had been two days since their lunch together, and he'd made no effort to see her. She'd spent some time on the beach right off her veranda, where she could sunbathe in private—with loads of sunscreen to protect her fair skin. She had ventured out to the restaurant for meals and had even visited the pool.

She had caught sight of Alex twice. Once she'd seen him walking toward the registration building, and another time, yesterday afternoon, she'd seen him leading a beach volleyball game. She'd watched him from a lawn chair just outside her hale. The group was way down the beach at a court designated for volleyball, but she would know those long, tanned legs and broad shoulders anywhere. She thought she could even hear him calling out encouragement to his teammates.

After an hour or so of play, the game ended, and they seemed to be reorganizing for another game. His head swung toward her hale. Her body froze, and she wasn't sure if she wanted to bury herself in the sand or stand up and wave him down. Could he see her from there? Her heart pounded.

Slowly, his arm lifted in greeting. She lifted her own and waved. He turned then and got his players back on the court. Her heart fluttered hard in her chest, and she scolded herself. For goodness' sake, it was just a wave. What was wrong with her?

But she couldn't deny the anticipation building in her chest. Would he come over when volleyball ended? She knew from his schedule in the newsletter that he was free until after dinner tonight. She felt embarrassed at even knowing that little tidbit. Why was she keeping up with his schedule like a secretary? If he knew that, he'd probably think she was some kind of weirdo stalking woman.

But all the anticipation had been for nothing, because Alex had not come over when the game ended. And he had not come over today either.

She dug her feet in the sand, enjoying the coolness down deep. She had finally concluded this morning that Alex had only wanted to draw her out of her hale to enjoy her vacation. He was only being kind, trying to help a guest enjoy herself. That was his job after all. But it didn't stop the heavy disappointment that settled in her belly like a glob of Play-doh. She felt silly, thinking he'd been interested in her, when he'd only been doing his job.

Further, she convinced herself that his invitation to the luau hadn't been personal. It had only been meant as a resort owner informing a guest about an event. He'd probably never even

211

planned to sit with her. Which was why, as she soaked in the last rays of the day, she decided not to attend the luau at all. The adventurer in her wanted to taste the roasted pig and watch the hula dancers and the Samoan fire-knife dance. The brochure had explained it all, and she'd looked forward to it for weeks.

But the thought of sitting alone, wishing Alex were sharing it with her, was more than her heart could take at the moment. After the disappointment of the canceled wedding, the last thing she needed was another heartbreak. Surely her heart wasn't mended enough from Shaun to even consider another man.

And yet here she was, doing just that.

Am I really that pathetic, God? How can I even consider another man when I've just had my heart broken by Shaun?

But had her heart really been broken by Shaun?

Of course it had. He practically jilted you at the altar.

Another part of her argued a different point. If she'd been in love with Shaun, why had her heart been so easily turned by Alex?

Shaun's words burned in her mind. *I know enough to see there's something missing from what you and I have.* Was that why she could be attracted to Alex so soon after Shaun? Had there been something missing? Had their relationship been wrong for marriage? She couldn't see how, when they knew each other so well, respected each other so much.

She laid her head against the chair and closed her eyes. The ocean roared as a wave crashed on the beach, and in the distance a seagull's screech pierced the wind. She had a lot of things to figure out. She was confused about her feelings, about what went wrong between her and Shaun, about what she was feeling for Alex. But, the optimist in her relished the fact that she had another three weeks in paradise to figure it all out.

Later that evening, after another room service meal, Callie slipped off her sandals and went to sit on the beach again. Darkness had descended, and there were only a few stragglers on the stretch of sand. Most, she figured, were at the luau.

She could hear the faint drumbeat of the Polynesian revue from across the resort and wished she could see it. It was a weekly event, though, and she could easily attend another one.

The stars overhead seemed unnaturally bright, and she wished she'd brought a towel so she could lie back in the sand. She pulled her knees up to her chest and hugged them with her arms, taking in the salty smell of the air. Behind her, the palms rustled in the breeze, and she closed her eyes, enjoying the tropical evening.

For the hundredth time of the evening, Alex scanned the crowd of tourists with eager eyes. Though, truth be known, the eagerness was rapidly morphing into disappointment. Where was Callie? Hadn't she said she'd be here? True, he'd asked her three days ago, and he'd not seen her since. Well, that wasn't true; he'd seen her, he just hadn't spoken to her.

And it hadn't been easy staying away. Especially when he'd spied her lounging by her hale yesterday. Everything in him wanted to go and talk to her. She'd obviously been watching him, otherwise she wouldn't have seen his greeting. Could it be she was interested in him too?

Yeah, right, Harrigan, right after a broken engagement?

So, it wasn't the most plausible thought, but a guy could dream, couldn't he?

And why are you wishing for it when she's going to leave you in three weeks?

Sometimes he hated this rational side of himself. It could take all the fun out of life.

The crowd had finished the roasted pig dinner and settled on mats as the Polynesian revue began to get underway. His brother Barnabas sat beside him with Liliana and their soon-to-be-adopted daughter, Abby, who loved attending the luaus.

Alex scanned the audience again, hoping for a glimpse of Callie.

"So, who is she?" Barnabas asked.

"Huh?" Alex didn't bother to stop his scanning, even though the drumbeats and swishing hula skirts announced the show had begun.

"You've been looking for someone all night."

Alex looked at his brother then. "So?"

Barnabas shrugged. "No need to get defensive. I was just making an observation."

His stomach felt heavy with disappointment, and his veins pumped with irritation. Why wasn't she here? Didn't she know he'd looked forward to this for three days?

And how would she know that when you've avoided her for those three days?

Barnabas leaned closer, talking over the rhythmic music. "You could always go find her, you know."

Alex sighed, but the sound was drowned by the drumbeat. He shook his head. "Doesn't matter. She'll be leaving in three weeks anyway."

Barnabas nodded thoughtfully. "That's what I thought about Liliana." He stretched his arm across his new wife's shoulders and turned his attention to the show.

The music played on, hula girls danced, but Alex was oblivious to it all. He thought about Barnabas and Liliana. He had married a tourist. Sometimes people did move here from far away. Why should Callie have to be any different?

Thoughts of Lana's departure filled his mind. He remembered well the weeks of sadness after she'd left. The disappointment. He'd written her letters and waited for hers, but they'd never come. He'd felt used.

Callie is not Lana, he reminded himself. They were as different as day from night. He'd been attracted to Lana, but he was drawn to Callie. So drawn, in fact, that sitting on the ground was getting harder by the moment. Was she at her hale? Walking the beach? His legs ached to get up and see.

Barnabas leaned over. "Would you go already? You're making me nervous."

It was all the impetus Alex needed.

Callie grabbed a handful of sand and let it filter through her fingers. In the distance, the drumbeat rhythm changed, and she wondered if the knife dance was starting. She also wondered if Alex had gone and with whom he was sitting. She hadn't missed the way the front desk girl had gone gaga when she and Alex had passed her on their way to the tennis courts several mornings ago.

A sick feeling pierced her stomach, and she recognized it as jealousy. It was absurd, really. What right did she have to be jealous? She thought of Shaun and the woman he'd met on a business trip to Chicago. The woman whose presence had made Shaun question their marriage. Callie had hardly had a moment's jealousy over her, and here she was sulking over some man she'd only met a week ago.

"Is there room for me?"

His voice made her heart lurch, and she knew it wasn't because he'd startled her. His question sank in and made her smile. "I think there's a small section here that's not reserved." She patted the sand beside her and went weak in the knees when his foot brushed hers.

"You're missing the luau," she heard herself say.

She felt rather than saw him look at her. "I could say the same for you."

She wondered if he'd gone at all. Had he been watching for her? Had he expected to sit with her? She couldn't find the nerve to ask. Instead, she looked up at the night sky. They were quiet for a moment, though the ocean's roar and the distant music filled the air with sounds of its own.

"I've never seen so many stars," she said.

"We have stargazing out here on Wednesday nights. It seems like all the ancient cultures had stories revolving around the stars and their origins. Hawaiians were no different."

"I find the history here fascinating. I've been reading about it in my guidebook."

He flipped off his sandals and dug his toes in the sand. "There's a lot to see in Hawaii. Are you visiting the other islands?"

She and Shaun had had a whole list of attractions and sites they'd wanted to see. But now. . . Somehow, the thought of sightseeing by herself made her feel lonely. She shrugged. "I'll probably hang around here mostly."

He rocked over and nudged her with his shoulder. "You can't do that. You traveled hundreds of miles to be here. You need to take advantage of it. At least see some of the sites on Maui."

"Maybe," she said, hedging the issue. She didn't want to tell him she was reluctant to wander around the island by herself. He'd only feel sorry for her, and that was the last thing she wanted.

She felt another nudge on the shoulder and looked at Alex. In the darkness, his eyes sparkled like the Pacific on a sunny day. The shadows of the night did wonderful things for the strong planes of his face. They caressed the hollows of his cheeks even as the wind caressed his hair. Her heart felt light, as if it could skitter away on the tiniest of breezes.

"Let me take you someplace." The way his gaze whispered along her face, she would have said yes to almost anything.

"You have to work."

He smiled, and a tiny shadow settled in his dimple. "Even Mr. Fun gets a day off every week."

She returned his smile, their gazes catching and holding for a poignant moment.

"I'm off all day Monday. What would you like to do?"

"Did I agree to this?" She allowed a flirtatious lilt to her voice.

"Do you think I'm going to take no for an answer?"

She laughed. Her first time in over a week. "Probably not."

He stood and dusted off the sand.

"Take a walk?"

"Sure." After brushing the sand from her legs, they began walking along the beach toward the bay. After asking about several tourist spots on the island, she decided she'd like to see Haleakala National Park on Monday. Alex insisted it was worth the drive.

Then Alex began asking about her family. After telling him of her younger sister and parents, she asked him if he had siblings.

"There are four of us here running the resort. You've probably seen most of them, but other than our trademark dimple, we don't look too much alike. Barnabas manages the resort, Connor is in charge of maintenance of grounds and equipment, and Steve is our accountant. You met him."

She tossed him a sideways glance. "I did?"

He gave her a little smile, and she nearly lost her footing. "Your first day here. At the front desk. . ."

She remembered the starchy-looking man who'd tried to help her. Her stomach clamped down at the memory. That had been Alex's brother? Oh, my, she knew how to make a first impression.

"You mean you didn't recognize the Harrigan dimple?"

She gave a wry grin. "He wasn't exactly smiling."

He chuckled then, and her heart grew lighter. With the distance of time, she was beginning to see her first day in Maui with a little amusement.

"Watch your step."

He grabbed her hand, and she realized they'd reached the rocky part of the shore. His hand felt warm and big around hers. He went first, leading her over the rocks, their hands still connected.

The darkness made their footing difficult, but it was the distraction of Alex's touch that was her biggest difficulty. When they reached the other side of the rocks, he let go of her hand.

Later that night, as they said good-bye outside her hale, Callie felt an emptiness that frightened her to the bone. If she felt this way about parting for only a day, how on earth would she feel about leaving him for good in three weeks?

Chapter 6

All the next day, Callie found her thoughts continuously on Alex. As she went back into her hale to retrieve her sunscreen, she realized she was anticipating Monday with more enthusiasm than was rational. *It's only a sight-seeing outing, Callie Andersen, so get a grip.*

But she couldn't seem to get a grip at all. She felt giddy with anticipation. After perusing "Harrigan's Happenings" that morning, she'd been tempted to join Alex's group for the fishing excursion. Then she remembered the time she and her dad had fished on Lake Erie, and she quickly ditched that idea. The only thing worse than being stuck on a boat and retching over the railing all day was being stuck on a boat and retching over the rail with Alex watching. No, she could do without that particular humiliation. Maybe she'd eat at the Hale Moana for dinner and run into him there.

Just as she snatched up the sunblock, the phone rang. Her first thought was of Alex, but she knew he was on the fishing trip, so it couldn't be him.

"Hello?" she greeted with enthusiasm.

She was ready to repeat the greeting when the caller finally responded.

"Callie?"

"Sarah!" Her sister's voice was a welcome sound. "I'm glad you called, but this'll cost a fortune."

"Are you all right, Cal?"

Concern laced her words, and Callie realized the last time she'd spoken with her sister, she'd been weeping all over her shoulder.

"Better all the time. Really, this trip is doing me a world of good."

"I was worried. Nobody's heard from you in a few days, and Mom said you were upset when she talked to you."

"I was."

"And Shaun said you'd forbade him to call back."

She cringed as she remembered her harsh words. "I just needed some time to think. Is he doing okay?"

"He's worried about you. He feels just awful—and he *should,* mind you. I'm not one bit happy with him myself."

Callie smiled at her sister's defense. "Do me a favor and let him know I'm doing all right, will you?"

"Don't you want to call him yourself?"

Callie thought for a moment. "No, not really. Just tell him, okay?"

They disconnected soon after that, but Callie made no mention of Alex or her growing feelings. Just the thought of admitting them, when she was supposed to have been married barely over a week ago, was embarrassing, to say the least.

Grabbing her sunblock from the cane table, she headed back out onto the beach to soak in some sun and undoubtedly daydream about Monday's excursion.

Monday arrived slowly, a sure sign of too much anticipation. On Sunday, she'd visited a little chapel down the road and had enjoyed the praise and worship. She had also come to a hard realization.

She had given little thought to God in regards to planning her future with Shaun. The two of them had hopped on what they'd thought was a good idea and asked God to bless it. How could she have left Him out of the most important decision of her life? She'd asked forgiveness for her selfishness right in her pew and vowed to seek God's counsel about her life decisions in the future. Clearly, she was not the best guide for her own life. If she'd sought His will to begin with, it would have saved a lot of pain and trouble.

Callie stepped into her sneakers and tied the shoestrings. Alex had called her the night before, and they'd planned for him to pick her up at seven. They planned to have breakfast on the road.

She looked at the digital alarm clock and realized the moment had arrived. When the knock sounded on her door, her heart tripped in excitement.

She opened the door to his heart-stopping grin and a cup of coffee. He handed it to her. "Ready to explore, Callie-girl?"

She smiled at the nickname and accepted the coffee.

"Thanks." After grabbing her money pouch and camera, she locked the door, and he led the way to his car.

They settled into a silver two-door car. When Alex got behind the wheel, she took a sip of the steaming java through the sipper lid. Two sugars and a French vanilla creamer.

"How did you know?" she asked him, realizing she hadn't had coffee during her one meal with him.

He wiggled his brows. "I have my sources."

She chuckled, the breeze from the open window ruffling her hair, and realized he must have found out from room service.

He pulled out two brochures and handed her one. "I thought we'd take the road to Hana down to Haleakala National Park. It's very scenic, and there are lots of places to shoot great photos."

"I've read about that. There's a black sand beach along the way, isn't there?"

"Yeah, in Waianapanapa State Park."

"Say that again?" she joked.

He humored her, and she shook her head. "Hawaii has some of the strangest words, and they roll off your tongue like you're a native. Have you lived here all your life?"

He explained that his mother and father had purchased the resort in the sixties. He and his brothers were all born in Hawaii, so they were, in fact, natives. They were interrupted briefly when they bought food at a drive-through to save time, but the conversation picked up easily afterward. She told him about her preschool classes and her work as a storyteller at the library; and before she knew it, they were at the Keanae Peninsula.

They got out of the car, and she took pictures of the peninsula jutting out into the deep blue ocean, while Alex explained that Keanae was a major growing area for taro. They followed the arboretum's paved path, which took them through plant displays with beautiful streams running alongside the path. The area was wet, and they didn't linger as the mosquitoes seemed to be particularly attracted to Callie.

"Sorry about that," Alex said as they made their way back to the car. "I've got some repellent in the trunk. Remind me to get it before we hike again."

He'd brought water bottles, and they sipped on them as he pulled out onto Hana Road again. "I really appreciate you taking me today, Alex. I hope you're not bored, seeing as how you've been here so many times."

He winked at her, and her stomach fluttered. "I'm here for the great company." They pulled off the road at a spot where a panoramic view of a valley greeted them. "And the views aren't bad either."

After taking a picture of the Wailua Lookout, they hit the road again, stopping for lunch at a cafe in Nahiku.

As they waited for their food, they discovered they'd both played baseball in high school. Then they discovered they were both huge Cincinnati Reds fans.

"I can't believe it," he said, when she'd told him it was her favorite team. "My dad was a big fan since he grew up in the Cincinnati area. When I was little, my room was filled with Reds paraphernalia. I think my dad and I are the only ones on the islands to give a hoot about the Reds. I even have a signed Chris Sabo card."

She smiled at his enthusiasm. She couldn't believe, this far away from home, she'd found another Reds fan. "I can beat that. I went to one of the World Series games when they played the Oakland A's."

His gaze swung to hers, his eyes wide. "No way."

"I did. Went with my dad."

"Which game?"

"The second. It was awesome."

His jaw dropped, and Callie wondered why he seemed so surprised. "Callie, I was there too."

Her heart knocked against her ribs, and she studied his face, not quite ready to believe the coincidence. "You're kidding. In October of 1990? Cincinnati won five to four—"

"—In the tenth inning. Barbara Bush threw the opening pitch—"

"And Tom Browning's wife went into labor during the game."

They both stared at each other in stunned silence. Alex wore a silly grin, and Callie suspected she did too.

She breathed a laugh. "That's amazing! What were you doing all the way in Cincinnati?"

"We made a trip back to the States to visit relatives. My uncle surprised my dad and me with tickets."

"Amazing. We were both there at the same time," she said. "All those years ago, all those miles away. . ."

"And here we are today." His gaze bore into hers, brown velvet softening the stare.

Her breath caught in her chest, and she couldn't tear her

gaze away from his. He seemed just as trapped as she, and she enjoyed the delicious sweetness of his attention.

The waiter picked that moment to bring their food, and the tension broke. Things were stirring up inside Callie that she couldn't put words to. *Is this the real thing, God? No matter how good it feels, I'm letting You guide this time. Direct our time together today and keep us on Your path.*

Chapter 7

O nce Callie and Alex arrived at Waianapanapa State Park, conversation was flowing and natural. When they stepped onto the black sand beach, she was awed by the sand and the half-submerged lavatube and caves.

"We could easily spend a few hours here," Alex said. "But if you still want to hike at Haleakala, we'll need to be going soon."

"Maybe I can come back here later this week."

"Or you could wait until next Monday, and we could go together."

His smile warmed her, as did his words. But she didn't want to take his day off for granted, so she just smiled and left the comment unanswered.

They drove through Hana, and Callie regretted that they couldn't stop and see the historic buildings and shops. But she knew it would take a few hours to tour the waterfalls and rain forests of Haleakala.

When they arrived at 'Ohe'o, also known as the Seven Pools, they parked the car in an unpaved lot outside the visitors' center. After spraying bug repellent on their clothes and grabbing their gear, they stopped by the center for trail maps.

They perused the maps and decided to take the trail across from the visitor's center. They found the break in the fence and started the uphill climb through the pasture. Callie's breath came hard, and sweat trickled down her back by the time they reached the trail fork that would take them to Makahiku Falls.

"Whew!" Alex said. "We should've started here this morning when it was cooler and made our way back in the heat of the day."

"Hot or not, this place is gorgeous."

He winked. "You ain't seen nothing yet."

After sipping some water, they followed the fork to the waterfall, and Callie was breathless at the sight of its 184-foot drop. The roar of the water was loud, and the tropical foliage surrounded them.

"It's beautiful," she said.

"Yes, it is," Alex said, but he was looking at her.

Her breath caught in her throat, then she looked away. It seemed as if they were alone on the island, and the thought thrilled her.

She took a picture, then posed as Alex took one of her with the waterfall in the background.

Back on the main trail, they hiked about a half mile through woodlands until they came to a bridge that crossed Palikea stream. The trail map warned them not to cross the stream on foot, and when they crossed the bridge and walked downstream, she saw why.

Looking carefully down a steep incline, Callie saw that the stream dropped suddenly into a towering waterfall.

"Wow," she said. Getting the heebie-jeebies from the drop-off, she stepped away from the edge.

"It's a four-hundred-foot drop, and if you think it's incredible from the top, wait until we get down there."

They walked again, and the lush forest became a beautiful array of edibles. Guavas, mountain apples, passion fruit, wild bananas, and coconuts grew all around them. At one spot, Alex plucked a yellow bloom from a plant, tore off the flower, and handed her the stem.

"Here, suck on the stem. There's nectar inside."

He broke off one for himself, and she tried it. "Ummm, it is sweet."

They drank some more water before continuing on their hike. Soon they entered the bamboo forest. A raised wooden walkway kept them from sinking into the mud, but Callie could hardly pull her gaze from the cool, dim forest.

"This is so neat," she said. "Kind of spooky too."

"Listen to the sounds."

They stopped and listened. As the winds from the sea tunneled up through the leafy tops of the bamboo, they swayed, and their poles knocked and scraped together.

"It's almost like a symphony." She smiled.

"The varying thicknesses of the bamboo trunks make different tones."

They moved on, enjoying for awhile the cooler air in the heat of the afternoon. When they left the bamboo forest, Callie could see a glimpse of Waimoku Falls ahead. The stream forked, and Alex took her hand as they crossed the nearer trunk to follow the farther one. It was not the first time he'd helped her by taking her hand on the hike; but each time he released it, she couldn't deny the letdown feeling that came over her.

She hadn't long to think about it this time, however, because a short distance ahead, the falls of Waimoku plunged down a horseshoe-shaped cliff into a pool. There were three people wading in the shallow waters, and she couldn't stop the stab of disappointment when she realized their privacy had been invaded.

Her gaze took in the scenery, and the site took her breath away. When they reached the edge of the pool, Callie stopped to look up the heights of the fall.

"That's the tallest waterfall I've ever seen in my life," she said over the crash of water.

"Want to get in?"

She smiled. "I wouldn't miss it."

They took off their shoes, as they had at the stream crossing, and left them on the shore. The air here was cooler, a relief after the long hike. Callie grabbed her camera and tucked it in her pocket as they stepped into the pool together. Alex took her hand to help her over the slippery rocks, and she welcomed the familiar strength of his grip.

The breeze blew a light mist near the falls. When they reached the middle, Callie backed up a bit until most of the falls could be captured in the frame. Alex had stepped out of the way. She lowered her camera.

"I'd like to get you in this shot if you don't mind."

He smiled and obliged.

Another woman took a shot of her family several feet away, then turned to Callie. The woman said words in a language Callie didn't understand, and at first she was confused. Then the woman pointed to her family and tried to hand Callie her camera.

"Oh," Callie said, getting it. "Sure, go on." She waved the woman over to her family and looked at the camera, a simple point-and-shoot job.

She snapped the shot, and when the woman came to get her camera, she reached for Callie's too, saying something else in her foreign tongue. "What?"

"I think she wants to take our picture for us," Alex said over the roaring water.

"Oh, thanks," she said to the smiling woman and handed her the camera.

Callie carefully joined Alex behind a short shelf of rock. When she reached his side, he draped an arm over her shoulder, and her heart fluttered like a butterfly in her chest.

Just then a little gust of wind blew through their private amphitheater, and the mist turned into a shower.

"Ahhh!" Callie ducked, turning her head into Alex's chest.

He pulled her into the curve of his arm, letting his broad shoulders protect her from the worst of it.

Callie heard his chest rumble with laughter. When the gust stopped, she looked up at him, laughing. "The trail map didn't warn us about that."

Drops of moisture clung to his dark hair, and rivulets of water ran down his face. Their gazes met and held, smiles wrapped around their faces like a ribbon on a package.

"You look like a drowned rat," she said, noticing that she'd escaped the worst of it.

Callie heard the woman with the camera and turned to see her holding up two fingers, gesturing to the camera, and saying something.

"Yes." Callie nodded. "Another one."

Alex wiped his face and brushed his damp hair off his forehead, then looped his arm around Callie. His hand settled on her upper arm. This time they stood shoulder to shoulder, hip to hip, and the smiles on their faces were as genuine as the waterfall behind them.

As the car pulled into the resort's drive, Callie gathered up her camera and moneybag. They'd stopped for dinner in Hana and made the drive back under the cover of darkness. The long drive had made her sleepy, but she and Alex had talked almost nonstop.

When they pulled up outside her hale, they exited the car, and Alex walked her to her door. She dug in her pouch for her key as they shuffled up the walk. A dim light glowed from a lantern beside the door, allowing her to see enough to slide the key in the door.

Once it was unlocked, she turned to face Alex. He stood with his hands in his pockets, that boyish smile lighting his eyes, his dimple coming out to play. Was it the golden glow from the lamp that made his eyes sparkle so?

It had been a long day, but the best one she'd had in longer than she could remember. She'd not once thought about her troubles back home. And spending time with Alex had been more special than she could have known. For a moment she was overcome with gratitude, wanting him to know how truly special the day had been for her, but not knowing the words to say. "Thank you for today." She hoped her eyes spoke the sincerity she felt.

"You already thanked me this morning."

"I mean it more now."

Her heart caught as his eyes grew serious. His gaze moved over her face with the gentleness of a whisper, and she wondered if her ribs would survive her heart's pummeling.

A breeze blew a strand of hair across her face, and before she could move, Alex pulled his hands from his pockets and swept the strand away, tucking it behind her ear. Her skin tingled along her cheek, and she felt his touch down to her toes.

"I had a wonderful time," he said.

"Me too." The words were not more than a whisper, and she was suddenly aware of her very dry throat. She wondered if he would kiss her and was surprised at how much she wanted him to.

Instead, he touched her face one last time. "Good night, Callie-girl." With a tiny smile, he turned and walked down the path that led to his car, and Callie wondered how a mere touch could make her legs feel like a bowl of gelatin.

Chapter 8

"Did you like the luau?" Alex asked as he and Callie strolled along the beach five days later. He'd never enjoyed anyone's company the way he'd enjoyed Callie's, but he was ever aware of the clock slowly ticking away their time together.

"It was even better than I expected. I've never had roasted hog before."

"You mean you Indiana folk don't just walk out to the hog pen and pick you a fat hog for supper?"

She laughed, and his soul thrilled at the sound. "Contrary to popular opinion, all Hoosiers don't own farms."

They approached the rocky part of the shore by the bay, and Alex took her hand to help her over the craggy surface. It was hard to manage in the dim moonlight, even as familiar as the rocks were. Her hand felt small in his, but it fit as no other woman's hand had.

Despite his reservations about the distance between their homes, a conversation with his brother Barnabas had convinced him to follow his heart.

If you don't give it a chance, she'll leave here, and you'll never know what could have been. His brother's words made sense, and besides, he didn't know if he had the strength to resist these feelings taking root in his heart.

When they reached the other side of the rocks, he made a decision. Rather than releasing her hand as he had done many times before, he shifted until their hands were locked together. Each of her dainty fingers dovetailed with his. His breath locked in his chest because he knew he'd just taken their relationship to a new level, made a statement he couldn't take back.

He looked at her as they walked, and her head turned. The moonlight glimmered in her eyes and rested in the sweet curve of her smile. The wind tugged her long hair over her shoulder, and he thought he'd never seen a more beautiful sight.

His feet stopped of their own volition, and he turned toward her. He clasped her other hand in his. They stood this way, hands joined, hearts united, while their faces hovered inches apart.

The wind rustled her hair, exposing her forehead, and he leaned just a breath away to place a kiss on her brow. Her skin was warm and soft, and she seemed to lean into him.

When Alex's lips touched her skin, Callie's breath caught and held in lungs that suddenly seemed incapable of expansion. Her eyes closed at the sweet touch, a mistake, since it suddenly made her lightheaded. She opened them again to find his gaze on hers, his face only a whisper away. The moon silhouetted his expression, but she didn't need the light to see that he was as affected as she.

Though he stood close, only their hands touched. They felt warm and strong in hers.

Something flickered in his eyes, but the darkness hid its meaning. When he turned and tugged her along with him, a fire of disappointment smoldered in her belly. They continued to walk, their hands intertwined, and they talked as the moon rose high in the sky.

That night in bed, Callie pondered how she could be feeling so close to a man she'd only met two weeks ago.

But you've spent so much time together, she rationalized. They'd spent hours together in the past few days. She met his brothers and dad. She'd joined several of his activities, including the snorkeling adventure on Tuesday. She'd enjoyed seeing him with the guests, seeing how he lit up in front of an audience. He was totally comfortable in the center of things, and people were drawn to him. Especially the women.

Callie frowned remembering the skimpy-suited women who'd flirted with him and requested needless assistance with their snorkeling equipment. But Alex, to his credit, had congenially done his job without leading them on. And, though he'd been available to every member of the group, he'd spent most of the snorkeling time with her.

Callie's fascination with the underwater world was what had led to their plans for Monday. She couldn't visit Maui without snorkeling at Molokini, he'd said.

Sometime later, she drifted to sleep. She wasn't sure at what point it happened, but she was certain her lips were curled in a smile.

✺

"Are you ready to go in?" Alex asked her as they pulled up to her hale. Their day at the island of Molokini had been fabulous and full, but she wasn't tired yet.

"No, not really. Walk on the beach?"

He smiled, then joined her on her side of the car. They walked down the slope to the sand and slipped off their sandals. It had become a habit, walking on the beach together in the evenings, and once again, her heart thrilled when he took her hand.

They talked about the possibility of a children's program as they walked. Alex's brothers liked the idea, and Steve was looking into the financial feasibility of it.

"Assuming it works out, what should we call it?" he asked over the ocean's roar.

"Hmm, haven't given that any thought."

"What do you think of Kiddie Klub? With the word club starting with a K."

"I like it. That's really cute."

He pulled her to a stop and faced her. "So are you." He smiled, and this time the moonlight shone on his face.

She read the intensity there as the smile faded in the shadow of deeper emotions.

He released one of her hands, and she felt his palm cup her face. She longed to turn into it and press a kiss into the soft flesh. Before she could, his thumb swept across her lower lip, leaving a trail of desire in its wake. Warmth kindled inside her

237

as his gaze burned into her own.

Her heart surged as he leaned closer, and his lips touched hers with a feather-light kiss. He was tentative and soft, and she responded with all the emotion she was feeling. The moment was over too soon, leaving her wanting more.

He straightened and turned away, and she wished she could read the expression in his eyes. Did he want to kiss her again? *Let it be so,* her heart cried. She'd never felt the stirring of her heart, her soul, in a simple kiss. Not with Shaun or anybody else. She had grown to believe such passion was for romance novels, not real life. But this kiss with Alex had shattered that belief.

He turned back to her, and his breath mingled with hers. His lips hovered near, and she desperately wanted him to kiss her again.

Instead, he spoke. "Callie. . ." Her name was soft as a rose petal on his lips. "I'm not sure this is wise."

Her thoughts were fuzzy, and she couldn't even fathom what he was thinking. Had their kiss not affected him as it had her? The thought brought a sting to her eyes.

"Callie," he said again. "This is crazy. You're just coming off a broken engagement."

What could she say? It was true. And yet. . .the feelings she had for Alex were there, strong and undeniable. "Are you reminding me—or you?"

He looked back at her then, and she read the sadness in his eyes. "Both of us, I guess."

She wanted to scream that this was different. That Shaun's embraces had merely invoked pleasant feelings, while Alex's shook her to the core. But she was only beginning to understand this herself. "I do have feelings for you, Alex."

His lips tipped in a sweet grin. "I think it goes without saying that you rock my world."

She breathed a laugh, relieved at his words.

"You live so far away." Sadness crept into his voice, the smile draining away.

It was on her mind too. She had less than two weeks left now and didn't relish the thought of leaving the man she was falling in love with.

"A lot can happen in a couple weeks," she said. "We're proof of that." She smiled, and he returned it.

"All right. We'll play it by ear."

Her heart clenched at the thought.

As she tossed and turned later that night, she couldn't help but wonder if she was setting herself up for a broken heart that would make her wedding fiasco pale in comparison.

Callie savored every moment of the next week, and time seemed to fly by. When she wasn't participating in Alex's activities or sharing time with him on his off hours, she was lounging on a bamboo mat, dreaming of their next encounter.

On his day off, they'd taken a whale-watching boat tour, and she'd gotten a great shot of a whale surfacing, shooting water through his blowhole.

As Callie swung in her hammock in the late afternoon heat, she didn't have to consult her calendar to realize she had only two more days with Alex. The thought was frightening, and she admitted something to herself that she'd avoided before.

She'd fallen in love with Alex. Although less than four weeks had passed since their first meeting, she knew her heart was gone for good. She suspected Alex felt the same way, though he'd not said as much. And she knew something else.

Shaun had been right. There had been something missing in their relationship. Something big. Theirs had not been the love of a husband and wife but of best friends. As much as she loved Shaun, there had been no passion, no spark. And eventually, they would have come to resent that.

One thing was sure, now that Callie had experienced the real thing, she could never imagine settling for less. Right now she couldn't imagine settling for anyone but Alex.

Which was a major problem, given that three days from now she would be traveling hundreds of miles away and not returning. Her heart squeezed at the thought, and a heavy ache started deep in her belly. Leaving would be like tearing away a part of herself. But what alternative was there?

The word that surfaced in her mind should have surprised her, but it rang too true to do so. Marriage. She wanted to be Alex's wife. Or at the very least, she wanted him to declare his interest. To ask her to stay, to make a serious commitment to her.

She shook her head in wonder. She was wanting a marriage proposal only a month after she was supposed to have been married to another man. It must be some kind of record.

She chuckled, joy filling her heart with love for Alex. *Thank You, God. You knew what You were doing all along.* She remembered her first day at the resort, all the emotions she'd experienced, the sadness and humiliation at having been jilted in front of her hometown. But it had all been for good purpose.

She thought she heard a ring and cocked her ear toward the French doors. It was hard to hear over the crashing waves, but she thought she heard her phone through the screen door. She rolled out of the hammock, almost falling on her face in her hurry, and grabbed the phone off the table.

As Alex made his way to Callie's hale, he could barely keep from breaking into a run. He only had a moment between activities; but he'd just met with Steve, and the kids' program was a go. He couldn't wait to share it with Callie, since it had been her idea and her expertise that had started the ball rolling. Though the prospect of improving their resort excited him, there was another idea brewing in his mind that really made this kids' program something special.

Callie. Somewhere along the way, he'd started thinking of her as the ideal person to run the program. Children were her calling, and he couldn't think of anyone better suited for the position. Not to mention, it would keep her in Maui, where he could pursue this relationship for all it was worth. His feelings for her were—well, he didn't want to think about that right now. There was no sense in admitting anything until he knew if she was willing to stay.

When he reached her front door, he knocked and waited. He was so excited about the possibility of her staying that he could hardly stand still. When a second knock brought no answer, he walked around her hale to the beach. When he rounded the corner, he saw the swaying hammock.

An impish grin spread across his mouth. He would sneak up behind her, cover her eyes, and maybe plant a big kiss across her sweet lips.

He took two steps before he heard her speak.

"What are you talking about, Shaun?"

His feet froze when he realized she was on the phone— and with whom she was speaking.

"And now you're saying you were wrong?" There was a note of exasperation in her voice.

Alex felt an unpleasant flutter in his gut. He should walk away. He shouldn't be eavesdropping.

"I can't believe you're saying this. What about everything you said before, that there was something missing between us—" There was strong emotion in her voice. Relief? Joy?

He couldn't tell. His heart stomped on his ribs, and the fluttering in his gut grew stronger. His feet moved in reverse, taking him to the corner of the hale. Soon the roaring ocean covered the sound of her voice, sheltering him from the words that were piercing his heart.

Chapter 9

Callie had been shocked by Shaun's change of heart, by his desire to continue with the wedding, but she couldn't do it. Now she knew it had been a mistake. Now she knew what real love felt like. She tried to let him down easily and told him she'd prayed about it and felt sure that it had never been God's will. He'd seemed sad when he realized how strongly she felt, but she knew he would come to realize eventually that he'd been right to cancel the wedding.

Callie was disappointed when she didn't run into Alex that night at the Hale Moana, where they'd been having casual dinners. She was further distressed when he didn't show up at the breakfast buffet the next day. She told herself she had no right to be upset. They hadn't had plans to meet, after all. But time was slipping away, and today was her last day in Maui.

One part of her wanted to seek him out after breakfast, but the other part of her worried that he didn't care as deeply as she did. Maybe he didn't dread the thought of her leaving. Maybe his kisses were casual.

But her fears were allayed when he called her after breakfast. His words had stirred up hope in her heart and set it to racing. *Let's have dinner at the Hale Samoa tonight. I have something important to ask you.*

She had yet to eat at the resort's fancy restaurant, and her heart could only think of one thing. He was going to ask her to stay. He was going to ask her to marry him. All afternoon, her spirits soared. She would say yes. She would move to Maui, leave her family and job if it meant a life with Alex. She hadn't thought it possible to love a man the way she did Alex, but she knew she would move to Timbuktu if it meant sharing a life with him.

Hoping she would be staying in Maui, she left her belongings scattered across the room. There was no sense packing if she wasn't going to be using those plane tickets in the morning. She would go back home eventually to pack her things and say good-bye to her friends and family, but she had all she needed for the time being.

She wore her nicest sundress, a coral affair that showed off her curves without clinging immodestly. Her face glowed with happiness as she carefully applied her makeup.

When Alex knocked on her door, her knees were weak with excitement. With trembling hands, she opened the door.

That easy smile that melted her heart spread across his face. An ivory shirt hugged his torso and tucked into pants, making his waist seem narrow in comparison to his shoulders. "Ready, Callie-girl?"

She smiled and nodded, a bit of her anxiety fleeing with the familiar nickname.

When they arrived at the restaurant, she noticed they were led to the nicest table, a small, secluded table in the corner that overlooked the beach. Candlelight flickered across the room from dainty white candles atop the tables. Once again, her heart worked overtime.

She perused the menu as the waiter poured water in tall crystal glasses. The words on the menu ran together. She couldn't think about food, didn't want to think about anything except the reason Alex had brought her here tonight.

When the waiter returned, she asked Alex to order for her, and he selected a trio of Hawaiian fish for each of them. When the waiter left, they talked about their afternoon, and Callie's nerves grew taut.

Service in the restaurant was slow and formal, and when Callie realized Alex must be waiting for the end of the meal, she wished the waiter had a fast-forward button.

Finally, the server cleared their plates and showed them a tray of desserts. Callie was going to refuse, but Alex insisted she try the Maui key lime pie, so she acquiesced.

Alex ordered a slice for himself, then leaned closer to her when the waiter left. "I have exciting news." His eyes brimmed with excitement. "Steve approved Kiddie Klub. It's a go."

"Alex! That's wonderful." She knew what it meant to him, and genuine joy rose in her heart. "I hope it's all the success we think it'll be."

He looked down at the table, then back to her, his expression changing, growing more intense somehow.

Her stomach lurched, and she wondered if the fish had

been such a good idea. Her insides fluttered and rolled, and she didn't know how much longer she could stand the antici-pation. *Heaven's sakes, Callie, you're like a schoolgirl.*

"I have something very important to ask you, Callie. I know it's not a decision to be made lightly, and you're supposed to be leaving in the morning. It's a lot to ask, but I've been thinking about it a lot the past couple of weeks—"

She laughed lightly. "What is it already?" she asked and wondered if he heard the quiver in her voice. "You're making me nervous."

He fiddled with the white cloth napkin and finally placed it on the table. The candlelight licked the strong planes of his face, and she thought for the hundredth time how handsome he was.

"I think you're the perfect person for the job." His eyes shone with fervor.

Job? Her thoughts raced.

"Who better than a preschool teacher to work with the kids here at the resort? You're fun and organized. Patient and creative. In short, you're exactly what this program needs." His gaze searched hers as she felt the smile on her face turn plastic. "What do you think?"

Alex was excited about the possibility of Callie taking the job, but mostly he was worried. Worried that she would go back to Indiana. Worried that she would marry Shaun. Ever since he'd overheard her conversation with him, he'd thought of little else.

"It would be perfect, Callie. I think you'd like working

here. The weather's great year-round, you'd live in tropical paradise and get paid for it. Just imagine. I know it'd be hard to leave your family." *Not to mention Shaun.* He pushed away the ugly thought. "But you could visit eventually, and they could visit you. And with today's technology, your family would be just an E-mail away." Gathering courage, he focused on her face for the first time since he had begun his speech.

His heart dropped at her expression. A smile seemed frozen on her face, and her eyes seemed determined to avoid his gaze.

Shaun. She wanted to go back home and marry her fiancé like she'd planned.

No, please, not that. He replayed his words in his mind. Had he left anything out? Anything that might convince her to stay and take the job?

Salary. Of course!

A smile found its way to his face again. "I'm sorry, I didn't even tell you how much we're prepared to offer." He named the sum Steve had agreed to, but even so, Callie seemed less than thrilled.

He took her hand and was rewarded with her gaze. She seemed to search his face. "What do you think, Callie? Will you stay?"

She opened her mouth, then shut it again. His lungs froze, though his heart seemed to be working double-time.

"I just—I don't know, Alex. It's a tempting offer, but—"

"Just think about it. Please." *Don't go home. Don't marry Shaun.*

A frown puckered between her brows. "I have to leave tomorrow, Alex. That doesn't give much time for thinking."

"I know. I'm sorry about that. I was hoping you wouldn't have to think about it."

The server brought the desserts then, and he and Callie ate in silence. The creamy confection glided tastelessly down his throat. Alex had been sure Callie had feelings for him. If only Shaun hadn't called. How can four weeks with Alex compare to the years of history those two shared?

Alex took care of the bill, noting that half of Callie's pie remained on the plate. They left the restaurant, and the darkness enveloped them.

"Walk on the beach?" he asked.

"Sure."

As they made their way across the resort to the sandy cove, Alex couldn't help but wish her answer to his previous question could have come easily.

Callie's heart was in turmoil as she and Alex walked and talked for over an hour. They discussed their faith and families and many other things. Except Alex's job offer.

When they reached the spot on the bay where the rocks poked up from the sand, they sat side by side, leaning against a rock shelf. For several moments they sat in silence, listening to the waves crash against the beach a short distance away.

The stab of disappointment she'd felt at Alex's job offer settled over her now like a heavy blanket. She couldn't move here for a mere job. Wouldn't consider leaving her home and her family for such a reason. If only he'd offer more. She'd thought perhaps the "more" would come later, as they'd walked.

But she saw now, there would be no "more." Alex didn't want her for his bride; he wanted her for his employee. The thought caused an ache in her belly and a sting behind her eyes.

A gust of wind tugged at her hair and raised gooseflesh on her skin. Alex wrapped his arm around her and pulled her close against him. He was warm and solid. Shivers of another kind ran through her.

She felt his fingers on her chin, pulling her face around to meet his gaze. His eyes sparkled in the moonlight. She allowed her gaze to flit over his face, burning the details into her mind for some lonely night in Grabill. The curves of his cheek, the hollows of his jaw. Her fingers traced the planes, relishing the softness of his clean-shaven chin, the sweet curve of his lower lip.

He leaned closer, and his lips met hers. Softly, gently they plied, until a fire kindled within her and spread its heat to the furthest reaches of her limbs. Oh, what he did to her. If only she could bottle it up and take it with her. If only he would ask her what she really wanted.

He pulled away, and she wondered when his hands had come around to cup her face.

His gaze burned into hers. "Stay, Callie," his voice rasped into her ear.

She drank in his words, his expression, his musky scent. And she waited. Waited for him to offer the something more she needed.

But he was waiting too. For her answer.

"I can't," she whispered.

His eyes closed, and his head bowed.

Ask me, her heart begged. *Tell me you love me. Tell me it's not just a job you want me for.*

She searched his face for something. Some clue that would give her cause to hope.

"Maybe you'll change your mind." His fingers caressed her face in a whisper-touch. "I don't have to fill the position right away."

She was tired of hearing about the job. She wanted to hear about his feelings for her. She wanted to hear that he would miss her, that her leaving would be unbearable.

She gave him a sad smile. "My plane leaves early." *These will be our last moments together.*

"I'll miss you."

Don't let me go. Her eyes stung, and she blinked away the moisture. How could she go back to life without Alex?

"There's always E-mail," he said.

"Sure." She returned his smile and thought hers probably looked as brittle as his.

He pulled her close to his side and laid his cheek on her head. They sat in silence for a long while. She was glad for the noisy ocean that covered her sniffles.

Covertly, she wiped at her cheeks when she sensed him straightening.

"It's getting late," he said.

The moon was high in the sky, and she knew it would be difficult to wake in the morning.

He stood and pulled her with him. On the walk back to her hale, he held her hand, and she noted that it would be for the last time. Each step brought them closer to the end, and she wondered how she would bear saying good-bye.

At the door, she turned to him. She wouldn't let his last memory of her be filled with tears.

She put a hand against his cheek, and he drew her into his arms. His lips covered hers, seeking and giving, giving and loving. She never wanted it to end, this painful torture of good-bye.

When he drew away, she wondered if his eyes sparkled with moisture or if the glow of the lamplight played tricks with her.

"Have a safe flight."

She nodded, not trusting her voice.

"You have my E-mail address."

She nodded again, and he pulled her into his chest. He held her tightly, and she knew he wanted her to stay. But not enough to say what she needed to hear.

He took her key and opened her door. She felt her throat tighten against the lump there as she turned to him on the threshold.

"Good-bye, Callie-girl." Gone were his twinkling eyes and playful dimple.

" 'Bye." It was all she could manage past the ache in her throat.

And with a final kiss, he was gone.

Chapter 10

Alex fell onto his couch, grabbed the remote, then flicked on the TV. The past two weeks had been unlike any he'd experienced before. He ached inside, and because of that, he felt miserable. What had happened to his playful personality? It seemed to have disappeared among all the pain. It was all he could do to get through his activities with the guests. He wondered if they saw through his plastic smile and injected enthusiasm.

He hadn't attempted to hide his depression from his brothers, and he knew they were getting tired of his moping.

He'd walked on the beach last night, remembering their moments together. Remembering the way her honey-blond hair whipped in the wind, remembering the way her blue eyes sparkled in the sun. He was tired of remembering. He wanted her here where he could touch her, kiss her, love her.

He was tired of checking his E-mail only to be disappointed when she hadn't written. Had she married Shaun? Was she even now with him?

He growled and tossed the remote control across the couch. His stomach knotted at the thought of his Callie with someone else. In his heart, she was his and he was hers. And whether he'd said the words aloud or not, he knew now it was true. He loved her.

Idiot! Why didn't you tell her that when you had the chance? When she'd been standing in his arms with her hands on his shoulders?

Because you wouldn't admit it until she was gone.

Now there was a fact. As much as he'd wanted her to stay, as much as he knew he cared for her, he hadn't realized the depth of his love until he'd lost her.

Lost her. The two little words stung like a stingray. He got up off the couch and walked to the window. And he'd thought losing Lana had been hard. That had been nothing. He'd only felt humiliated about having been used, he realized now that he knew what real heartbreak felt like.

A knock sounded at the door, and he scowled. He wasn't in the mood for company, but he made his way toward the door anyway.

When he opened it, Barnabas's face greeted him. "We need to talk, Bro."

As Callie drove to her parents' house for a picnic dinner, she let out a tired sigh. She knew they meant well, but she wasn't in the mood for an evening barbecue. Instead of getting her mind off Alex, the dark night air and gentle summer breezes would only remind her of him. She'd thought it would get easier, being away from him, but it had been almost three weeks now, and today had been the hardest.

This afternoon, at her mother's prodding, she picked up her developed pictures on the way to her library reading. She'd sat in the car and flipped through the stack.

The one of her and Alex by the waterfall caught her heart. Her lungs seized in her chest, and an achy lump formed in her throat. The one of them being doused by water made her laugh, but at the same time, tears clogged her throat and glazed her vision. Finally, she'd put the pictures aside and gone into the library to do her reading, only to find it was Hawaiian week.

Leis and orchids splashed across all the bulletin boards, and Hawaiian books decorated the tables and shelves. *Great,* she thought. *Just what I need.* Then Gretchen handed her the book she was to read to the children: *"A" is for Aloha.*

By the time she got home, she was ready to stare at her pictures of Alex and have a good cry session. But her dad was barbecuing chicken, so her pity party had to wait.

She parked the car in her parents' drive, grabbed the Maui photos off the seat, and walked around back. She thought of the picture of her and Alex posing by the waterfall. He was so handsome in his rugged hiking clothes. His arm was wrapped around her shoulder, and his hair was damp and raked off his forehead. They were laughing. She could almost hear his deep, throaty laugh. She could almost hear the crashing waves of the Pacific. She could almost hear the Polynesian music.

Wait a minute. She *did* hear Polynesian music.

She rounded the corner of the house to her mom's garden

and stopped in her tracks. Tiki poles dotted the landscape, their flickering flames lighting the patio area. Sand covered the pathways between the foliage, and indeed, Polynesian music was wafting through the night air.

But what caught and held her attention was the man standing on the bricked patio. A tall, handsome man wearing a Hawaiian shirt and colorful lei.

"Alex!" Her heart skipped a beat, then caught up, doing double-time. "What are you doing here?"

His hands in his pockets, his feet shuffled on the brick flooring. He looked adorably unsure of himself. From across the patio, his gaze seemed to caress her face. "I missed you, Callie-girl."

Her heart thudded heavily at his tone. The look in his eyes stole her breath from her lungs. He stepped closer, her heart pounding with each pace, until she felt his breath on her face. She looked into his eyes and wanted to drown in the brown depths. He touched her face with gentle fingers, and she closed her eyes. "I missed you too."

"I know."

She opened her eyes.

"Your mom told me."

"How did you find my parents?"

He shrugged. "They're the only *Andersen* listed in the Grabill directory."

"Is that so?"

"Mmm-hmm." He nuzzled her face with his. "Once I told them how much I missed you, your mom was very helpful in setting this up." He looked around at the Hawaiian scenery. "I was hoping it'd make you homesick for Hawaii." His palm cupped her cheek.

"It's working." Her senses were swimming with his touch.

His finger tipped up her chin. "Did you miss me as much as I missed you?"

"Worse," she whispered as he lowered his head.

His lips claimed hers, gently, probing and promising. She felt it to the core of her body, and her legs went weak.

Slowly he drew away. She wanted to pull him back, though only inches separated them. His gaze roamed her face, bathing her with love. "There's a position open in Hawaii with your name on it," he whispered.

Her heart plummeted, but before she could speak, he withdrew something from his pocket and held it between them.

A ring. A brilliant diamond ring set in a gold band winked at her in the evening light.

"You're the only one who can fill this position," he said. His gaze bore into hers with urgency. "I love you, Callie. Don't make me go home without you."

Joy filled her heart at his words. He loved her. He wanted to marry her. Her vision blurred as tears swam in her eyes. "Now, that's an offer I can't refuse," she whispered. And he wiped the smile from her face with a satisfying kiss.

DENISE HUNTER

Denise lives in Indiana with her husband and three active, young sons. As the only female of the household, every day is a new adventure, but Denise holds on to the belief that her most important responsibility in this life is to raise her children in such a way that they will love and fear the Lord. The message Denise wants her writing to convey is that "God needs to be the center of our lives. If He isn't, everything else is out of kilter."

It All Adds Up to Love

by Gail Sattler

Chapter 1

S teve Harrigan righted his glasses on his nose as he stepped closer to his brother's desk. He leaned forward, rested one palm on the desktop, and cleared his throat.

"Barnabas, remember when that special shipment came in with the stuff for the new koi pond, and you were the only one around because of the odd time it came in? I have to know the exact amount you gave the delivery person. Paying more than the minimum required for delivery constitutes a partial payment. By doing that you've changed our payment schedule and our discount. In addition to that, changing the payment alters my budget projections because I have to allocate the expense for this purchase order into three different liability accounts. That also affects my bank reconciliation, with the change in payments. I also can't believe you'd carry around that much cash."

His brother merely shrugged his shoulders. "I knew how important it was to keep the pond project on schedule. I didn't have a check with me in the middle of the grounds, so I had to pay cash. Since I didn't have enough cash on me to pay the amount required, Liliana emptied her wallet too. She gave him everything she had, thinking she was helping, that we'd get charged less interest by making a larger down payment. She was only trying to help. We had no idea we were supposed to stick to the minimum. And sorry about the receipt. We were busy with Abby, so Connor handled it."

"You mean you've got personal funds involved here too?"

"Is that a problem? Can't you just reimburse me in my next paycheck? You're the accountant. You know how to do that kind of stuff. Once you figure out how much I paid, that is."

Steve stood straight, gritted his teeth, and ran his fingers through his hair. Barnabas had always been the most responsible of his brothers, yet Barnabas had increasingly allowed his relationship with Liliana to affect his performance in the management of their resort. Barnabas had told him that being married wouldn't change anything, but this latest blunder confirmed Steve's fears. Liliana was in fact a distraction—and a major one at that. This time they were not talking pocket change, but an allocation of nearly a thousand dollars.

Fortunately for Steve, despite Barnabas's inaccurate handling of the payment for the new pond liner and all the equipment that went with the filtration system, he knew he could depend on Connor to have the receipt, since Connor had been the one to actually accept the delivery.

Steve opened his mouth to ask Barnabas if he knew where Connor was, but the electronic tone of Barnabas's cell phone interrupted him.

"Hello?" Barnabas paused, and the sappiest grin came over

his face. "Hi, Honey. I miss you too."

"Never mind," Steve grumbled. "Just remember for next time, okay?"

Steve turned around and stomped into Connor's office across the hall. As expected, Steve didn't find Connor actually in his office. Eventually he found Connor outside near the pump house for their new pond adjusting one of the connections.

Steve rammed both hands into his pockets and forced himself to smile. "Hi, Connor. Do you remember when you and Barnabas accepted delivery for the pond liner? Where did you put the receipt? I need it."

Connor laid the wrench down on the large pipe, straightened, and scratched the top of his head. "I don't know. That was weeks ago. Maybe it's in my drawer. No, wait. I remember now. Beth needed me, so I gave it to Alex. Didn't he give it to you?"

Steve dragged his palm down his face. Connor had always been a little absentminded once he got started on a project, but since he'd married Beth, he'd gone from bad to worse. "If he gave it to me, I wouldn't be asking now, would I?"

Connor picked up his wrench and returned to his tinkering. "Sorry, Bro. Can't help you. I think Alex is making up the new rec schedule. Why don't you ask him?"

"I never would have thought of that without your suggestion," Steve grumbled between gritted teeth. "Thank you so much." He didn't care about the sarcasm dripping in his words.

Connor raised his head and smiled, obviously not realizing that Steve was so annoyed. "No problem. By the way, Beth and I are going to join the guests on the patio and watch that new singer after supper. Barn and Lil are going to be there too, and I think so are Alex and Callie. You want to join us?"

The last thing Steve wanted to do was to spend time surrounded by couples, especially since he knew the biggest topic of conversation was going to be Alex and Callie's future wedding. "No, thanks. I plan to be busy. Fixing up all my spreadsheets. If I can ever get the right data to input."

Connor shrugged his shoulders. "Suit yourself. You don't know what you're missing."

"I think I do," Steve mumbled as he strode off in the direction of the activity center.

He found Alex making a few adjustments to the next week's activity calendar. While Alex was working, he was also humming some wedding song.

Steve shook his head and squeezed his eyes shut for a brief second. "Alex, do you remember when the new pond liner was delivered? Do you by any chance have the receipt? Connor says he gave it to you."

Alex didn't look up. "I dunno. When was that? I don't remember him giving me any receipts."

"Two weeks ago last Wednesday."

Alex paged back in his activity book, then rested the pencil on the afternoon's list of activities. "That was the day Callie had the idea to do a special teen marshmallow roast and sing-along. All Connor gave me was a handful of scrap papers, because I remember that I didn't have to go to the shed for old newspapers. There weren't any receipts in there. We used the pile to light the fire."

"Light the. . ." Steve let his voice trail off. He wondered what other critical paperwork was in the pile of "scrap" papers.

"Sorry, Bro," Alex said with a smile, then returned his attention to his schedule book. "Did you ask Barnabas? I remember he and Liliana paid the delivery guy."

Steve opened his mouth, but no words came out, which was not a bad thing. In his present mood, he wasn't sure the words almost coming out of his mouth were appropriate for a Christian man to say aloud or even to think.

"Never mind," he mumbled. "I'll think of something. I have to."

Without another word, Steve spun on his toes and strode back to his office in the main building. He plopped himself behind his desk, straightened his glasses, gritted his teeth, and stared at the accumulation of papers atop the desk. In the back of his mind, he tried to remember what color the surface of his desk was. He hadn't seen the top of it since Brittany, his part-time assistant, had begun her leave of absence.

Steve had talked to Brittany only yesterday. Unfortunately, instead of telling him how happy she was to be returning to work, Brittany had asked for yet another extension to her leave. Steve didn't want to be hard-hearted. After all, her baby had medical problems, and Brittany needed the time off. However, what had begun as a few weeks had extended into months. With her latest request for even more time off, he still didn't know when she'd return.

He knew Brittany sensed his frustration during their last phone call. Not only did she promise that after exactly one month she would return no matter what, Brittany had also joked about bringing the baby back to work with her if she couldn't get a reliable sitter who could administer the child's medication. At this point Steve wouldn't have cared if she brought the baby with her. He just wanted his reliable helper back.

For now, he couldn't do anything about Brittany, but one thing Steve did know. He would never become a besotted fool like any of his brothers. With the addition of the women in their lives, all three of his brothers had been giving more attention to their ladies and less to the affairs of the resort. Every week things fell further and further behind, which they could ill afford during this, the peak of tourist season.

Between his brothers' mistakes and now with Brittany off for another month, Steve was so far behind, he still hadn't balanced the previous season's fiscal year.

He shook his head, sighed, and picked up the next invoice from the top of the pile to discover that it, too, was missing the receipt.

Steve squeezed his eyes shut at the thought of chasing Barnabas, Connor, and Alex for the details of yet another unbalanced transaction. When he finally opened his eyes, all he could do was stare blankly at his computer, which had been inactive for so long the screen-saver had come on.

He watched the multicolored patterns flicker and change for a few minutes before he moved the mouse to reactivate his program. However, Steve couldn't bring himself to make an entry. He no longer had the strength or the will to fight with everyone and everything, including his computer. He didn't know what accountants did in the days before computers; but if this was what he faced with the most modern technology, he didn't want to think of having to rely on manual records or calculations.

Steve let out a sigh and pushed in the keyboard tray. He normally didn't give up so readily; but for today, he was too frustrated to be productive, and he was too far behind for a couple of hours to make any difference. Tomorrow he would start early, when he could face his problems with a fresh mind, a clear head, and a couple gallons of coffee.

He started to slide the chair backward, but as he wheeled away, he caught sight of an unopened brown envelope from the pile of yesterday's mail. He rolled the chair back up to the desk, picked up the envelope, and opened it.

As soon as he read the first paragraph, the letter dropped from his numb fingers.

Slowly, Steve lowered his elbows to rest on top of the mounds of paperwork and buried his face in his hands. "No. . . ," he muttered. "Not now."

A blast of hot air lifted Tasha Struchenkowich's bangs off her forehead as she stepped outside the airport and walked to the area to await the shuttle bus. She was no longer in the shelter of the building, and the brightness of the sun made her eyes water. She shuffled her suitcases under the shade of the canopy along with the other tourists and prepared herself to wait.

Instead of standing in the middle of a hot tarmac in the blazing sun, Tasha tried to imagine herself at home, taking a walk on the shady nature trail at the city park after a cool fall rain. However, no matter how hard she tried to think about anything other than the heat that attempted to stifle her, she broke out into a sweat anyway.

An airport shuttle pulled up to the shelter, and a family of six piled out. "Enjoy your vacation, people!" the driver of the bus called out as the last person got off. "The buses for the resorts will all be here in a few minutes to whisk you off to vacation paradise."

Tasha forced herself to smile along with the rest of the tourists under the canopy. Not that she didn't want, or need, a vacation. It was just that if she could have picked a place to vacation by herself, she would not have chosen Hawaii. She would have chosen someplace cooler—and something not so commercial. She would have chosen someplace where she could get away from the crowd, not simply get lost in one, as in a sea of strangers. A one-month vacation was only a vacation if it was possible to put aside the rigors and stresses of the other forty-eight weeks of the year. To Tasha, that meant being alone.

One more time, she looked at the brochure in her hand. Her aunt had fallen in love with the picture on the front, which Tasha supposed was the mark of successful advertising. The picture portrayed an endless sandy beach running alongside a strip of crystal blue water, the shore dotted with tall and beautiful palm trees swaying in the ocean breeze.

Tasha knew when she arrived at Harrigan's Cove what she saw wouldn't look like the brochure in her hand. She didn't know of anywhere in this current decade that wouldn't be crowded with throngs of people, especially in a state whose major industry was tourism.

Once more, she flipped through the brochure depicting a grand selection of digitally enhanced photographs of beaches and the amenities of the resort in all their splendor. She'd never seen anyone who had been to Hawaii come home with such vivid pictures, even if they stood in the same place as the paid photographer. While the settings were beautiful and the flora and fauna divine, they weren't quite real.

Her only consolation was that this resort would be different from the rest, not by the nature of the surroundings, but the nature of the management. This was the resort owned by the Harrigans. Tasha didn't like the heat, she hated the crowds, and too much sun wasn't good for her skin, but she knew Steve Harrigan from her college days. While that specifically wasn't a good enough reason to come here, it was the best reason she had to tell herself she might possibly enjoy this vacation.

Four small buses painted with various logos for different resorts rumbled up to the shelter. Tasha sucked in a deep breath, picked up her suitcases, and joined the rest of the people destined for Harrigan's Cove.

Chapter 2

"A loha!" A very pregnant woman in a bright flowery dress and a tall, good-looking man who had to be one of Steve's brothers placed a lei around the neck of every person as they stepped off the shuttle bus, Tasha included.

"My name is Barnabas Harrigan, and welcome to Harrigan's Cove. Please see me and I'll give you the key for your hale, a schedule of events, and a map of the resort, then a steward will drive you to your hale. If you have any questions, my door is always open. You can find me almost any time at the registration center in the middle of Harrigan's Cove. Please feel free to ask me anything, any time."

As Barnabas's smile swept over the small crowd, pausing briefly on each new arrival, Tasha's heart nearly stopped. She forced herself to smile back like everyone around her, hoping no one had noticed her odd reaction to a man who should have been a stranger.

It had been a few years since she'd seen Steve, but his brother shared the one thing she would never forget. That little dimple in his left cheek. It reminded her so much of Steve that she wanted to drop her suitcases and run to find him.

Instead, Tasha blinked and stared, transfixed, at his brother's face, so much like Steve's, with the addition of a few years. Seeing an older version of Steve, including the gorgeous blue eyes, minus the glasses, brought her back to the last time she'd seen him, four years ago. At the suggestion of her dear old grandmother, Tasha had taken what she thought would be her last chance to travel for many years. She'd mixed business with pleasure and traveled to sunny California to finish her university degree before returning home to North Dakota to settle down with a job as a career accountant.

Likewise, Steve had achieved his bachelor of science degree at home, which for him was Hawaii. Similar prompting by his family had sent him packing his bags and heading to California to get his master of business administration degree before he settled in to take over the financial transactions of his family's resort, which would tie him to home for years to come, likely with little chance of vacation.

Like two country cousins both away from home for the first time and as the only two Christians in their graduating class, they had sought the quiet places away from the crowds. In doing so, they had become fast friends. Over the years since graduation, their written communications had dwindled to birthday cards only, but they did tend to send a lot of E-mail.

Tasha stepped forward to receive the necessary paperwork from Steve's brother. "Excuse me. Is there any place here on your resort where I can just go sit by myself, like under a tree or something, not on the beach, but in the shade?"

Barnabas's warm smile again made Tasha see visions of Steve. "Actually, yes. We're in the finishing stages of making a large koi pond in one of our areas away from the main activities. It's not quite done, so we haven't had our maps reprinted yet, but if you'll come to the registration center after you're settled in, I'll gladly give you directions. If you don't mind a few workers or the gardener coming by, you're welcome to use the facilities."

Tasha couldn't help but smile back. "That sounds perfect. I'll see you later."

For the first time since boarding the plane, Tasha started to feel at peace. She knew she would spend some time on the beach; after all, this was Hawaii. But, she didn't want to spend an entire month on the beach lost in a sea of sunburned tourists. Spending some quiet time in the shade with a good book beside a pond full of fish sounded just about perfect.

Rather than a high-rise hotel, accommodations here consisted of individual hutlike cabins called hales, most of them single occupancy, although a few of the larger buildings were duplex types. The steward loaded her two suitcases into a brightly painted golf cart and drove her to her hale, which would be her home-away-from-home for the next month. Tasha listened politely while he gave her an overview of the resort and its features, then carried her suitcases inside and gave her a quick tour of the one-bedroom accommodation. As soon as he left, Tasha hurried to the reservation center so she could talk to Barnabas.

When she arrived, an elderly couple dressed in loud-patterned matching shirts was monopolizing his attention. While she waited for her turn, Tasha checked out the building. The main area consisted of one large room decorated in a casual style. Many open windows allowed the ocean breeze to blow through the room, giving it a true tropical feel. Bulletin boards around the room featured brochures of activities and pictures of different areas of the resort.

Instead of focusing on the advertising, Tasha's attention wandered to the doorway leading down a hallway, where a posted sign said STAFF ONLY.

She smiled. She could picture Steve happily working at his computer, typing furiously, a calculator at his side, and his paperwork meticulously organized, sorted into color-coded folders, arranged neatly by date and priority.

"I'll be right with you, Miss."

Tasha turned back to Barnabas, who was pointing something out on one of the boards to the same elderly couple.

"No rush. Can you tell me if Steve is here? We're old friends."

Barnabas's smile widened as he pointed down the Staff Only hallway. "He's in his office. Go right in. I'm sure he'll be happy to see you. He's been in there a long time and could probably use a break."

Tasha's insides quivered as she took her first step down the hallway. She hadn't told Steve she was coming. Her trip to Hawaii was a vacation for her, but for Steve, the height of tourist season was his busiest time of year. While sitting on the plane, she'd rolled over and over in her mind what she was going to say to him and decided to simply say a quick hello and go back to her little hut. She would let Steve decide how much or how little time they'd spend together, because she wouldn't be a burden or an inconvenience to him when he was working.

The door to the first office she passed was closed and had Barnabas's name on it. Tasha slowed her pace and checked the door across the hall, which had Connor's name on it, and was also closed. As she continued on, the next door had Steve's name on it, and it was wide open.

Tasha didn't hear any sound emanating from the room, so instead of walking straight in, she stopped and peeked her head in first. The small room barely housed two desks. The larger desk faced the wall at an open window overlooking the courtyard, and a smaller desk was pushed up beside it with the front of the small desk facing the side of the larger desk.

The smaller desk was vacant, but a man sat working at the larger desk. With his back to her, it gave Tasha the opportunity to see Steve before he could see her. She opened her mouth to speak, but her words caught in her throat at the sight before her.

Unlike Steve's pristine work and study habits that she'd witnessed in college, both desks were piled with stacks and stacks of papers so high and so jumbled she couldn't see the surface of either desk. The larger desk was worse, with the only low spot of the mountain of papers being around the mouse pad, which was crooked, and if she wasn't mistaken, marred by a coffee stain. Scribbled sticky notes surrounded the computer monitor. A stack of papers had obviously overflowed the desk and lay littered about the floor.

Tasha wondered if maybe she had the wrong office. She glanced quickly back to the sign on the door, which definitely stated "Steve Harrigan." Again, she studied the man behind the desk. Even though she couldn't see his face, Tasha recognized Steve's sun-streaked brown hair.

A breeze wafting through the window swiped a paper from the top of one of many piles to the floor. Tasha watched as Steve slouched so far forward that his forehead pressed into the stack of papers closest to the edge of the desk. With one arm extended, he slowly reached down and groped in the air toward the paper now lying on the floor. At the same time, his other hand reached for and connected with the handle of a large coffee mug with his name on it, which was sitting on the corner of the desk, halfway onto the mouse pad, which explained the coffee stain.

From the back, she could see Steve's chest expand, and then his whole body sagged as he let out a huge sigh. He didn't move, but remained rooted with his forehead on the desk. Instead of picking up the fallen paperwork, his arm went limp, dangling aimlessly with his fingertips dragging on the floor. His other hand remained fixed on the handle of his mug.

She didn't know what had happened to the Steve she knew, but one thing she did know—his brother was right. This Steve certainly could use a break.

Tasha cleared her throat. "Steve?"

He sat up and turned around so fast more papers fluttered to the floor, accompanied by the *thunk* of the mouse as it fell too, hitting the desk drawer on its way down.

Continuing in one motion, Steve bolted out of the chair, maintaining a firm grip on the handle of the mug. Coffee sloshed over the rim and onto the floor as Steve straightened. His eyes widened, and he reached up with his free hand to straighten his glasses. "Tasha? Is that you? Am I dreaming? What are you doing here?"

Tasha struggled to speak normally, but her words came out in a tight squeak. "I'm on vacation. I got in on short notice with a cancellation."

"Why didn't you tell me you were coming? Or did you e-mail and I haven't answered? I'm a little behind on things, as you can tell."

"I didn't want to disrupt your schedule, so I thought I'd surprise you. From the look of things, I succeeded."

He turned around, haphazardly pushed aside some of the papers to make room for his coffee mug, then turned back to her. He stood tall, spread his arms wide, and smiled. "Never mind the mess. Come here. This is no way for old friends to greet each other. Aloha!"

"I. . ." Tasha let her voice trail off as she stared at him. She hadn't had any trouble with the quick shoulder hugs and air kisses bestowed on tourists as they deplaned and then arrived at their reserved destinations. This was Hawaii, where greetings were given to all with utmost enthusiasm, even to strangers. But Steve was no stranger, and this was no token greeting—at least it wasn't to her.

"Come on, Tasha. What are you waiting for?" With his arms still wide open, Steve flexed his fingers in a "come hither" motion.

She couldn't not go to him. Trying to appear nonchalant, Tasha shrugged her shoulders, pasted a smile on her face, and walked into his arms. Instead of giving him a big hug, she raised her palms and rested them lightly on his chest, meaning to keep the contact brief and casual.

Steve didn't respond in the same manner. He wrapped his arms around her and pulled her in close. He said nothing as he held her.

Tasha didn't know what to do. She'd only been in Steve's arms once before, and that day was nothing like this.

On the day of their graduation, everyone had just received their diplomas and the moment had come for them to flip the tassels on their caps to the other side. With a cheer, the entire graduating class threw their grad caps in the air, then laughed, cried, and hugged each other. However, neither she nor Steve had done much hugging, except with each other. Steve had wrapped his arms around her and not let go until all the hooting and hollering was over. The entire time, while surrounded by family, friends, and fellow classmates, with all the noise around them, only three words passed between them. "*We did it*," he'd whispered in her ear, and then the moment was over.

Unlike that day three years ago, today Steve was completely silent.

Today he held her firmly pressed against him. As good as it felt to be held by him, after his words of greeting had been said, there was no joy in his embrace. The way he held her so close felt almost sad, somewhat desperate, and mostly. . .defeated.

Because her palms were still resting on his chest, as well as her cheek, Tasha felt the movement as Steve inhaled deeply, then exhaled in a long sigh. It was almost like feeling him deflate and sag.

She tilted her head back, but from up against him, all she could see was the bottom of his chin.

"What's wrong?"

He sighed again. "I'm sorry. I don't mean to be such a downer, but I've got big problems." His chest rose and fell as he took in another deep breath. "I'm nowhere near ready to turn over our books to the auditor, and the deadline to file our taxes is just about a month away."

Tasha pushed gently on his chest. At the pressure, he quickly released her and stood back, allowing her to finally see him properly and think without the distraction of his touch. When she looked into his eyes, Steve turned away. He rammed one hand in his pocket, adjusted his glasses with the other, and faced the mountain of papers on the desks.

"Since the very early days of the resort, an outside auditing firm has come in to examine and certify our books before we file our taxes each year. After I got my degree and took over doing the books from the service Pop used before, we decided it would be a good idea to keep up the external audit, you know, as a safeguard, since this is a family-owned business and all."

"That's a good idea," Tasha mumbled, also turning to study the mounds of paperwork, wondering where he was going with his story.

"Anyway, today I received a letter telling me that the stateside auditor has already purchased his airline ticket. He's arriving in thirty days. Actually, I think I got his letter and flight confirmation a few days ago, but this is the first time I've seen it." He shook his head slowly from side to side. "Even if I wanted to, I can't just phone him up and ask him to reschedule, because the tax-filing deadline comes just three days after he leaves."

She cleared her throat and ran her fingers through her hair. "Audits aren't so bad if all your transactions are in order and balanced."

Steve shuffled sideways, extending one arm in the direction of the two desks buried so deep with papers that she couldn't tell where one desk stopped and the other began. With his arm stretched out, he turned his head to face her as he spoke. "I don't think I need to elaborate. That disaster speaks for itself. Without my assistant, Brittany, I'll never be ready for either the auditor or the tax-filing deadline. I have less than a month to get that in order and balance last year's fiscal year-end reports. I'm so far behind, I don't know where to start."

"What about your brothers? Can't they help you?"

"Not a chance. Cupid's arrow has turned all their brains to mush. I'm on my own. Worse than on my own. Every time I have to ask one of them for something to fix up one more disaster, whatever they've done makes two more appear. Instead of turning in receipts, they're starting to burn them."

Tasha almost wanted to laugh, except that she had a feeling he wasn't joking. Again, she studied the desks and the volume of paperwork.

"Before I got my corporate job, I used to freelance my services. I've had people bring me all their company records for an entire year in a shoebox. It really can be sorted out. It just takes time."

"What you see here is only the tip of the iceberg. This is somewhat bigger than a shoebox. The auditor won't be able to make sense of this. I can't make sense of this mess, and it's my mess. I wonder if I turned myself in to the tax authorities without the audit or anything in order, if the IRS would just throw me in jail and spare me the agony of working through all this?"

"No one is going to throw you in jail." However, she didn't want to mention the fine for late filing, which would likely be considerable for a place with cash flow for a large Hawaiian resort such as Harrigan's Cove.

She looked at the mess, specifically at the smaller, obviously vacant desk. "You said in your E-mails that Brittany was on a leave of absence. When is she coming back?"

"She's extended her leave so many times, I can't say for certain. Definitely not within the next thirty days."

"Isn't there anyone else you can call?"

"No one knows our system like Brittany. Besides, I'd never get anyone qualified to handle a disaster like this on short notice. Not only that, I don't want someone I hire on a temporary basis to see all our confidential files and then perhaps be next hired full time by our competition."

Tasha nodded. "I never thought of that."

She continued to study the mounds of paper overflowing

both desks. If what she saw was just the "tip," as Steve said, then it would take months for a certified accountant to get through everything accurately.

Or. . .half that time if *two* certified accountants tackled it.

"Exactly what day is the auditor coming?"

Steve walked to his desk and held up the page on the calendar. From where she stood, Tasha noticed a day with a picture of a skull and crossbones drawn on it before Steve covered up his artwork with his finger.

"Right here. The auditor is coming at one. And the deadline to file with the IRS is three days after that."

Tasha sucked in a deep breath. It was the day she was returning home, except her flight left at nine in the morning.

Even though she knew she would enjoy sitting at the side of the koi pond and reading, it wasn't something she could do every day for four weeks. Besides, she'd only brought a handful of books, not the whole library. Before she left home, she worried that being in a strange place with nothing constructive to do would drive her crazy. While Steve's situation was less than ideal, it was the perfect solution.

She shuffled her feet, stiffened her back, and crossed her arms. "That's the day I'm leaving. That's lots of time. I can help you."

"What? That's ridiculous. I can't ask that of you. This is your vacation. You're here to relax before you have to get back to the old grind."

Tasha shook her head. "Remember how I've been looking after my aunt Sally while she was sick? I didn't tell you, but the last time I asked to extend my leave of absence to care for her, they said no and that if I didn't come back by a certain date, I was fired. We'll just say I didn't give them the chance to fire me. I quit."

Steve dropped the calendar page and was standing in front of her before she barely had time to blink.

"You didn't tell me that. I thought you went back to work a couple of weeks ago."

"Nope. In fact, that's why I'm here. Aunt Sally was so grateful that I took all that time off to stay with her and then she felt so bad that I quit my job that she gave me this vacation package as a gift. I couldn't hurt her feelings. I had to come here."

Steve crossed his arms, knotted his brows, and stared down at her. "What do you mean *had* to come here? Harrigan's Cove is a great place. People pay big bucks to come here, and many of them have their vacations booked a year in advance, you know."

Tasha shook her head. "That's not what I meant, and you know it. I think you know my point."

"Not really."

"I didn't want a vacation. I wanted to find another job and get back to work. But Aunt Sally thought this was such a good idea. I didn't have the heart to turn her down. I know you're going to take this the wrong way, but the bottom line is that I'm stuck here for four weeks, whether I like it or not. So, I might as well do something constructive and help you get ready for that audit."

Steve blinked a few times, rested his fists on his hips, and

n turned sideways to study the disaster on his desk. Tasha
ted a full two minutes before he finally spoke.

"Brittany just had a year of business college. You're not only
PA, you've got your MBA, just like me. Since I don't pay
self a regular nine-to-five salary, I'll have to find out what
're worth."

"What I'm worth?" Tasha gritted her teeth and shuffled
r to position herself directly in front of Steve. To make sure
had his full attention, she jabbed him in the chest with her
ex finger. "If you think you're going to pay me, you've got
ther think coming. If I don't do this on a volunteer basis, I
't do it at all."

Steve waved one hand in the air. "But you're on vacation!"

"This is not a vacation, and I refuse to repeat myself. I've
ady been through that."

"Then only under one condition. I insist you also spend
he time vacationing, even if I have to watch you do it. You
't come to Hawaii and not spend time on the beach or go
rkeling or stuff like that."

"As long as you don't make me go to any of the commer-
tourist traps, you've got yourself a deal."

Steve extended his hand forward for a handshake to cement
ur agreement.

Tasha stared at his hand, then placed her hand in his. Slowly,
fingers closed over hers, and his other hand covered their
ed hands. Instead of a real handshake, he ran his thumb over
wrist.

If it had been anyone other than Steve, she would have

considered the gesture a little suggestive. However, Steve
simply an old college friend and nothing more, even tho
she'd always liked him in a special way.

Because of the distance between them, knowing they co
never have more, she had, instead, used Steve as the stand
when she met and dated men in various degrees of casua
serious relationships. Every time she had found them lack
She consoled herself by telling herself that, one day, (
would put an accessible good Christian man like Steve in
path and that it would happen so fast she wouldn't know w
hit her.

Until that happened, she would be patient and wait
God's timing. But for now, she was stuck on this stu
Hawaiian vacation, and she would make the best of her t
with Steve.

When Steve finally spoke, his voice came out in a
rumble. "Then we have a deal. I guess I'll see you back her
the morning. In the meantime, since it's almost suppertime
me close up here and we can go out to dinner and catch up
old times."

Tasha gulped and nodded, hoping she hadn't just d
something she would regret.

Chapter 3

Steve turned on both computers. "I'll give you Brittany's log-in code and password, and then we can get started. The computers are linked together so we can both input at the me time, as well as see what the other is doing. The only trans-tions up to date are the deposits and payments for our guests' cations and the employees' salaries. All else is fair game."

While he waited for the computers to boot up, Steve arched the desk for his highlighting pen, which he knew he d yesterday. He saw the end of it poking out from between o piles, and as he reached for it, he glanced up at Tasha.

Tasha didn't look back at him. Instead, she tucked a lock of ir behind her ear and thumbed through the pile of paper arest to her right hand.

Steve froze midreach. He hadn't seen her for years, yet he membered the gesture from their college days. He wondered w much else hadn't changed. Corresponding off and on via mail in no way compared to the direct contact of speaking e-to-face.

Physically, Tasha hadn't changed much over the past fo
years. She still had the same delicate features, and she was st
as short as ever. She'd put on a couple of pounds, but then, s
had he, probably from sitting behind a desk all day. Even wi
the small bit of added weight, Tasha still looked as goo
maybe even better than she had then.

The only change he could see was her hair, which was no
past her shoulders, compared to the practical and carefr
short style she'd worn four years ago.

Another thing that hadn't changed was that, despite her la
of stature, she still made her presence known. She was more cu
than pretty, but last night in the restaurant, he'd noticed oth
men taking second glances at Tasha. He didn't know if th
were just tourists checking out other tourists or men enjoyir
the indoor scenery. Either way, it had felt strange when, inste
of looking away or acting coy, she'd stared right back, the
waved, forcing the lookers to become embarrassed and retu
their attention to the ladies they were with.

"Hmm. . . These really are all mixed up," she muttered as s
ran one finger along a number of the papers, stopping on t
dates, then moving the oldest ones to the top of the pile. "You'
made payments to suppliers without first entering these pu
chase orders."

"I know. There aren't enough hours in the day, especia
when I'm doing this alone. It's driving me crazy."

She continued to sort through the never-ending stacks
paper while he entered the log-ins and passwords, pausing or
to listen and memorize them, then continuing her quest looki

through the piles of various unrecorded transactions.

The disorganization disturbed him, and the current mess embarrassed Steve beyond measure, both personally and professionally.

Back in college, he had always had all his files in good order, and he didn't want Tasha to see him like this. Tasha had been the most organized person in their graduating class, which said a lot considering the status and standing of their peers.

She held up one of the papers, read it twice, and shook her head. "You weren't exaggerating when you said this would take months. You must really be missing Brittany."

He cleared his throat, but otherwise didn't move. "Yes. I'll never take her for granted again."

"The sooner we get started, the sooner we'll finish. Let's get to it."

No more words were spoken as they made it their first priority to sort, categorize, and prioritize every piece of paper to deal with everything in the most efficient manner.

Their first break came when Steve's stomach reminded them that it was past lunchtime. If the noise wasn't embarrassing enough, Tasha's giggle made his cheeks burn.

Steve cleared his throat, stood, and stiffened his posture in a vain attempt to regain his dignity. "I don't know if we made any progress, but it's time for a break."

Tasha nodded in response. "Yes, I agree. I'm hungry too. My stomach just isn't as obvious about it."

At her little grin, his stomach gave a strange lurch, making him think he was hungrier than he realized.

He covered his stomach with his palm. "We can go grab something from the buffet, which you'll enjoy. We put all the munchies on ice to help the guests cool down. Most people aren't used to the heat when they first arrive, and it takes a few days to adjust. We serve local fruits and vegetables, as well as a nice variety of local seafood."

Tasha also rose. "That sounds great. Let's go."

Most days Steve merely left both windows open, as well as the door to his office, to let the breeze cool the room. However, with the paper even more spread out than usual, today he had closed everything up and turned on the air-conditioning to prevent papers being blown, as sometimes happened. He didn't like to use the air-conditioning, not only because of the expense to keep the unit running in the heat, but because of the shock when walking out of the coolness and into the midday Hawaii heat.

As soon as he opened the door, Tasha stepped outside his office and into the hallway, where it had become stuffy with the three doors closed. Her step hesitated slightly. She inhaled sharply and gave a short cough. Then she quickened her pace until she reached the main, open area of the reservation center, where all the windows and doorways were wide open. The air was cooler with the midday breeze, which had already picked up.

"The buffet lunch is over there, in the courtyard. Most days I go to the kitchen and make myself a plate to carry back to my office, but today we're going to mingle with the tourists. Remember, you are a tourist. And most of all, you're my guest. Since you'll be spending so much time in the office, I think we should take all our lunches outside so you can at least see a little of the beauty Hawaii and Harrigan's Cove have to offer."

"I won't argue with having lunch outside."

The second Tasha stepped outside the shelter of the building and into the afternoon sun, her eyes widened, her step faltered, and she swayed. In a split second, he wrapped his hand around her arm and cupped her elbow with his other hand, forcing her to stand still while she became accustomed to the sudden change in temperature.

"You have to walk into the heat slowly. Sometimes it takes a little getting used to."

Tasha lowered her head, and with her free hand, she rubbed her eyes.

"Less than twenty-four hours ago I was in my driveway shoveling snow with my neighbor so we could get the car out and drive to the airport. The snowstorm made the roads so bad that I almost missed my flight."

"I've seen pictures of snow. It looks so pretty and so peaceful."

"It's only peaceful when you don't have to go anywhere in it. I'm okay now. Let's go get that lunch."

As they walked, Steve made a mental note to turn the air-conditioning onto a warmer setting so the difference when going outside wouldn't be so much of a shock for Tasha. Or, maybe he could do what he'd done before—leave the windows open and bring in some rocks from outside to weigh down the stacks against the ocean breeze and not turn on the air-conditioning at all.

Her eyes widened as they neared the buffet tables, this time not from heat shock but from what she saw. "This is unbelievable! Is it like this every day?"

He nodded. "Yes. And for supper we do barbecues in the pit. Every Friday night we have a luau, complete with a roasted pig."

He didn't think it was possible, but her eyes widened even more. "You eat like this all the time?"

Steve smiled ear to ear. "Every day. Jealous?"

"Never. Where are the plates?"

He couldn't hold back his grin as Tasha eagerly filled her plate with what the rest of the world termed exotic fare. He had to admit that he might have been a little spoiled with regards to his dietary habits, but he and his brothers had worked very hard over the years to make the resort the way it was today. He'd also be working just as hard for the resort in the years to come until the day he retired.

Last night he'd taken her off the resort to a restaurant, but for today, even though Tasha told him she didn't want to get lost in a crowd, he made sure they stayed with everyone else. After all, she was a guest and had paid to receive everything their resort had to offer. In lieu of a salary, he'd tried to offer her a partial refund since she would be spending most of her time in the office working, but all he'd accomplished was to make her angry.

While they ate, Steve gave her a rundown of the usual activities and options offered. He made a mental note of everything he said that seemed to pique her interest, intending to take a few days to show her the sights of Hawaii after they managed to catch up a bit.

"Your brother told me about a koi pond that wasn't finished yet. Can we have our lunch there tomorrow?"

"Yes. I love it there. The landscaping isn't quite finished, but we've already got the fish in the pond. They're not very big, but I picked a variety with large fins. They're really nice to watch."

Another couple who recognized him as a staff member stopped to ask Steve questions, preventing him from finding out more of what Tasha might be interested in. Rather than linger, as soon as they finished eating, Steve excused himself and returned with Tasha to his office.

Once back at the office, they restricted all conversation to business only in order to give them a real possibility of meeting their deadline. Like the morning, the afternoon passed so quickly, they were both surprised when suppertime came.

As promised, Steve took Tasha to the courtyard for the supper, where the featured entree was barbecued chicken with rice and local vegetables.

Unlike lunchtime, this time they didn't remain alone. Instead, his three brothers and their ladies all joined them. As well, Barnabas and Liliana had brought Abby. Steve introduced them all, but before he had a chance to open the conversation, Alex spoke up.

"Steve told us an old friend had arrived and was going to help him get ready for the audit. Old friends or not, I can't believe you'd rather spend your time cooped up in that office with him instead of taking advantage of the resort's activities. On Wednesday night we're going to show everyone the constellations and have a contest for who can remember the most. And if you need a break from Steve during the daytime, tomorrow we're going to make sand candles for our arts-and-crafts activity. That was

Callie's idea." He paused long enough to exchange a doting smile with Callie, then turned back to Tasha. "Would you like to join us?"

"I don't know. We're awful busy."

Alex leaned to one side and pulled a crumpled brochure out of his back pocket. "Steve says you're going to be with us for four weeks. That's a long time. Surely you can get away at least a few times. Maybe you can make a miracle happen and convince Steve to participate. I just happen to have this week's list handy. We have package tours and outings to almost everything interesting on the island. We can also arrange transportation if you want to go to any of the other islands for the day."

Steve leaned back in his chair, crossed his arms, and cleared his throat. "That's enough already, Alex. You can turn off your salesman mode. I've already tried to convince Tasha to take advantage of all we have to offer our guests. Maybe she will when we get our heads above water. Until then, don't expect to see much of her."

He wanted to say more to Alex about how his responsibilities around the resort had fallen behind, but he couldn't. Since Alex and Callie had become engaged, he had noticed a difference in his youngest brother, some things better and some things worse.

Tasha shook her head and waved one hand in the air while she swallowed her mouthful. "Please, Alex. I know Harrigan's Cove has all sorts of wonderful things for your guests. Maybe I'll do some when we're caught up, but for the next while, Steve and I simply have too much work to do."

"Well, you know where to find me when the time is right. My door is always open."

She smiled so sweetly at Alex, then at Barnabas, that something funny happened in Steve's stomach again; only this time he knew he wasn't hungry, because he was already halfway finished with his supper.

"I've heard that same line already from Barnabas. I must say you're very friendly here. I can see why your resort is so successful."

Alex smiled back, pausing to let Liliana and Beth regale Tasha with more tales of the resort—as if she needed convincing.

Steve opened his mouth to add to something Beth was saying, but before he could get a word out, something jabbed him in the ribs. He turned to see Connor, who was sitting beside him, grinning from ear to ear.

"Hey, Bro. You said 'old friend.' I didn't know you had old friends like that. Got any more secrets you've been holding out on us?"

"I don't know what you mean. Tasha and I are old friends from college."

"Yeah, right."

Alex turned to Connor. "Forget it, Connor. Of course she's just an old friend. This is Steve we're dealing with."

"Oh, right. I nearly forgot."

Steve narrowed his eyes. "Pardon me?"

Barnabas tapped his fingers on the table, not loud enough to create a disturbance, but loud enough to get Connor and Alex's attention. "Knock it off, you guys. The important thing is that we be ready for the audit. I don't know how we could have gotten so far behind that it's become a crisis situation."

Steve rested his palms on the table and leaned forward. "I can tell you, easily."

A gentle touch on Steve's other side stopped his words.

"The dessert cart is coming, Steve," Tasha said quietly. "Can you recommend something for me?"

Steve sighed, then smiled back at Tasha. He didn't know if she was aware of what was happening on his side of the table, but he was grateful beyond words that she'd stopped him from saying more. Finally, things were looking up, and now was not the time to berate his brothers for their part in the trouble they were in. He could do so later, when all was balanced and Tasha had gone home.

By the time they finished dessert and conversation had dwindled, the sun had set and many of the guests had left the patio.

Steve turned to Tasha as Barnabas and Liliana rose to take Abby home. "I don't think you've seen much of the cove yet. I know it's dark, but it's a full moon tonight. You've never seen anything quite so beautiful as the full moon over the bay. Do you have a camera that can take night pictures? If you don't, I do. I can send you copies when you get home, or I can scan them and e-mail them to you."

Tasha stood, so Steve did too.

"Yes, I do have a good camera. That sounds like a good idea." She turned to Connor and Beth and Alex and Callie. "If you'll excuse us, I think I have a little sightseeing to do."

Chapter 4

Tasha slung her camera's strap over her shoulder and turned to Steve, who had just appeared in the doorway of her hut. "I'm almost ready. I just have to find another roll of film. I took so many pictures out the plane window yesterday, I only have a couple left in my camera."

"You can't go like that. This is Hawaii. We're going for a walk on the beach at night. You still have your sandals on."

Tasha lowered her gaze to Steve's feet. He had changed from shorts into cotton pants, but he had them rolled sloppily to halfway up to his knees. He rocked back on his heels and wiggled his bare toes for effect, then patted his camera bag, which was slung over his shoulder, as was hers. She noticed he also had a tripod case along with his camera. "See? I'm ready for a walk on a moonlit beach. I always have a couple of extra rolls of film in my bag, so don't worry about digging through your suitcases. Let's go."

Tasha shrugged her shoulders and kicked off her sandals. "When in Rome, I guess. . ." She wiggled the doorknob to make sure it was locked, and a few steps later they were on the beach.

Steve walked straight into the water until he was ankle deep. "Come on. You've got to tell your friends back home that you went wading in the ocean after sunset."

She waded in to find the water still quite warm, despite the darkness. As soon as she reached Steve, they started walking slowly down the shoreline. Between the glowing light of the full moon, the gentle lapping of the waves on the sandy shore, and the peace and tranquility of the beauty around her, Tasha thought the night would have been quite romantic, if she'd been with anyone else.

"It's so beautiful and peaceful here. Are all the huts in your resort on the beach?"

"Most of them, yes. Of course the most expensive run right along the water; and as you can see, they're staggered three deep so everyone gets an ocean view. We also have a small lake on our property, and we have hales circling that. Since you're going to be working with some of the guests' records, you'll soon figure out the pricing structure."

Since her vacation was a gift, she really didn't want to know the price, although she supposed she would find out anyway because of their arrangement. The only thing Aunt Sally would tell her was that she'd gotten a considerable discount on a last-minute cancellation.

Instead of thinking anymore about money and risk spoiling her vacation, Tasha turned her attention to the beach. A few couples sat in deck chairs in front of their huts, but only two couples had ventured out onto the beach. Even though it was dark, the light of the moon lit the sky enough for a swim, yet no one was in the water except them, and they were only in up to their ankles.

"Where is everyone? I thought you were booked to capacity, but there's hardly anyone out here. It's not even very late. We just finished supper not long ago. I can't believe it's dark out already."

"Many of our visitors say the same thing. Here in Hawaii the days and nights are pretty much around twelve hours each, all year long. Sunrise and sunset aren't much different in summer than winter, with only about an hour variance either way. Not that we really have winter here, by your terms."

"Thanks for reminding me of what's back home waiting for me. You haven't explained why we're practically the only ones out here."

"This resort is fairly upscale. We don't attract the party crowd. Most of our guests tend to go to bed early and then get up early with the sunrise, which right now is around seven."

Tasha shook her head. "I don't get up at seven, even when I'm going to work."

"I get up at six, five-thirty in the summer, so I'm ready to begin working at sunrise. The restaurant opens for breakfast at seven-fifteen. Many people are up and circulating well before then."

Tasha pretended to shudder. "Ugh. That's too early for me."

"We're at the spot I wanted. Let's stop here and take some pictures. See how the moon reflects across the water, next to the outcropping? Won't that make a great picture?"

The beauty of the perfectly round moon reflecting over the water took Tasha's breath away.

Thoughts of postcards and the brochure with the digitally enhanced photos danced through her mind. Even though she knew her photo wouldn't do the beauty before them any justice, Tasha had to try her luck.

They waded out of the water to stand on the beach, where she removed her camera from its case, planted her feet firmly apart, and took one quick picture. She tilted the camera sideways and was about to press the button again when Steve spoke.

"What are you doing?"

She lowered the camera. "I'm taking pictures of the moon over the water. It's every bit as beautiful as you said."

"You'll never get a clear shot that way. That's why I brought my tripod and an extender so you don't have to touch the camera. A lot also depends on your aperture setting, as well, which I haven't seen you change."

"Oh. I don't know anything about that camera stuff. I just aim and hit the button."

Steve smiled. Almost like from the pages of a romantic storybook, his eyes caught the light of the moon and actually seemed to sparkle. Tasha had to remind herself that this was Steve.

"Let me see your camera. I'm pretty good with cameras. Maybe I can figure out some of your settings for you."

He tilted and tipped it, squinted, brought it closer to his face, then adjusted his glasses on his nose while he did his best to use the light of the moon to make out all those numbers and symbols that Tasha never did take the time to read the owner's manual about in order to interpret.

"I've opened your aperture, but you can't add an extender. We can solve that problem by putting it on the tripod and using the timer. This will still take a decent photo. You've got a fairly decent little camera."

She stood and watched as Steve set up her camera. When he was done, he shuffled to the side, bowed, and extended one arm, inviting her to be the one to actually push the button, which, judging from the whole process, was the least important step.

After the delay, one click signified the shutter opening, then another one a few seconds later told them her picture had been taken. Tasha unscrewed her camera from Steve's tripod and tucked it back into the case. "Are you going to take a picture now?"

Steve nodded as he removed a very expensive-looking, professional camera from his case. Everything he'd ever said about taking pictures, both today and as short mentions in E-mails, came to mind.

"Those pictures on your brochure. By any chance, did you take them?"

"Yup," he mumbled as he very carefully turned the knob to fasten his camera to the tripod. "Photography is a hobby of mine. This is the best moon shot I've seen in years. This may make it into next year's brochure."

"So that means my picture should look exactly the same as the one in the brochure."

"Don't count on it. A lot more work goes into those photos than mere photography. The bare photo will look much the same, but the graphics people touch it up before it goes to the printer."

"If this is going to be a preview of your next brochure, I'd like to see what it looks like before I go home. Where can I get my pictures developed?"

"We make it so our guests don't have to leave the resort unless they want to. We have a one-hour photo center in the gift shop, which I sometimes run. It's kind of fun and a nice change from being stuck behind my desk six days a week."

"You guys think of everything, don't you?"

"We try. All four of us have worked for the resort all our lives, but when Pop retired a few years ago, he left it all in our hands. We've all made a few changes and additions. I think the resort is better than it's ever been. Pop was great, but he was a little old-fashioned."

Tasha remained silent while Steve took his pictures. As diligently as he set it up, he carefully packed everything away. She thought the whole process rather long and involved for one simple scene. However, if this picture was going to make it into their international advertising, she supposed she couldn't compare it to her finished photos that she looked at once, then tucked in a box, never to be seen again.

"Speaking of the resort and its operations, shouldn't we be back in your office? You weren't exaggerating when you said it would take months."

"I know. But this is your first day. I didn't want to overwhelm you. You're also on vacation."

"We already went over that vacation stuff. I had enough time off looking after my aunt Sally. What I really want is to get back to work."

"We'll do that tomorrow. Remember, you promised that you'd do vacation things too. Otherwise, the deal's off."

"You're in no position for this deal to be off."

Steve grumbled something under his breath, but Tasha ignored him as they slung their cameras and accessories over their shoulders and kept walking.

When they reached the end of the Harrigan property, Steve stopped.

"This is it. The reservation building is in the center of the property. Tomorrow night we can walk in the other direction. I'll have to take you to the lake during the daytime, as it doesn't have a sandy beach and the trees around it shield the moonlight. It's not the kind of thing you'd walk around at night."

"What I'd really like to see is your new koi pond. I've already seen some of the invoices. Of course there are no purchase orders to go with them. Yet."

"Yes. I promised we'd have our lunch there tomorrow."

Tasha smiled. She didn't know why she hadn't been looking forward to an exotic Hawaiian vacation. Now that she had something constructive to do all day and she was going to spend her evenings, if there were any free evenings, with Steve, she found herself looking forward to what was left of the remaining four weeks.

They walked even more slowly on their return trip than they had on the way to the edge of the property. Just like their days together back in college, they didn't say much, but simply felt at ease in each other's company.

Too soon, Steve had her back to her hut. While she unlocked the door, she heard him try to stifle a yawn behind her.

"I guess it's your bedtime soon, since you get up so early. I hope you don't expect me to get up at six too."

"You said you were here to work."

"You're using my own words the way they suit you best. Yes, I said I wanted to work. No, I didn't say I was going to get up at the crack of dawn."

"But I always get up before dawn. Sorry," he said, but his sly little grin told her that he really wasn't.

"I didn't bring an alarm clock, you know. I really am supposed to be on vacation."

Steve unfastened his wristwatch and dangled it in front of her. "I have my watch set for six, even though I'm usually awake by then and simply cancel the alarm. You, on the other hand, might need it. And if you're thinking of not taking it, I could always knock on the door at 6:01 and catch you in your pajamas."

Tasha grabbed the watch.

"Good night, Tasha. See you in the morning."

He'd turned away and started walking before Tasha could think. For some reason, she'd almost expected him to lean forward and give her a peck on the cheek.

Tasha rubbed her eyes and watched Steve disappear into the night. She was obviously more tired than she thought.

Chapter 5

"I thought you said you weren't going to knock on my door."

Steve's little grin almost made Tasha want to swat him with the towel she had in her hand, except she didn't have the energy.

"I never said I wasn't going to knock on your door. In fact, I remember offering to knock at 6:01. I gave you a full twenty-nine minutes extra. That's plenty of time."

Tasha turned around, leaving Steve standing in the doorway. "Very funny. Just let me get my purse, and I'll be right out."

The sun had not yet risen, but the sky was aglow with the predawn. Even though it was light enough to see where they were going, Steve carried a flashlight. The entire trip from her hut to his office, Tasha found his upbeat disposition incredibly annoying. If there was anything to learn from an exotic vacation, it was the value of sleeping in.

Immediately upon arriving at Steve's office, he tucked the flashlight into a drawer and booted up his computer.

"Don't we get to eat first?" Tasha grumbled.

"The dining room staff doesn't start to put the food out until seven, but I guess we could go raid the kitchen if you can't wait."

She stood without hesitation. Once at the kitchen, she waited only long enough to be polite while he introduced her around as his friend and temporary assistant before she filled a plate with two pieces of toast and a selection of fruit. Rather than carry two mugs of coffee, Steve swiped a full carafe of coffee and a container of cream, and they quickly returned to Steve's office. They paused for a short prayer and began to eat without the need to make pleasant conversation.

After half a piece of toast, some nibbles of the assorted sweet fruit, and a few cautious sips of the hot coffee, Tasha started to feel more human. "This is good," she muttered around the food in her mouth. "I could eat like this every day. I don't even mind eating in here. At least it's quiet."

Steve picked up his plate from his lap and started to push a stack of paper, hesitated, then laid his plate on top of the pile while he called up his accounting program. "I hope tomorrow it won't be so much of a struggle to make room for the plates."

Tasha shook her head. "Shouldn't be. See how much progress we made yesterday?"

"Quite frankly, no, I don't."

"Well, we did. And we're going to make just as much progress today and every day following. You'll see."

"I still have my doubts, but I know I have to do whatever it takes to be ready. I think the first thing we should do today is just enter the job projects, and then we can enter the purchase orders."

"Good idea."

By mutual agreement, they only stopped briefly for lunch and supper. Rather than going to the buffet, they raided the kitchen and again brought their meals into Steve's office to eat while they painstakingly entered all the projects and events of the past six months. It was well past sunset and they were both yawning by the time they finished.

Steve lifted his glasses and rubbed his eyes. "I know we're still missing a number of things, but I think it's time to quit for the night. We've been at it for fourteen hours. I hope you don't mind if I don't take you for a walk to the other end of the beach like I promised. I'm afraid I'm too tired to be good company. I'll make it up to you tomorrow."

"No, I don't mind. I'm quite tired myself. I think I'd just like to go back to my hut and crawl into bed."

"Hale. It's called a hale."

"It's a glorified hut."

Steve smiled. Even though his eyes seemed to droop at the corners, it was still a lovely smile. "Whatever. I'm not going to argue with you."

This time, since they were under the shelter of the lush vegetation instead of on the open beach, they needed the flash-light to see where they were going. Tasha walked close beside Steve so they could both walk in the same circle of light.

Being so close to him, it suddenly struck her that she hadn't realized how tall he was before. She looked up at him as they reached the sand and the wide-open area of the beach.

There was now a lot of room and plenty of light, but she

suddenly didn't want to move away from him.

Too soon, they reached her hut. He stood close by and held the flashlight over her purse while she fished for her keys, and then he shone the light on the doorknob as she inserted the key and turned it.

For Steve, it was the most romantic thing she thought he could do.

At the thought of combining Steve and romance in one sentence, Tasha fumbled with her key chain and dropped it.

They both squatted and reached for the fallen keys at the same time. Since they were both too tired to think quickly, they both touched the keys at the same time, overlapping hands. At the touch, they both froze. Their eyes met, only inches apart.

Tasha swallowed hard. Given the length of their relationship, this was the place where he should have kissed her. If it was anyone other than Steve.

Tasha yanked the keys from out of Steve's fingers, bolted upright, and shook her head. "I'm really tired. I think I'm going to go straight to bed. It's been a long day."

Steve stood more slowly. "I'm sorry, Tasha. I didn't mean to overwork you. This is supposed to be your vacation. Would you like to take tomorrow off?"

She shook her head. "No. As lovely as it is here on your resort, I need to slow down gradually. I would go crazy with nothing to do. I'll see you tomorrow morning. Bright and early."

He smiled, and Tasha nearly forgot to breathe. "Watch it. I just might take you at your word on that."

"Yeah, well, whatever. Good night, Steve."

Tasha hustled inside and shut the door soundly behind her.

She knew she would go straight to bed, but suddenly, she wasn't so sure she would sleep.

Steve raised his fist to knock on the door of Tasha's hale, then froze with his fist in midair. At his feet lay a coconut, the resort's symbol for "do not disturb."

He rested his fists on his hips and stared down at the coconut, at the same time feeling himself grinning, anticipating Tasha's response to his intrusion.

He'd been looking forward to seeing Tasha again from the moment he got up. Because of that, he'd been ready in record time and had had to restrain himself to take the full twenty-nine minutes to arrive at her door.

It seemed his whole life had changed in just a few short days.

For weeks now, he'd felt himself sinking deeper and deeper into the quagmire of unbalanced transactions and unreconciled accounts to the point of wondering if he would ever be able to see the light of day. He'd never been one to lack motivation, but in the past month, for the first time ever, he'd had to force himself to go to work in the morning. But now he found he'd never looked so forward to spending the day at his computer.

The difference was Tasha. Because of his current dilemma, they could only focus on work these days; but some time before she left, Steve looked forward to doing more with her than simply swapping data files. He thought of all the places he'd been over the years and all the things he enjoyed doing, both on and off the resort. He wanted to do those things with Tasha, to share in the joy of his homeland.

Admittedly, between his busy schedule and his lack of a sense of adventure, he didn't have much of a social life. He gladly left the social interplay up to Alex and the guest interaction required in the running of the resort to Barnabas. Steve simply enjoyed standing back and doing his own thing. He was doing what he liked best, and that was spending most of his time by himself and getting lost in his work.

Over the past year, his brothers had found mates, and their work had begun to suffer increasingly as they traded one responsibility for another. Fortunately for Steve, he was too sensible to fall into that trap. But, since the work his brothers didn't do still had to be done, he was forced to take up the slack. Until he felt himself drowning in work and past the point of no return, he hadn't minded spending almost every waking minute at his computer. Spending more time on the computer gave him more opportunity to e-mail and chat with friends like Tasha.

Now Tasha was here with him, in person. Even though they were working and working hard, he couldn't remember the last time he'd felt so good about life in general.

Not caring that he was grinning like an idiot for no apparent reason, Steve raised his fist and knocked. Loudly.

A bang came from inside the hale, then a scraping sound, then the sound of muffled footsteps. The door swung open and Tasha stood in the doorway, dressed and almost ready to go, except for her bare feet and the towel on her head.

"Can't you read your own coconut?"

"I'm exempt from the coconut." He tapped his name badge with his index finger. "Says right here in the fine print. Gotta read that fine print."

She whipped the towel off her head, exposing her wet hair. "Okay, fine. But when my hair goes all frizzy from not drying it properly, you're the one who has to look at me."

Quite frankly, he didn't think there was anything wrong with her hair, frizzy or not. "I don't care about your hair. You ready to go now? Breakfast awaits."

"Right. You mean you've prewarned the kitchen staff that we're going to go on another raid this morning."

"Something like that."

She slipped her feet into her sandals and slung the towel over the closet doorknob. "I'm too hungry to argue. Let's go."

All the way to the kitchen, Steve wanted to talk, but Tasha's only "comments" were monosyllabic grunts given only when he asked a question that required a reply.

Upon arrival at the kitchen, Tasha smiled politely, took a plate, and filled it to capacity with toast and fruit. Steve wondered if he should have been honored that she spoke to him in complete sentences when she asked if he was again going to bring a carafe of coffee and cream to his office.

The whole process took only minutes, and they were back in his office. Just as the day before, Steve watched her grumpy mood dissipate in stages with each additional bite of her breakfast. Inversely, the more coffee she drank, the more she appeared to relax.

Therefore, today Steve knew better than to say anything, and he just let her eat.

When she was done, she smiled, sighed, and, for lack of any empty desk space, set the plate down on the floor. She sat up, sighed again, and took a long, slow sip of her cooled coffee.

"That was wonderful," she said airily.

"You're not a morning person, are you?"

"What do you mean?"

"Forget it. We have a lot to do today. I want to be able to make room for our breakfast plates on the desks tomorrow morning instead of eating out of our laps."

"That's motivation, if you ask me. Let's get to it."

The entire morning, Steve found himself stealing glances at Tasha. As her hair dried, it may have gone a little wild, but he would never have called it frizzy. In all the time he'd known Tasha, he'd never seen her hair the way it was today, not in school and especially not in the pictures she'd sent him over the years. He never would have known there was effort involved in keeping her hair mildly wavy, in comparison to the uncontrolled curls he now observed.

In a way, he liked her styleless style. He knew she hated to be called cute, but the untamed locks made her look cuter than ever. Therefore, he knew he couldn't tell her how much he liked it and especially not why. He wondered if he would be catching her with unprocessed hair other mornings or if she would be waking earlier to have it tamed down before he arrived at six-thirty. The possibility made Steve contemplate knocking on her door a little earlier in days to come.

As the morning neared its end, instead of waiting for his stomach to tell him it was lunchtime, Steve kept one eye on the clock. At precisely 11:55, he pushed in the keyboard tray.

"I have a surprise for you. I asked Kaila to make up a picnic lunch for us so we can go hide away at the koi pond. At noon the landscapers will be off for lunch for an hour, so we'll have the place all to ourselves. Just you, me, and a dozen koi."

Her smile made all his planning and giving the landscapers extra time for lunch worth the effort. "That's great! Are we going now?"

"Yup."

They made a short stop at the kitchen and headed down the path to the koi pond. Carrying the tote containing their lunches over his shoulder and a blanket under his arm, Steve took the lead. Tasha followed behind him with a large bottle of fruit juice.

"These plants are beautiful. Is this all wild, or did your father plant this? What are they?"

"Those are bird-of-paradise bushes, and it's all wild. All of Hawaii is like this. The only parts of the islands you'll see without this lush vegetation are on the lava flows and on the beaches. Remind me to make a note to schedule regular maintenance to keep the path the proper width for two people to walk side by side. For now, it's too narrow because it's only been our employees using it. It should be wide enough for a couple to walk side by side and hold hands."

Behind him, Tasha sighed. "That sounds so romantic."

"Yes. Often couples come to Hawaii for their honeymoon.

Many even plan their entire weddings here. We have packages set up for both options. Featuring the secluded pond as a get-away would be a nice addition to the brochure. I'm going to have to take some pictures of the pond for the next one."

The path opened to a small clearing, in the center of which was the koi pond that had been his dream. One day, when all was back to normal and he didn't have to work from sunrise to sunset, Steve looked forward to lounging by the pond without having to worry about how much time he was wasting by not doing anything constructive.

He'd had the idea for years, but when Connor built his fountain in the main area, that was all the encouragement Steve needed to begin planning the koi pond in the last undeveloped piece of the Harrigan property.

"It's beautiful. I know your guests will love it here."

"The only things missing are a couple of benches for people to sit on. I personally think that will spoil the natural *feel* of it a bit, but I have to make it available and comfortable for everybody. Even though the pond is hand dug with a rubber liner and the water is pumped in and filtered, it still looks like a natural setting."

"Rubber liner?"

"You don't think you can keep up something man-made like this without a little help, do you? You can't just dig a hole and fill it with water because the water will soak into the ground. The koi aren't indigenous to Hawaii either. I picked them because they're hardy fish for such an application."

Tasha studied his pond, then turned her head to take in

the trees and flowers and, finally, the landscaping of the professionally placed rocks and bushes around the pond. "That makes this nothing more than a glorified outdoor aquarium."

Steve grinned as he set the tote down and spread the blanket on the ground. "I guess. But I like it anyway."

"I'm sorry. I didn't mean to sound so condescending. You've done a beautiful job. By the way, just how much work did you actually do?"

Steve sat on the blanket, removed the food containers from the tote Kaila had prepared, and began to open them. "I was obligated to do the resort's business first, and you can see what kind of job I'm doing with Brittany gone. I designed the pond and surrounding area, planted some of the shrubbery, and helped position the liner. If your real question is did I get down and dirty and actually dig, the answer is *no*. We pay people to do that. Now come here and sit down so we can eat. I want to enjoy this break, and then we have to get back to work."

Chapter 6

Tasha had just dropped her toothbrush back into the holder when three sharp raps sounded on the hale door. She glanced quickly at Steve's watch, which had made its permanent home on her wrist, to see that the time read 6:25.

It had taken nearly a week, but she'd finally managed to be ready with her hair properly dry and tamed two days in a row, ready for Steve's arrival at six-thirty. Today, since Steve was unexpectedly five minutes early, her hair was dry, but not tamed.

She grumbled under her breath, yanked the cord for the curling iron out of the wall, and stomped to the door.

She opened her mouth to scold him, but Steve raised one finger in the air to silence her, giving him the opportunity to speak first.

"I know what you're going to say. I know I'm early. But the sun is up a few minutes earlier than it was last week, and I wanted to take advantage of the extra time."

"But. . ." Tasha let her voice trail off, wondering why in the world he thought it important to get up earlier, since it was still half an hour before sunrise. He didn't need to keep anything close to office hours, although she knew that self-employed people tended to work longer and harder than someone who worked a nine-to-five job. Or was he still considered self-employed if the four brothers owned the resort and worked for each other and no one was really the boss?

Tasha pressed her fingertips to her temples and shook her head. Thinking of such complicated issues hurt her brain so early in the morning. If she had to look on the bright side, which Steve had been encouraging her to do in the mornings, getting up five minutes earlier meant she could eat breakfast five minutes earlier.

"Fine. Let me find my sandals, and I'll be right out."

After their daily kitchen raid, they hurried to Steve's office, where they laid their plates on the desks. They said a short prayer of thanks for their meals and for God's blessings on their day and began to eat.

As he did every day, Steve didn't say a word while they ate. Even though she'd wondered why he never spoke during breakfast, Tasha enjoyed the silence.

He finally spoke after she set her plate aside and took another sip of her coffee.

"This really feels good to be able to use the top of the desks for something besides storage areas for unprocessed paperwork."

"I know. We've made a lot of progress in a week."

"I think we deserve a break from all this hard work. What do you say we take an extra-long lunch and go for a walk around the lake? I feel so guilty that you haven't seen anything but the koi pond during the daytime, and we're back here until dark."

"Do we have the time for that? There's still so much work."

"If we can't spare a couple of hours over the course of a month, then we might as well give up now."

Since Tasha wasn't about to concede, she agreed. Besides, she was almost positive that they would make Steve's deadline. "All right. Now let's get to work, or we really won't have time to walk around at lunchtime."

At 11:55 Steve went alone to the kitchen to pick up their lunch, which they ate quickly at the desks, then headed to the lake.

The shoreline wasn't a sandy beach like she expected, but a mulch-covered path that surrounded the entire lake. Tasha compared what she thought the view would be like from the huts surrounding the lake and couldn't decide which was more relaxing, being surrounded by the lush plant life and small lake or being more in the open and watching the ocean.

All the way around, Steve told her about the bushes and plants and colorful birds they saw. He told her tales of the nene birds, Hawaii's national bird, and explained their habit of having a midafternoon snack of *naupaka* berries, which explained why the bushes were stripped of berries to a height of two feet above ground.

Despite the fact that she was working, Tasha couldn't remember the last time she'd had such a wonderful vacation.

Steve gritted his teeth when Tasha winced at his touch. "I'm so sorry. This is all my fault."

She sucked in a deep breath and stiffened from head to toe. "No, it's my fault. I knew I should have put on sunscreen. Keep going. I know it will feel better when you're done."

Steve stuck his fingers in the jar of cool creme and once more attempted to apply a liberal dose to Tasha's shoulder with the lightest possible touch. "If you can get past the sunburn, you have to admit that snorkeling was fun."

Tasha nodded too quickly. Even from behind her, he could tell that she had gritted her teeth against his touch, despite his best efforts to be gentle. "Yes," she said tightly, confirming his suspicions about gritted teeth. "It was fun. I'm so glad you had that little disposable underwater camera. Now that I think of it, I've seen purchase orders for those. You sell a lot of them in the gift shop, don't you?"

"Yup."

She turned and smiled at him, which made him feel even worse. Living in the middle of a tropical tourist mecca had conditioned his skin to a year-round tan. Tasha, however, had come from the middle of winter in North Dakota. Her skin was so white that if he didn't know better, he would have asked if she had been sick. It was also his fault for keeping her inside so much that she hadn't built up a tan to protect her from the sun for an afternoon outing.

She turned forward again and lifted her hair with both hands so he could continue. "Since we're getting this stuff on right away, I bet the effects of the burn will be less painful."

"I don't know. I never get sunburns. Not only do I have a

year-round tan, but I'm usually careful to use sunscreen. I don't know why I forgot."

Not only did he not know why he forgot the sunscreen, over the last two weeks he'd found himself losing his train of thought on even the most basic things when all he was doing was simply watching Tasha do some little task he'd seen her do a thousand times. Either that or when they talked, he remembered the strangest things, things he hadn't thought about for years.

He wondered if the stress of preparing for the audit had affected his mental capacities, because these things had never happened before. Either that or Barnabas was right—he really was overdue for a vacation, as if he could really take one with Brittany gone indefinitely and everything else hanging over his head.

Tasha turned her head so she made eye contact, still holding up her hair with both hands. "Since we were goofing off all afternoon, maybe we should grab something for dinner, bring it in here, and do a little more work before we pack it in for the night."

Steve opened his mouth to protest, wanting to tell her that it wasn't necessary to keep working, but he snapped it shut. The way she was feeling, he knew she would be more likely to go to bed early or spend the evening alone in her hale than to spend the evening with him. He'd already asked her a number of times to participate in evening activities, but she'd turned him down. However, every time he suggested that they catch up on "just a few more things" at the office, she always said yes.

"I guess we can keep working. I just don't want you to get overtired."

"If you're worried about me getting overtired, you could always let me sleep later in the mornings."

"But the morning is the most productive time of day. Maybe I should take you back to your hale, and you can go to bed early."

"Forget it. Give me the inventory list for the third quarter and let's get back to work."

Steve kept a careful eye on the time, and when he figured she'd had enough, he ignored her protests and took her back to her hale for the night. As usual, he returned at 6:25 sharp, finding Tasha with a towel once again wrapped around her hair.

"You keep ignoring that coconut."

"And I keep telling you I'm exempt."

He tried not to laugh as Tasha grumbled and muttered under her breath the entire way to the kitchen. She continued to gripe and complain the entire time she filled her plate, much to the surprise of the kitchen staff, who had always seen her totally silent in the morning. Steve gave everyone a big smile and shrugged his shoulders while he filled the usual coffee carafe, then he hurried to the office after Tasha had selected her usual breakfast fare.

The morning passed quickly—so quickly that Steve lost track of the time and missed his chance to pick up the lunch tote from Kaila before the lunch-rush crowd.

They had almost reached the staff entrance to the kitchen when a little voice stopped them.

"Steve! Look what I found!"

Steve glanced up to see Barnabas standing at a distance, smiling. Steve smiled back, then squatted down to greet Abby. "Hi, Abby. What have you got there? It looks like a feather."

"Yes!" she squealed and held the feather higher.

"Yes, I wonder if you have a nene feather? See the stripes?"

Abby tipped her head up and held the feather out to Tasha. "Would you like to see my nene feather, Miss Schroo-chek-oh, uh, Stew-chenk-er, uh. . ."

Tasha smiled. "That's Struchenkowich. Please, just call me Tasha. It's easier."

"Tasha is a pretty name. I gotta go find Api and show her my feather. Bye!"

"She's a sweet little girl, isn't she? What is she, about five? I wonder if she's excited about being a big sister soon?"

"I don't know. I haven't had much time to talk to Barnabas. Lately it seems we've only had time to talk business. But I think Liliana's due shortly after tax D-Day."

"So you're going to be an uncle two times over, then."

He shrugged his shoulders. "I guess that's what it means."

"You know I don't have any brothers or sisters, but some of my cousins have kids. It's kind of neat being an auntie. It means I get to spoil them rotten, then send them home to Mom and Dad."

Steve grinned. "You're bad. Now let's go get our lunch and sneak off to the pond."

Because they had to walk single file down the path, Steve had time to think.

It wasn't merely being an uncle that he'd been thinking

about lately. Since he saw Liliana almost every day, even if he didn't always talk to her beyond a quick greeting, he'd watched her grow with the baby she was carrying. More than watching Liliana, he'd watched his brother. During the short courtship before Barnabas and Liliana married, he'd seen Barnabas change in ways he could never have foreseen. Barnabas had always been the most responsible of his other three brothers, but there had been a shift in Barnabas's priorities. He'd even changed the way he handled things at the resort in order to accommodate Liliana and Abby. While Steve knew that being the father of a newborn would change Barnabas even more, Steve found, as their due date came closer, he'd been thinking of something else.

Watching Barnabas get ready for the baby had made Steve wonder what it would be like to become a father. He knew many people who were parents, and many of the guests at their resort brought their children. The decision to have children was usually a natural progression from getting married. However, seeing the baby and Liliana grow under Barnabas's watchful eye had given Steve a different outlook on prospective parenthood and on love in general.

He had to be realistic and know that one day he, too, would fall in love like his brothers. However, when he did, he knew it would be with careful planning and that he would not allow his responsibilities to slide.

When he reached the grassy section by the pond, Steve spread out the blanket he'd been carrying over his arm and set the tote down on it. "Your banquet awaits."

"Don't move. I have a surprise for you."

Without waiting for him, Tasha nudged Steve aside and began rummaging through the tote. "Here it is. I asked Kaila to pack us something special today."

"You did? I'm touched."

Instead of giving the container to him, Tasha walked to the edge of the pond.

"What are you doing?"

"I've seen this done in Japanese restaurants at home. Have you ever been to a Japanese restaurant?"

"Not that I can recall. I don't leave the resort very often."

"That's what I thought. Watch."

Very slowly, Tasha tossed in a couple of raw, peeled shrimp and stood stock-still. A couple of the koi swam slowly toward her, grabbed the shrimp, and disappeared back into the depths of the center of the pond.

"What are you doing? I have special koi food shipped in for my fish."

"I checked this out on the Internet when you went to talk to Alex this morning. Back home, there's a Japanese restaurant where the waitresses feed the koi by hand every day. You don't have a dog or cat or anything, so I figure these things are the closest you're going to have to pets. You should at least commune with them."

Tasha tossed in a few more shrimp, this time closer to the edge where she stood. "If you put in a couple every day and get closer and closer, then you should be able to just drop them in and they'll come right up to you. Before you know it, you'll be able to put the shrimp in your hand, and the koi will eat right out of your hand."

"Really?"

"As long as you work at it slowly and every day, you should have them eating out of your hand in no time. Literally."

Steve joined Tasha at the edge and watched as she tossed the shrimp in, one at a time, each shrimp a little closer than the one before. "See?"

He couldn't hold back his smile. "I'm impressed."

Tasha turned to him and smiled back. "My sources say that this works best when they're hungry."

Steve froze. In only two short weeks, Tasha seemed to have touched so many parts of his life, even down to sharing his enjoyment of the koi pond he'd dreamed about for years.

In only two short weeks, she would be gone.

He couldn't believe how fast the last two weeks had disappeared.

He had to find some way to make the most of the short time they had left together. While E-mails had been fine for the last four years, Steve had a bad feeling it wouldn't be good enough anymore.

"I have an idea. Let's finish up early tonight and go into the city. Not that I'm into the night life, but you can at least see a little of what Hawaii is like off of our resort."

"But I've already seen the city. On Sunday morning, when you took me to that big, old church."

"Then I have a better idea. Let's take the whole day off tomorrow, and I'll take you on a tour of some of the other islands. First we can go to Ka'upulehu, on the big island, and see Mokuaikaua church. It was built in 1823 of lava stone and koa wood and it's the oldest Christian place of worship in the Hawaiian Islands. I can also take you to some of the museums and maybe even the shopping mall. Or if you're not into that, we can go Kahuwai Bay to see the sea turtles. Or we can take a whole day and go on a hike up one of the smaller mountains. Have you ever seen a wild donkey?"

"Those all sound like good ideas, and maybe we can do them another time, and definitely we'll have to go do something on the weekend. For now, let's just eat and get back to work."

Chapter 7

Tasha watched as Steve knelt by the edge of his koi pond. Slowly, he lowered his hand, filled with shrimp, into the water.

Just as they had done for the past few days, the larger koi swam to him to grab as much as they could out of his hand, while the smaller koi swam to the sides and below his hand, catching the smaller pieces as they floated away.

They only had a few hours' work to do and they would be done, with every transaction balanced and accounted for, all receipts located or duplicated, and every account reconciled.

Tomorrow the auditor was coming.

Tomorrow she was going home.

Tasha shook her head to clear her thoughts. "I don't know what's wrong with me. I shouldn't be so melancholy. Look at what we accomplished. With only a few minutes' work, you're going to be ready for whatever that auditor throws at you."

At first she hadn't wanted to come. Now, she didn't want to leave.

Steve looked up, his hand still submerged. "I really think you should be doing this too. After all, it was your idea. You don't want to blow your last chance."

At his reminder, something strange happened in the pit of her stomach, and it had nothing to do with her hunger.

Tasha cleared her throat. "Last night after you dropped me off at my hut, I looked at that brochure Alex gave me. Before I go, I'd like to go on the dinner cruise. I don't get to go on many dinner cruises in North Dakota, especially in the middle of winter. The only mode of travel this time of year on the lakes is via snowmobile."

"Snowmobile? I've heard of those, but never seen one."

"Think of a Jet Ski, except it has treads like a tractor so it can go over snow and on the frozen lake. My uncle's snowmobile can seat four people, and the ice is thick enough to support the combined weight from mid-January until spring, when it starts to thaw. Once a year my uncle and his friends go ice fishing with it. They drive out to the middle of the lake, cut a hole in the ice, and go fishing, and every year it's the same. For as long as I can remember, they've never caught anything. I don't know why they keep trying year after year."

"Wow. I can't imagine fishing from the lake's own surface. I wonder if your uncle feels like Peter did when he walked on the water to meet Jesus on the way to Gennesaret."

"Walking on the frozen lake isn't much different than a skating rink, except without the special machinery, the surface isn't quite as flat because it isn't so processed."

Steve's eyes widened. Tasha struggled not to smile, wondering if he was imagining himself walking across a frozen version of the lake in the middle of their resort. She, too, was imagining him doing the same thing, only he was dressed in the way she was now used to seeing him—in a loud Aloha shirt and baggy shorts.

"I have no idea what natural ice is like. When it's a natural lake, can you see through the ice? The only ice I've ever touched was in the form of ice cubes from a dispenser, and they're clear. I've seen ice rinks on television, though, and the ice is very white. Also, before the hockey game, they put out a carpet runner for the person who is singing the anthem to walk on, so it must be hard to walk on."

"You mean you've never been skating?"

"Tasha, this is Hawaii. There are no skating rinks here. I have in-line skates, though, and the cement isn't the least bit slippery. It's actually kind of a hot landing if you happen to fall."

Tasha thought of Steve's reaction to real cold, knowing his only experience with a non-Hawaii winter was California's coast. To her, that alleged winter in California had felt like summer turned back to an extended spring with nothing in between. "One year you'll have to take a vacation and come to North Dakota in the winter."

"That's backwards. People from the colder climates come here in the winter."

"Then just think of the great off-season rates you'll get. I bet my uncle would love taking you on the snowmobile."

"As fun as it sounds, I think I'll pass." He stood and wiped his hands on his pants. "I'm starving. The fish have been fed, so now we can eat."

Tasha handed him the packages of wipes to clean his hands after feeding the fish and spread their lunch out on the blanket. "I'm really going to miss Kaila's wonderful lunches. I won't be eating like this at home."

For the first time, they ate in silence slowly, not rushing, sitting side by side and soaking in the beauty of their surroundings. For once, neither of them had anything to say, which was fine with Tasha. She didn't know if she could speak without crying.

They still didn't speak as they packed up for the last time. Fortunately when they returned to the office, she was able to get lost in her work as they made a final check of all the details. They traded files and talked just as they had every other day, which was exactly what Tasha needed to do.

As could be expected, they uncovered a few things that needed to be investigated, so they weren't finished as early as they wanted. It was dark out by the time Tasha's stomach grumbling brought them both to a stop.

Steve's hands froze over his keyboard. "I think that's a sign. You said you wanted to go on the dinner cruise tonight, and you don't want to miss it. It will only take me a minute to finish up these last few things. Why don't you go home and freshen up or do whatever it is that women do before going out."

"I don't know how to dress. What are you going to wear?"

"I'm going to change into long pants." He rubbed his fingers over his chin. "I think I'll shave too. The cruise is meant to be casual, but not scruffy."

Tasha looked down at her cut-off shorts. "I'd better change into a skirt, then. How much time have we got?"

"I don't know. You've got my watch. The boat leaves shore at seven-thirty whether we're on it or not."

"It's seven-fourteen. That should give us just enough time. I'll meet you at the dock." She walked around to Steve's desk, removed the flashlight out of his drawer, and started toward the door.

"What are you doing?"

She'd always known that Steve lived on the grounds, but she only learned after her arrival that the fourth door in the hallway with the offices wasn't a fourth office—it was marked PRIVATE because it was Steve's apartment. Now that she'd been working with him for a month, his work ethics perfectly explained an E-mail he'd sent a few months ago. One night he couldn't sleep, and he'd gotten out of bed to work on something that suddenly crossed his mind. Before he could forget, he'd crossed the hall and begun working on it. Daylight had snuck up on him, and he had been embarrassed when one of the guests had peeked into the staff-only hallway and caught him sneaking from his office back to his apartment in his pajamas.

Tasha stepped toward the door, speaking over her shoulder. "When we're pressed for time, it's silly for you to walk all the way to my hut and back again, especially when it's going to take you longer to get ready than me. I'm quite capable of walking to my hut alone. I'll see you on the boat."

"But—"

Before he could finish his sentence, and knowing he would need time to lock up, Tasha hurried out the door. She jogged all the way to her hut, even though she knew that he wouldn't chase her once she put enough distance between them.

With the door closed behind her, Tasha breathed a sigh of relief. Her long-distance relationship with Steve had been comfortable. Now that they had been side by side for almost every waking moment of the past month, everything had changed. She was no longer comfortable.

Tasha squeezed her eyes shut. She'd dreamed of what it would be like to fall in love and do the happily-ever-after thing with a good Christian man like Steve. She hadn't realized until recently that every time she met a man, either at church or on the job, she'd compared him to Steve to help her decide what she wanted in her future mate.

Naturally, every man she'd ever met had fallen short. And now that she'd been with Steve for so long, she knew she didn't have a hope in the universe of meeting another man who could match Steve's standards. Steve was unique. She loved working with him. He was efficient and organized, and he carefully thought every situation through thoroughly and intelligently to the most logical conclusion. He was a demanding boss, yet he asked nothing of anyone that he wouldn't be prepared to do himself.

She'd never worked so smoothly or so in tune with another living soul.

But when they weren't working, being with him made her heart race and her brain freeze.

Tasha leaned her forehead against the door and pressed her palms to the cool wood surface. Whatever was happening to her was wrong. Anything new she felt for Steve could only be an aberration of a summer romance—except it was winter. This was a vacation fling, except that she was working—even if it was for free. Knowing this, such relationships were always over as quickly as they began. If she didn't have to consider that she'd known Steve for years.

Clearly Steve didn't feel the same way she did. Steve was still good old analytical Steve, always doing the proper thing, down to picking the right clothing and being right on time, exactly to the minute.

Thinking of those minutes, Tasha hurried to change, then jogged to the boat dock in the center of the resort's beach. She found Steve standing on the shore.

He smiled, which set her insides into more of a tizzy. "I know you said to meet on the boat, but I didn't want to take the chance that you wouldn't make it, and you nearly didn't. They're sailing in exactly one minute. Let's go get our table."

He bent his arm and patted it, encouraging her to slip her hand through the crook as they walked up the ramp and onto the boat. Without preamble, they sat at a cozy table for two on the side of the deck.

"We'll be traveling slowly. The captain will take a scenic tour lasting just long enough for everyone to enjoy a leisurely supper, and we'll be back ashore. It's timed that way so people don't get up and walk around, as the boat isn't big enough for that."

Tasha glanced around as much as possible without moving

her head. Except for a path only wide enough to go single file along the center, all available deck space was filled with tables.

Each table was barely lit by a candle, which was somehow fastened to the center of each table. Between being on the water, the twinkle of the camera, and the obvious table-for-two theme, the whole setup was far too romantic.

"Will we be seeing the lights on shore? I wish I had brought my camera."

Steve smiled, which only made her stomach feel worse. "You can't take pictures at night from a moving boat. You should know that."

"I guess. What's for dinner? I'm starving."

"It was a choice between a seafood combo or chicken, which we were supposed to reserve at least fifteen minutes before we boarded. I phoned after you dashed out on me and got in at the last minute. I picked chicken for you."

Right on cue, a waiter appeared with their selections.

For something preordered and obviously not cooked on board, the food on the boat was as wonderful as the rest of the food served at the resort. They paused for a prayer of thanks for the food and for the beauty of their surroundings, and Tasha delicately sampled her first nibble.

"This is delicious!" she mumbled around the food in her mouth. She closed her eyes, savored it, then swallowed. "I can't believe you eat like this every day and you don't weigh four hundred pounds."

"If you think about it, everything we serve is quite healthy. Most of what we have is fresh fruit or flame-broiled entrees, which means nothing is cooked with any extra fat. Since the seafood is all fresh and not deep-fried, that's good for you too. You've been here nearly a month now, and you haven't put on any weight. At least I don't think you have." Even in the dark, the flickering light of the candle gave Tasha enough light to see Steve's cheeks darken. "Not that I've been looking that closely."

"I have no idea. And since I'm on vacation, I don't care either. There will be plenty of time to diet when I get home."

Home. Back to E-mail only.

She wanted to tell him how much she would miss him, but she didn't want to hear that he wouldn't miss her the same way.

Tasha shook her head to clear her thoughts. "I don't know what's wrong with me. I shouldn't be so melancholy. We should be celebrating. Look at what we accomplished. With only a few minutes more work, you're going to be ready for whatever question the auditor may throw at you."

"Yes. I know."

She waited for Steve to say something, but he remained silent.

The boat shifted slightly as it nudged the dock.

They were back.

All she had left was the evening with Steve, and her time with him was over.

Never in her whole life had four weeks gone by so quickly.

"I guess you're going to have to be up early tomorrow. Your flight leaves at nine. If you want, I can take you to the airport."

She couldn't believe he was so quick to make plans to let her go.

Tasha tried to stop the sinking feeling inside. As much as it hurt to know he didn't want her to stay, she had to take him up on his offer, since it was the last time she might ever see him again. She wasn't likely to ever come back to Hawaii, knowing what awaited her.

She stood when the people in the table beside them began to file off the boat. "Yes. I'd like that. Now I think I'd like to go back to my hut. I should pack some of my stuff so I can be ready early."

Chapter 8

Steve couldn't stop the numb feeling in the pit of his stomach. He couldn't believe that she was going, yet the reality was that she'd been there for four weeks, and her time was up.

He'd never walked so slowly as he did from the dock to Tasha's hale. Either Tasha didn't notice, or she didn't say anything, because she followed his lead and walked just as slowly.

They arrived too soon. His heart sank when she reached for her purse to get her key.

"Wait. Let's just walk a bit. It's your last night here. Why don't we kick off our sandals and walk on the shore? The moon is almost full, and it's a clear night. It'll be almost like when you first got here, only we won't have our cameras."

"Sure. I think that's a great idea. We can leave our sandals here. Then we won't have anything to carry."

Because they were both barefoot, all it took was a quick glance at each other, and without a word between them, they raced to the ocean. They ran, laughing, splashing, and kicking up water before they settled down to just walk over the sandy shore and let the constant waves sloshing back and forth lick at their ankles.

As they walked, Steve had the strangest urge to hold her hand, but he couldn't. In the past month they'd talked about anything and everything, except for one issue. He hadn't asked if she had a special someone back home because if she did, he didn't want to know. He knew it wasn't being fair to think that way. Above all, he wanted Tasha to be happy. He had to be realistic and know that one day she would meet her Mr. Right and settle down and get married and have children back home in North Dakota.

A cold sensation settled over him at the thought of Tasha with another man. He forced himself to push aside his jealousy of a man who, so far, probably didn't exist.

As for himself, he supposed that one day he would meet someone as well. Although, he couldn't see any woman measuring up to Tasha with her intelligence, her beauty, her charm, her unshakable Christian walk, her unselfishness, their common interests and values, or the quality of the friendship they'd developed over the years, even if the last four years of it had been long distance.

Instead of talking about what awaited her back home, they talked about all the things they'd done together in the past four weeks and all the fun they'd had together. When conversation lagged, Tasha reminded him of a few things she wasn't sure he would remember when the auditor arrived. Before they knew it, they'd been to both ends of the Harrigan property and back to her hale, and it was well after midnight. Steve knew he would never think of hale number 37 the same way again.

"I guess I'll pick you up at the regular time, except we won't be going to the office, we'll be going to the airport."

Tasha's voice came out strained, like she was losing her voice. "Yes," she whispered.

"Good night, Tasha," Steve said, finding that his voice wasn't coming out quite normal either. He started to step to the side to pick up his sandals, but the sudden touch of Tasha's fingers on his arm stopped him.

"Wait." Before he could figure out what she was doing, she cupped his cheeks with both hands, raised herself up on her bare tiptoes, and pressed her mouth to his.

It took a couple of seconds for the shock to wear off and to remember to breathe. But when he did, Steve wrapped his arms around her and kissed her right back. His head swam and his heart raced. Holding her and kissing her felt so right that he didn't want to ever stop.

Of course, they had to stop at some point, so Steve reluctantly stopped kissing her, but he didn't let her go. He held her even more tightly.

He bent his head forward and buried his face in her hair. "I'll miss you so much," he mumbled.

"I'll miss you too," she muttered into his chest.

They stood wrapped in each other's arms until the sound of the approach of the family from the next hale forced them to separate for propriety's sake.

Tasha backed up, picked her purse up out of the sand, and

fished out her key. "I'll see you in the morning then. Good night, Steve."

"Good night, Tasha."

He didn't move until the door closed behind her and the light came on inside.

Steve squeezed his eyes shut. Once she left, he knew his life would never be the same again. It hadn't been the same since Tasha arrived four short weeks ago.

Steve stood to the side as Tasha checked in at the ticket counter. He'd never thought much about airports before, whether he'd been greeting someone or dropping them off. Today, the constant noise and the bustle around him annoyed him.

He wanted to savor every last second he could have with Tasha, and he couldn't do it in a crowd. There were a million things he wanted to say to her, but not surrounded by a throng of people all heading for the same small opening. Even if the crowd was more widely dispersed, it wasn't good enough. He only had a few minutes before she would walk through the gate, never to return.

A voice came over the paging system announcing that it was time for Tasha's flight to board.

He realized that he had never told her how much he appreciated her help.

Steve lifted one of Tasha's suitcases up to the belt so the clerk could weigh it and tag it, then lifted her other suitcase as soon as the first one began its path on the conveyor belt to the loading bay.

He never told her how much he enjoyed bugging her in the morning when she hadn't yet fixed her hair.

Tasha stepped aside so the next person in line could begin checking in.

He never told her how special it had been when she helped train his fish to eat out of his hand.

"I guess this is it. It's time for me to go to the passengers' waiting area."

He never told her how much he enjoyed her laughter and how much she brightened every day.

"I didn't get a window seat, but I guess I took enough pictures on the way here to do me."

He never told her how her smiles filled his dreams at night.

Tasha's voice started to shake. "I should go now before I do something stupid and embarrass myself. Good-bye, Steve. It's been fun."

He never told her how much he loved her.

She leaned toward him. As Steve stood, his feet frozen to the floor, Tasha leaned upward, gave him a quick peck on the cheek, and turned around.

Steve suddenly thought of his brother Alex, how he'd seen Callie off, how his normally carefree brother had become miserable and agitated at every little thing. Suddenly, two weeks after Callie left, Alex dropped everything and disappeared. He'd come back a happy man with Callie on his arm, where she had stayed, figuratively, at least.

Alex had found out the hard way that he couldn't live without Callie.

Could Steve live without Tasha?

In only three steps, Tasha was already halfway to the gate—where she would be past the point of no return.

Steve couldn't see himself living without Tasha, and he knew it wouldn't take him two weeks to confirm it. He could see himself boarding the very next plane, only he wouldn't be going to warm Indiana. He would be braving the North Dakota winter to tell Tasha what he should have said when he had the chance.

"Wait!" Steve called out. He ran the six steps toward her, reached out his hand, and grabbed her arm, preventing her from taking that last step into the boarding area.

"Steve? What are you—"

He gave her a gentle nudge to escort her out of the way of the other people waiting to board. "Don't go."

She wiggled her arm, but he tightened his grip. "What are you doing? They've called my flight."

"Please don't get on that plane. Stay with me. Forever. Marry me."

Tasha's mouth opened, but no words came out. She snapped it shut, squeezed her eyes shut, and shook her head.

"I should have said this sooner. I love you, Tasha. I can't live without you, and I hope you feel the same way about me."

She opened her eyes wider than he'd ever seen. "Are you serious?"

"If you go, I'm going to follow you. I'll even get on this same plane if I can, even without a winter jacket. Then you'll be responsible for me if I freeze to death when we land. Save my life and marry me now."

The corners of her mouth quivered, her eyes became glassy, and she tipped her head up. "I don't know what to say."

"You could always say you love me too and say yes, you'll marry me."

She turned her head toward the people filing toward the plane, then turned back to him.

Her voice dropped to a husky whisper. "I love you, and yes, I'll stay and marry you."

"Thank You, God!" Steve murmured, and bent to kiss Tasha, the love of his life, his future wife.

From somewhere behind him, someone started to applaud. The applause spread until all the people around them were either applauding or cheering, and a few women were crying.

Steve separated from Tasha and grasped her hand. Together they gave a short bow, at which everyone smiled and started to go back about their own business.

"What about my luggage?"

"It's probably too late to catch it. We can buy you something new. In the meantime, let's go home. We have an audit to supervise."

She squeezed his hand and smiled up at him. "Yes. Let's go home."

GAIL SATTLER

Despite the overabundance of rain, Gail Sattler enjoys living on the West Coast with her husband, three sons, two dogs, five lizards, and countless fish, many of which have names. Gail Sattler loves to write tales of romance that can be complete only with God in their center. She's had many books out with Heartsong Presents and Barbour Publishing. In 2001 and 2000, Gail was voted as the Favorite Heartsong Author. Visit Gail's webpage at www.gailsattler.com.

A Letter to Our Readers

Dear Readers:

In order that we might better contribute to your reading enjoyment, we would appreciate you taking a few minutes to respond to the following questions. When completed, please return to the following: Fiction Editor, Barbour Publishing, Inc., P.O. Box 719, Uhrichsville, OH 44683.

1. Did you enjoy reading *Aloha?*
   ❏ Very much—I would like to see more books like this.
   ❏ Moderately—I would have enjoyed it more if _____
   _____
   _____

2. What influenced your decision to purchase this book?
   (Check those that apply.)
   ❏ Cover   ❏ Back cover copy   ❏ Title   ❏ Price
   ❏ Friends   ❏ Publicity   ❏ Other

3. Which story was your favorite?
   ❏ *Love, Suite Love*   ❏ *Game of Love*
   ❏ *Fixed by Love*   ❏ *It All Adds Up to Love*

4. Please check your age range:
   ❏ Under 18   ❏ 18–24   ❏ 25–34
   ❏ 35–45   ❏ 46–55   ❏ Over 55

5. How many hours per week do you read? _____

Name _____

Occupation _____

Address _____

City _____ State _____ Zip _____

If you enjoyed

Aloha

then read:

LOVE AFLOAT

*Drifting Hearts Find Safe Harbor
in Four Romantic Novellas*

The Matchmakers by Kimberley Comeaux
Troubled Waters by Linda Goodnight
By the Silvery Moon by JoAnn A. Grote
Healing Voyage by Diann Hunt

If you enjoyed

Aloha

then read:

the Sewing Circle

One Woman's Mentoring Shapes Lives in Four Stories of Love

Tumbling Blocks by Andrea Boeshaar
Old Maid's Choice by Cathy Marie Hake
Jacob's Ladder by Pamela Kaye Tracy
Four Hearts by Sally Laity

If you enjoyed

Aloha

then read:

Prairie

BRIDES

Four New Inspirational
Love Stories from the North American Prairie

The Bride's Song by Linda Ford
The Barefoot Bride by Linda Goodnight
A Homesteader, a Bride, and a Baby by JoAnn A. Grote
A Vow Unbroken by Amy Rognlie

$\mathcal{H}$EARTSONG 💜 PRESENTS

Love Stories
Are Rated G!

That's for godly, gratifying, and of course, great! If you love a thrilling love story but don't appreciate the sordidness of some popular paperback romances, **Heartsong Presents** is for you. In fact, **Heartsong Presents** is the only inspirational romance book club featuring love stories where Christian faith is the primary ingredient in a marriage relationship.

Sign up today to receive your first set of four, never-before-published Christian romances. Send no money now; you will receive a bill with the first shipment. You may cancel at any time without obligation, and if you aren't completely satisfied with any selection, you may return the books for an immediate refund!

Imagine. . .four new romances every four weeks—two historical, two contemporary—with men and women like you who long to meet the one God has chosen as the love of their lives. . .all for the low price of $10.99 postpaid.

To join, simply complete the coupon below and mail to the address provided. **Heartsong Presents** romances are rated G for another reason: They'll arrive Godspeed!

YES! Sign me up for Heartsong!

NEW MEMBERSHIPS WILL BE SHIPPED IMMEDIATELY!
Send no money now. We'll bill you only $10.99 postpaid with your first shipment of four books. Or for faster action, call toll free 1-800-847-8270.

NAME _____

ADDRESS _____

CITY _____ STATE_____ ZIP_____

MAIL TO: HEARTSONG PRESENTS, P.O. Box 721, Uhrichsville, Ohio 44683
or visit www.heartsongpresents.com

If you enjoyed

Aloha

then read:

American
DREAM

*Four Historical Love Stories
Celebrating the Faith of American Immigrants*

I Take Thee, a Stranger by Kristy Dykes
Blessed Land by Nancy J. Farrier
Promises Kept by Sally Laity
Freedom's Ring by Judith McCoy Miller

Available wherever books are sold.

Or order from:
Barbour Publishing, Inc.
P.O. Box 721
Uhrichsville, Ohio 44683
www.barbourbooks.com

You may order by mail for $6.99 and add $2.00 to your order for shipping.
Prices subject to change without notice.